MW01228809

HUNT YOUR OWN

a novel

VICTORIA LYALL

© 2019

Lyall, Victoria Lynn, 1969–
Hunt Your Own : a novel / Victoria Lyall
ISBN 978-1-6534-1964-7 (pbk)

Cover art and design by author.

Printed in the U.S.A.
First Edition December 2019

To the wanderers and the homebodies.

It is said that a good Hopi is one who has a quiet heart and takes part in all the dances.
– Tony Hillerman

I told them people on my grandpa's mountain,
'You can lock the gate,
but you can't keep me
from crawlin' under it.'
– Milas Rathbone,
3rd generation ginseng hunter

Everything worthwhile is a sort of secret anyway, not to be bought or sold, just rooted out painstakingly, one little life at a time.
– Elisa Albert

1
Shelley Morgan

"You're just makin' it worse," said a female voice beside the car.

Stan jumped, and went from worried to angry in one smooth motion. He didn't like to be caught looking foolish. His foot left the gas pedal and the tires spun to a halt in the red mud. He peered up out the window at a young woman in jeans and a black Aerosmith T-shirt, with her hands on her hips, her brown ponytail swinging as she shook her head at him. She had a face like a doll, if you had just insulted the doll's mother.

"I suppose you have a better idea."

"Yeah, and if you stop spraying dirt all over the place I'll tell it to you. What're you doing out here, anyway?" They were deep in Pisgah National Forest, a half mile beyond where the gravel ended on a road without a name. Besides their voices, the only sound was the rhythmic thrumming of insects, which came from everywhere and nowhere at once.

"My *job*," he said in a steely voice.

Shelley noticed the National Forest Service seal on the clipboard in the passenger seat. "Oh, I get it. You're the new ginseng police. Nice undercover. I thought you were a hippie in this raggedy car." She looked at the holes under the tires. "You've been spinning for a while. Don't they teach you this stuff in ginseng police school?"

Stan placed his hands on the wheel in the 10 and 2 o'clock positions and drew a steadying breath. He was driving his personal vehicle until his requisitioned pickup truck arrived. In ginseng police school, also known as Wildlife Preservation Ranger Training, they taught you to handle interpersonal conflicts in a conciliatory but assertive manner. He sighed and said, "Ma'am, if there is a way that you can help me get out of here, I would be very grateful."

I'd be grateful if you got out of here, too, thought Shelley. But she said, "Well, *sir*, this mud is here because you are near a river. Also near the river are lots of rocks. You get a bunch of them, you put them in the holes behind your tires, pack them into a little ramp shape, and you back out *slowly*. If that doesn't work, you put more in the front, and then you kind of rock back and forth until you can get out on your momentum."

Stan hesitated. *Pack rocks around his already-stuck tires?*

"Really, that's how you do it," said Shelley. "Come winter when you get stuck in the snow, same thing." She laughed and moved away from the car.

In the trunk, Stan found a plastic bin he could use as a bucket and headed toward the opening in the trees ahead. When he returned to the car, the August sun twinkling through the leaves overhead had raised a sweat that fogged his sunglasses. The woman was sitting nearby on a fallen log, watching him. He dumped the rocks behind one tire and stalked off again. When he reached the river again he heard the car's engine crank. He dropped the bin and raced back to see the woman getting out of the driver's seat. She said something he couldn't hear, and two large young men in camouflage pants came around the back of the car, laughing. The car had moved about a foot forward; its tires rested on fresh, unfurrowed ground.

"What the–" he began, more assertive than conciliatory.

"Oh yeah, I forgot to mention," Shelley said. "Another way to get out is if you have a couple of people to push." The three of them turned and disappeared down a barely-visible trail into the woods.

Stan turned off the car and took the keys with him to retrieve his plastic bin. It had floated into midstream, and his regulation boots would be wet for two days.

"You should have seen the look on his face," Shelley said, plopping the third spoonful of mashed potatoes onto her plate. She handed the bowl off with her left hand while picking up a fork with the right. She grinned across the table at her aunt Sue, mother of her two cousins who had shoved the ranger's car onto safe ground. Ricky took the mashed potato bowl and chuckled.

"He was picturing spending the night out there by himself and telling his new supervisor that the car got stolen!" he added. Ricky was over 6 feet tall, with wide shoulders well-shaped by the use of construction tools, but the boisterous adolescent he had been a decade ago was still apparent.

Sue put her hand over her mouth to cover a laugh, and a starburst of faint lines crinkled at the outside corners of her black-brown eyes. After her parents were killed in the wreck, Shelley had watched those crinkles form over the decade that she had grown up in this house alongside her cousins. Those lines that she never got to see around her mother's eyes reassured Shelley that she herself might last long enough for the family resemblance to show through on her own face.

In spite of the laugh, Sue meant it when she said, "You all are just makin' trouble for yourselves. You're no smarter than that man gunnin' his motor and trying to force his way out of a mudhole."

"It ain't goin' to make a difference, mama," said Tim, whose teenaged charm was long gone, his continuing fascination with race cars notwithstanding. "If he catches somebody, he catches somebody. He looks like a Wyatt-Earp type. Whether he's pissed off before he catches them or not, he'll send 'em in either way."

The table was quiet for a moment while they all remembered the last Wildlife Preservation Ranger. Bob Mackey had grown up in the next county over, and moved to Cinderton to work after his divorce. "Just couldn't stand all the memories, everywhere I went," he had once told Sue, in a conversation that was half romance, half therapy session. Bob had been known to accept a few pounds of fresh deer meat and consider it clear evidence that nothing illegal had happened.

"Remember when Bob ran me in that time for gettin' a 4-point out of season, and then next season he went hunting with me and gave me that whole box of thirty-aught-six Springfield cartridges that he got in Morganton?" recalled Ricky.

"They was nice cartridges," put in Tim. "Didn't tear up the meat."

When the Rangers were ordered to monitor the ginseng and goldenseal as closely as the deer and trout, Bob had moved farther, to Morganton, and stayed. "I'm not ready to start arrestin' people for flower-pickin'," he told Sue. She didn't know if she missed him more as a suitor or patient.

"I heard he's a supervisor in a furniture factory now," Sue said.

"At least he still works with *trees*," said Shelley, in the hard calm voice she might one day use to acknowledge that her husband's cheating gave her more free time. The rest of dinner was quiet.

Lightning bugs sparkled in the yard as Shelley drove away from her cousins' home, headed to a night class. From her IPod, the Kentucky Headhunters invited all listeners to party by the river as she slid expertly around the curves on Green Branch Road.

"The cops are gone, it's almost dawn, let's all get Dixie-fried," sang Mark Orr, and she found herself thinking again about the new ranger. She knew that Ricky and Tim counted on their annual take of ginseng to cover the property taxes on Sue's house, and she suspected a portion of last year's earnings had gone toward her tuition at the community college. Her cell phone rang.

"Hey, Shelley," said the manager of the Quikstop gas station.

"Ohhhh. Hi, Louise."

"Whatcha doin'?"

"Oh, well, I was just thinking that if Sue paid for any of my classes with money from 'sang that came out of Pisgah, then I'm going to college on organized crime, just like if I lived in the city and my heroin-dealing pimp brother paid for it. What do you think of that?"

Louise laughed. "I guess you got a point, Shelley. I can help you with that. You can make your own money down here, working Jack's shift tomorrow. They're playing tomorrow night."

Shelley rolled her eyes. "That's okay, Louise. You don't have to do that. I didn't say I minded."

"Ha. You better have your butt down there at four o'clock."

"Alright, Louise."

"Thanks, girl. I knew I could count on you."

Damn, thought Shelley. Saturday night again. She would have to turn away at least one well-past-glowing man wanting to buy beer, and by the time the shift ended, it would be too late to go hear the band. But Louise was right, and they both knew it. Shelley was not in a position to say no to extra money.

2
Sophia

The man in the long flowered skirt whirled to his right. His eyes searched her out, and suddenly his hand was in hers. They smiled, stepped lightly around each other, and he was gone again. She barely had time to think, *left hand star*, and nod to the woman on the other side. She spun and wove through the crowd, her hands brushing from partner to partner. Crimson triangles and lemon-yellow hexagons in the quilts hanging on the walls swirled through her line of sight as she tried to match her steps to the music. Two hundred people moving on the wooden gymnasium floor sent the heat and smells of their bodies drifting up and out the high windows to the squirrels sleeping in the oaks.

The Thursday night dance ended well before midnight because most of the dancers had to work the next day. Sophia found herself, sweaty and red-cheeked, having late-night coffee with her equally flushed friend Gale. She blew a puff of air up into her wispy gray-blond bangs, hoping to un-stick them from her face.

"What good exercise! You don't know you're working that hard, but you are."

"I know, it's my best workout all week," Gale said. She set her coffee carefully on the bamboo-topped table with arching metal legs.

"You know what else I love about it?" Sophia asked. "That

everybody dances together – old people, young people... You never have to look for a partner, someone's always ready to jump in with you."

"And you don't have to make small talk afterward," Gale added. "Nobody hits on you."

"Do you think that kid in the skirt would hit on old women like us?" Sophia teased.

"Oh, he's a student, he's 'defying gender roles.'" Gale made air quotes. "Isn't it fun?" She blew on her coffee and slurped in a small mouthful. "So lively and inclusive."

Sophia leaned back in her bamboo-and-metal chair and remembered the city she left to come here. Up north, people used their horns in traffic in place of their own voices. They dressed in clothes that were too nice for the dirty subway cars, or even the taxis, where the last person to ride may have dropped mustard from the hot dog she grabbed as she hurried to her next meeting. But the clothes allowed them to believe that they had perfected their lives. With the right banking decisions and a talented dry cleaner, they barred themselves from dangers, like mustard stains or a bad investment. To avoid heart attacks, they exercised in air-conditioned gyms on electric bicycles. They warded off crime by installing security systems satellite-linked to the police department. They insured themselves against unemployment by keeping up-to-date resumes in a cloud that never blessed the ground with rain.

Eventually the effort of keeping up this barrier exhausted them, or at least it drained Sophia. After a vacation spent in the mountains of North Carolina, torn between the beeping of her cell phone and the singing of crickets, she disassembled her life and hauled it south. She met Gale a week after arriving. They clung to each other, two rat-race runaways in an enchanting foreign land. They overheard the locals calling them "transplants," and they intended to thrive in this unfamiliar soil.

Now Sophia wore old comfortable clothes and drove a second-hand SUV, not because she couldn't afford better, but because it relaxed her. She could park outside the door of anywhere she needed to go, and still buy quality coffee in shops run by other urban expatriates. People on the street here said hello, and even though that was nearly *all* they ever said to her, it was plenty.

3
Analía Raymunda Cuevas Alvarado

If she had read *Walden,* she would have recognized it here. Life had returned to its essential elements, where every daily need was an adventure. Laundry, food, a phone call home -- all required courage, attention, and research.

The difficulties were not for lack of conveniences. Everywhere she looked were machines of every sort, and everyone seemed to have, and expect to have, everything they wanted within moments of wanting it. All the Americans moved very fast, and she could not see in their faces any doubts about their destinations. Analía had followed her brother here from Mexico, but she hadn't found him yet.

"He is in Cinderton, North Carolina," her mother said. In the last of the many buses of her trip, Analía had gotten to know the driver, and the woman had pointed out a motel near the bus station. That was six days ago, and now her money was shrinking faster than the distance between Jaime and her.

Today she got out of bed and without expectation dialed the cell phone number that had been disconnected for months. This had become her ritual, a way of recommitting herself to searching even though everywhere she looked was emptiness. Sometimes what you have lost turns out to be in a place where you have been many times.

So once more she got dressed and had one of the sweet

breads from the motel lobby with the weak coffee. But this time she stopped at the desk and asked the man with the curly reddish hair, "Where can I rent an apartment?"

"You don't want to stay with us anymore?" he said, pretending to be offended.

His playfulness was encouraging. "Of course! It is very nice. You are going to let me stay for free?"

He raised his eyebrows briefly. "Yeah, I see what you mean. I reckon the thing to do is look in the papers. The Iwanna is the best. There's one in the corner, there. You can have it. And we have a Craigslist site, too."

So far Analía had looked for Jaime by exploring the town and inquiring of every Latino face that she had spotted. By now there was a thin but far-reaching web of dishwashers, hotel workers, and construction helpers asking about him. The red-haired man would be the first American to know about her quest.

"If you were looking for someone here, how could you find that person?"

"Um, what kind of person?" While Analía weighed the nobility of truth against the necessity of privacy, he sensed her discomfort and suggested, "Like an old friend?"

"Yes."

"Does this person have family here?"

"I don't think so," she evaded.

"There's always the phone book." He was happy to have her presence explained, having watched this mysterious stranger come and go all week without a phone call or visitor.

"And if he's not found in the phone book?"

He looked at the ceiling and the doorknob and the wainscoting, the searching in his mind acted out with his eyes. "Well...then it gets a lot harder...have you tried the internet?"

Analía sighed. "I tried that before I got here. There are too many people with the same names." She looked around the lobby. Even this inexpensive motel had a computer in the corner and a note posted with its WiFi password. "He...does not use the computer much," she said, although that didn't begin to describe it.

The red-haired man leaned on the counter and propped his foot on the rung of the stool beside him, settling into the problem. "Are you sure he's still here?" he asked, and immediately regretted it.

Analía had held tightly to her mother's words as if they were the key to a family chest in a faraway place, and she had never considered that the key might not fit, or that the chest might have been moved. In all of the buses and six days of relying on the kindness of countrymen abroad she had never wavered in her sense that Jaime was nearby, that like at the laundrymat and the ATM, all she had to do was find the magic code and he would appear. The secret to Jaime might be, 1400 Cinderton Highway, Apt 4C, or even, "the food prep guy at Margarita's Bar and Grill," but he would be there, working or drinking and waiting. Were all those people asking about Jaime wasting their time?

The red-haired man could see that she was about to cry. He started to reach across the counter, but his hands halted in a prayer-like gesture at the far edge of the counter. He went on.

"Hold on, it's not impossible. What kind of work does this person do?"

"I...don't know," she said, feeling that summed up most of her recent past. "Before, he collected eggs from farmers and sold them to stores, but...I don't think he could do that here."

The red-haired man smiled. "Probably not. Here they put all the chickens in one great big farm. I'm glad I don't have to clean that place!" He winked, hoping to distract her from being upset.

Analía looked at the counter and sighed. What good is privacy when one is utterly alone? "He is my brother. I don't know what kind of work he would do here."

"Your brother!" He stood up straighter. "You don't have his address or anything?"

"Not exactly. But I think he is here."

"So he would be a Mexican guy, right?" She nodded. "Does he speak English?"

"Only a little. I went to school for English, but he did not."

"Hmmm. Without English, he would probably work in, let's see, a restaurant, or construction. Maybe in a Mexican restaurant."

But Analía had been to all the Mexican restaurants. She could not understand how no one had ever known a Jaime Cuevas. She had told everyone where to find her, and the red-haired man seemed genuinely concerned. "It is possible that after I move to an apartment, someone will bring me a message here about my brother. Can you keep the message and I will come back for it? For a little while, only?"

"Oh yeah, of course, sure," he said, and Analía turned to go.

"Don't forget the paper, there, in the corner." She grabbed a copy of the thick paper made up of classified ads.

She sat with it in one of the now-familiar Mexican restaurants and pondered the strange abbreviations. From the prices, FP's and W/D's were good to have. She did the math to convert square feet to metric and was surprised at the spaciousness of even the smallest apartments advertised. She was shocked to see advertisements for churches, and even more shocked to realize that today was Sunday. Perhaps that was what she had been doing wrong. She had not asked for help since she left Mexico.

It was not hard to find a church. It was hard to choose from the multitude offering salvation, redemption, joy, and/or peace. Analía ruled out any of the places that advertised in the paper, because if a church needed to advertise, there must be a reason people didn't want to go there. Within walking distance of her motel, there were four churches, none of them Catholic. Three claimed variations on Baptist principles and she chose one of these. It was a white rectangular building, simple and tall. The façade displayed none of the splendor of her church at home, but the yellow pansies out front were welcoming and fresh in the already-hot morning. The people going in seemed happy to see each other. Their chatter was soft.

Analía stood behind a small crowd easing its way in the door. An older woman with fluffy hair smiled at her.

"Hello. Are you joining us this morning?"

"Yes, it is my first time here."

"You'll like it. This here's my husband George." She pulled on the arm of a man who was telling a story about a transmission.

"George, George, we have company this morning. This is – what's your name, dear?"

"Analía Raisa Cuevas." One's own name will always sound from one's own language, and this one rolled off just the way it had since her first day of school in Aguascalientes. The fluffy-haired woman blinked until she could pick out something familiar.

"Um, this is Anna, George."

"Well, hello! Welcome." George shook her hand roughly and turned back to his friend who was asking about first gear. The small group suddenly surged inward and Analía had no chance to take back her decision.

Inside, the people sat quietly under a cloud of Avon-scented humidity. At the end of the pew next to George and his wife, Analía sat and inhaled the flowery heat. She understood bits of the service, and followed the crowd as they stood and sang, stood and prayed, sat and fanned themselves. During the prayers she asked in her mind for a sign of where Jaime could be.

Please lead me from your house to him, she asked. *Please let him be okay when I find him.*

When she opened her eyes after the last prayer, the crowd

was already working its way toward the door. Once outside, released from the weight of piety, children were running in the parking lot and the adults' voices were louder and harder. There was talk of food and yard work.

"Are you going to come back, dear?" The fluffy-haired woman beamed at her from the church steps.

"Well, yes, I think so. It was very nice."

"We're having a church supper Saturday after next. You're welcome to come. It's at 6:00. Bring your family." Analía tried to keep her face pleasant as her heart screamed out, *yes, if only I could.*

"At 6:00? I will try." Another woman with sparkling gold-rimmed glasses was listening. She spoke up.

"Yes, you come back. We love to have new people. You have a lovely accent."

"Thank you." Analía smiled.

"Where are you from?" asked the fluffy-haired woman.

"From Mexico."

"Do you live in Cinderton?" asked the woman with the glasses. Her makeup glittered, too, and her earrings. She was crisp and tinkly, a bird crackling with internal energy. Still Analía was not sure she wanted to answer all the questions. She was finding that most conversations with Americans got confusing quickly, as her English ran out and her answers never seemed to be what people expected.

"I just got here. I am looking for a place to live." Her heart shouted at her again, complaining that it did not want to live here, it would not take that long to find Jaime.

"You just came from Mexico? Where are you staying now?" said the sparkling woman. Analía was reminded of the way her aunts had fussed over her when she announced that, after months without a word from Jaime, she was going alone to the U.S. to look for him.

"In a motel there." She pointed down the street.

"Oh my, you can't do that for very long. Let me show you something." The fluffy-haired woman put a hand on her shoulder and ushered her back into the tropics of the church building. In a corner near the restroom hung a bulletin board.

"God, it's hot in here," the woman said to herself. "But I guess he knows that, it being his house. Maybe he likes it that way. Here you go. Sometimes there's signs here from people that have rooms." She tilted her head back and examined the board. After a moment she shook her head once.

"Hm, maybe next week. What are you doing for money?"

"What I do for money?"

"I mean, do you have enough? Have you found a job?"

Analía had been offered a number of jobs in her rounds of restaurants and hotels. She declined all of them, thinking they would distract her from her search. In this dark corner of the church she wondered how long she would be looking for Jaime.

"No…I think…can be a good idea."

"Do you know how to run a cash register?"

"Cash register?"

"Doesn't matter. You strike me as a smart girl. I run a little store and I need a cashier about 20 hours a week. Do you think you might be interested?"

"Maybe. Is it far?"

"Not at all. Here." The woman took a blank notecard from the corner of the bulletin board and wrote an address. "You just keep going past your motel and it's on the other side of the road about a mile down. The QuikStop gas station."

"What is your name, please?"

"Oh, I'm sorry, honey. I'm Louise Dillingham. You just come down to the store about 5:00 tomorrow."

"Thank you very much." Louise led the way out of the

church. Analía picked her way through the crowd, anxious to escape. The sparkling woman spotted her.

"We hope we'll see you next Saturday!" she called out.

Analía smiled and kept moving. Louise watched her go and turned to her husband. "George, I think she's walking back to that motel. Should we give her a ride?"

George shielded his eyes from the sun with his hand and peered after Analía, who had already reached the curb at the edge of the church parking lot. "She's fine, Louise. Let her be."

Monday at 4:00 Analía set out from the motel in the other direction, along a cracked sidewalk where she had to duck the guidewires of electric poles set along its edge. A stone retaining wall butted to the sidewalk held back the mountain that had been sliced to make the road. Speeding cars pushed gusts of air toward her, and the trapped gusts protested by tossing discarded fast food wrappers against her ankles. She scanned down the street, looking for an escape: open asphalt with gas pumps, bright logos, and big numbers. She located the QuikStop and hurried toward its parking lot, relieved to get away from the road and the wind. Inside, she smiled at the girl behind the counter, and quietly examined every aisle.

"Can I help you find something?"

"I am waiting for someone." The girl nodded and went back to stocking cigarettes.

A moment later the girl said, "Oh! You must be the person that Louise is hiring!" She came out from behind the counter and held out her hand. Analía took it delicately. "I'm Shelley. I'm going to train you."

"My name is Analía."

"You're from Mexico, right?" Analía nodded. "Louise is

happy about that. We get a lot of Mexican customers. I bet she'll want you to work Friday nights, when they all buy beer. Have you worked in a store before?" Analía shook her head. "That's okay. It's just like shopping in a store, only backward." Shelley gave a small snort of a laugh at her own joke.

The two girls were standing in the toiletries, cat food, and motor oil aisle of the convenience store, and Shelley loomed over Analía by a good six inches. But they were about to become colleagues in providing road snacks and emergency aspirin to the needy of Route 25. Analía felt strangely comfortable.

"So tell me about yourself. How long have you been in America?" Shelley asked.

"This is my day...seven." It sounded like a lot to Analía.

"Seventh day! Wow, your English is good. You must've been learning it in Mexico."

"Yes, in school. But it sounds different here."

Shelley laughed again. "This part of America is the South. They say we talk funny. But you can understand me, right?"

"Most of the time."

"So what do you think of America so far?"

"The air is free!" A cheerful voice cut in as the glass door to the parking lot opened. Louise entered while shouting over her shoulder to a customer suffering from a flat tire outside.

"So you found it." She swooped over to Analía and patted her shoulder. "Hey, Shelley. Y'all getting to know each other?"

And thus Analía began learning to shop backward, the first of many things in the United States that would feel entirely counterintuitive.

4
Personal Best

"It's such a wonderful thing, the way they are keeping traditional cultural forms alive. I wish it could be bigger somehow, that more people could experience it," said Sophia to Gale, a few days after the dance, as they picked their way up the rocky path to the Devil's Courthouse off the Blue Ridge Parkway. "You know what I mean – if there were money available for a better location, or a marketing plan."

"I don't know if that band even gets paid," said Gale. "I know they all have day jobs."

"As welldiggers and things like that!" marveled Sophia. "I would love to help them out. I wonder who I should talk to, who's in charge of the whole thing?"

"Who knows?" muttered Gale, preoccupied with placing one Teva-booted foot after another. Sophia paused to look off the side of the trail, through the upper branches of trees rooted further down the slope. A soft mist blurred the distant views, hanging thick in the valleys and dancing in thin swirls at its upper edges. The same mist was sticking her clothes to her body, and she imagined that the added weight in the damp fabric was dragging her back down the mountain. She wished she could just roll like a drop of water all the way to that icy clear creek at the bottom, tumble over the boulders that lined it, bounce into the stream, and finally let go.

This desire to simply lie down had followed her for months, like that ridiculous cloud in the antidepressant commercials. In Boston she had agreed to take the pills after three doctors had refused to listen anymore to her stories of exhaustion and indefinite pain. She couldn't make them understand this drive toward passivity, the something-like-nausea that kept telling her to *stop*. Absolutely nothing seemed important or interesting enough to be worth the effort of lifting her arms to take hold of it.

Yet here she was, traipsing a path of bare dirt, small boulders, and tree roots to the top of a mountain. Down in her stomach with the something-like-nausea was a thimbleful of fear that she would not make it back to the parking lot. Even from partway up the mountain the cars looked like, not so much ants, they were too colorful for ants, but maybe the buses the ants rode to work in the morning. She smiled to herself, wondering if the ants' buses would be full of the detritus of previous ants, the way the buses in Boston had been full of disassembled newspapers and abandoned coffee cups. How small would an ant's coffee cup be, she wondered, and which section of the newspaper would interest them? The restaurant section, of course, she answered herself and smiled again.

The doctor in North Carolina had let her go slowly off the antidepressants, and she hadn't noticed any difference. It was hard to compare, she thought, because maybe it was those buses, or the places they took her, that had caused whatever it was that the doctors had given up on and labeled "emotional." There had been no steep mountain paths in Boston to test herself against.

And she had bested this one, or at least the uphill half of it. She and Gale stepped out of the arch of tree branches shading the path and onto stone steps slick with dew. The view opened up. They were standing on the rim of a jagged bowl, a few thousand feet deep and forty-plus miles across, lined with undulating forest. A plaque beside the coin-operated binoculars informed them that they could see four states.

Sophia took in these mountains laid before her. She squinted, unable to make out individual trees in the fog. But she could feel it from here: under that fog, that bowl of mountains contained an extraordinary healing force, a knowing ancient presence that could guide her away from her toxic past.

Somewhere down there, she thought eagerly, *it's growing*.

5
Southern Cures

"The root of *Panax quinquefolia* has been prized for its medicinal value since ancient times. Since ginseng is believed to relieve many different ailments, some with essentially opposite symptoms, such as depression *and* anxiety, it is often taken as a general tonic or preventive, even when no symptoms are present. It was said to rejuvenate the tired and calm the nervous," explained Shelley's botany professor to the class.

"Like vitamins?" asked a girl in the front row.

"In a way," said the professor. "Pay attention, folks, do you see the same Latin root in *Panax* and *panacea?* Who knows what a panacea is?"

"Let's get to the root of the root," mumbled Hal Dorsey suggestively, a few seats over. Shelley turned her head away from him and made a face. She couldn't believe he still sat in class. He hadn't paid attention since junior year of high school.

Driving away from campus after class, Shelley thought about the lecture she'd heard. When she was small, her grandmother sometimes told her that her grandfather was out hunting ginseng, and for years she thought it was an animal, like the rabbits or squirrels he sometimes brought home. She knew it couldn't be as big as a deer, because she never saw anything in the back of the truck when he came home. And she couldn't miss seeing the deer, their limp bodies folded into the bed of the truck. She had been allowed to watch her grandfather skin a squirrel once. While she watched, she sobbed and placed her grandfather under a thousand curses. She didn't walk away until he took it into the kitchen to her grandmother, having transformed it from a fluffy-tailed Disney character into a creature out of a horror movie. Later she ate her grandmother's squirrel gravy over homemade biscuits.

Now she sometimes hung around Ricky when he dressed deer, taking short glances at his work, feeling glad he was willing to do it. Unlike other hunters she knew, Ricky always butchered his deer studiously, without beer or music, sorting the sections for eating soon, freezing, and giving to the dogs. She and Ricky had spent their lives together, jumping in rivers, exploring caves with flashlights. She'd even piloted his four-wheeler back when he had one. When he cleaned a deer was the only time he felt foreign to her. There was a part of him she didn't understand, even having lived in parallel to him since they were toddlers. She didn't know, hadn't learned to know, what it was to take an animal apart for dinner.

Something else the professor said in class: most American ginseng was sold to the Chinese, and most ginseng sold in America was imported from Asia. No one wanted the ginseng-next-door. Each side of the world placed mystic value in the plants from the other side of the world, as if the mere difficulty of obtaining them added to their power. Gnarled, dried roots went back and forth around the planet in container ships alongside plastic toys and silicon chips. Each side was happy to have the other side of the world kill and dress their ginseng for them.

What a waste of fossil fuel to move it all around, Shelley thought, and that made her angry all over again.

Shelley yanked open the door to the convenience store and marched behind the counter, flinging her backpack into the closet-sized office behind the cigarette rack.

"Havin' a good day?" asked Louise warily from behind the ancient metal desk.

"What? Oh, sorry, Louise, just a little pissed that some of us can get daddy to pay for college they don't even take seriously while the rest of us have to bust our asses to pay for books *and* car insurance."

Louise stood up. "I know, Shelley, I know." She picked up her purse and extracted herself from the nook between the desk and the stacks of boxes. She paused in front of Shelley and patted her arm. "I know it's a lot to keep up with. Just remember that hard work will make your graduation day even prouder, honey. Someday we're gonna miss you around this gas station while you're off doing big things."

Shelley gave her a quick shy hug.

"You won't be missing me, Louise. I'll still need gas to do big things."

Louise's eyebrows shot up. "Now you're not going to get that far and then just turn around and come back to nowheresville! No, ma'am. But for now, get out there and train that girl some more. She's out there organizing the plastic spoons and straightening the paper cups. She just won't set still."

Analía was sorting the jumbled flavors of individual coffee creamers in the kitchenette where customers could microwave pre-made sandwiches and single-serving frozen pizzas. Shelley watched her for a minute, envying the meditative quality of her motions. The focus apparent in Analía's face made it seem as if hazelnut and vanilla were the entire world, as if nothing else clamored for her attention.

"You keep that up and you'll make me look bad," Shelley

said. When Analía looked chastised Shelley quickly added, "Just kidding. It's about time somebody got to that," enjoying her own sarcasm even if no one else did. No one cared if the creamers were mingled, they just dug through the bins with their dirty fingers and grabbed what they wanted.

"I did not know what else to do."

"Well, I think you pretty much know where everything is from the other day. Why don't you sit with me at the cash register?" suggested Shelley. She nodded goodbye as Louise went out the door, waving over her shoulder.

Analía put the small boxes containing each flavor back into the rack and looked at the remaining pile of unsorted creamers that she had dumped onto the counter. "What I do with these?"

"Just bring 'em. We can sort 'em while we're sitting." Shelley stretched the bottom of her T-shirt out into a basket and brushed the pile into it. As they moved behind the counter, she added, "Now might be a good time to tell you. Once in a while the health department guy stops by. They don't look at much here, since we don't cook anything. I get the feeling that when you're here, it'll be clean enough already. If a guy in a dress shirt with a clipboard comes in, just let him poke around. He's supposed to show you his ID first; make sure it says Health Department."

"I can do that."

The two girls settled in behind the cash register, perched on tall wooden stools, and began making little piles of creamer cups along the countertop. After a bit Shelley said, "This reminds me of kindergarten. You know – can you put all the red blocks together?" she imitated a friendly teacher. Analía smiled.

"Speaking of school, Analía, you seem awfully smart and educated to come all the way to the U.S. to work in a gas station. They must have gas stations in Mexico. I don't mean to be nosy, but why did you want to leave Mexico?"

Analía froze for a moment, and Shelley wanted to squirm, feeling she had asked the wrong question. She could see that Analía was deciding what to say. She began scrabbling mentally for sensitive replies, fearing she was about to hear "My whole family was shot by drug dealers," or "I was raped," or even, "I joined the wrong political party and a civil war broke out."

Finally Analía said, "I did not want to leave Mexico for nothing. My brother is here in the U.S. somewhere and I am looking for him."

Shelley managed not to say, *Oh thank god.*

Analía took a deep breath. Explaining her quest in English felt like clumsily handing a precious relic to a stranger, without knowing whether it would be treated gently. "He was a good boy. And was just a boy. He was sixteen when he left. For three years he never missed a single week to send us money, no matter how small a money. Maybe only $20. But every week. When he stopped, I wanted to come after the second week, but everyone said, no, no, he is just busy in America, maybe he is enjoying too many beers and forgot us for a minute, but he will remember soon. Then still we do not hear from him for more weeks and I was so mad at everyone in the family for making me wait. I scream at them. Then it took me eight more months to get a permission to come here. He is gone for almost a year." Her dark eyes filled with liquid and she looked away, touching her fingers to her eyes with a quick gesture and throwing the drops to the floor.

"I'm sorry, I cannot talk about this now," she shook her head and snatched at the creamer cups, furiously plopping them into their correct piles.

"I'm sorry, Analía," Shelley whispered. "Stay right here," she said, and sprang from her stool. She strode to the wall of refrigerators and pulled out two cans of the other southern panacea, Diet Coke.

At closing time, Shelley watched Analía put her bag over her shoulder crosswise and smooth her clothes, preparing for the walk back to her motel. Analía still had that look of peaceful readiness for whatever was in front of her, even if it was a half-mile walk in the dark. She went out the glass door, waving a small goodbye from the parking lot. Shelley grabbed her own backpack and raced out, slapping at the automated lock panel beside the door. She caught up to Analía and practically shoved her toward the old Ford.

"You need a ride home," she declared.

"Okay – okay!" Analía laughed. "Yes, mama." Shelley dropped into the driver's seat and had the engine running, the music selected, and the car in gear by the time Analía closed the passenger door.

"Ready?" Shelley asked, and Analía blinked as the car surged onto the empty road. A few empty plastic bottles clunked as they were thrown against the side doors in the back.

"I am being kidnapped?"

"Ha. Yeah, first I made you cry and now I'm kidnapping you. Listen, don't you want some help with your brother? I mean, I know this is a small town, but how can you work and look for him, too?"

Analía couldn't tell if Shelley was helping or discouraging her. These Americans insisted on inserting themselves into every struggle they noticed. She had been riding a wave from the bus driver to getting the job to now this. Would this wave dump her in front of Jaime or was it all a big distraction?

They swerved into the parking lot of the motel. Shelley turned sideways in her seat. The gears burred as she threw the car into Park.

"I was hoping to have more time to convince you," she began. "You've got a big job playing detective. I know a lot of people. I might be able to help."

Through the windshield, even with the lights in the parking lot, Analía could see a few stars speckling the deepest blue sky, the sky she knew stretched all the way to Aguascalientes, where at this time of evening her mother would be clearing the table from dinner. Now there were two empty spaces at that table.

Analía let go of the breath she'd been holding. "Okay," she said. "Thank you."

"I haven't done anything yet," Shelley demurred. "What do you know about his life here? Do you know where he worked? Or where he lived?"

Analía shook her head. "We do not know anything. He said he had a job as a manager of a restaurant, but I went to so many restaurants and no one has ever heard of him. I think he just said that so we would be proud of him. We just picked up the money every week." She shook her head as a swell of guilt washed over her.

"Didn't he call you? Did he say anything about his friends, or people he knew?"

"He just called them guys, you know, 'a guy at work this and that.'"

"There has to be some place to start," said Shelley, scowling at the dashboard.

"I feel like I am with the police," said Analía, but she smiled. Shelley's brow wrinkled.

"Well, you know, that's not a bad idea." Analía's eyes widened and she shook her head forcefully. Shelley persisted. "We don't have to go to the police. But we can see if they found him – we can check his criminal record and see if it has an address."

"We cannot make the police look for him." Analía sat up straighter. She would have to sacrifice Shelley's assistance if she insisted on this path.

"No, no, they won't even know. My cousin knows how to look. He has a criminal record." Seeing Analía's face, she continued, "It's no big deal. He likes to hunt out of season."

"What does that mean?"

"Huh? Oh – here you can only hunt certain animals at certain times of the year, deer season or turkey season, and if you shoot one outside those times, it's against the law."

"But if you need to eat?" asked Analía.

"I guess that's what the grocery store is for," said Shelley. "Anyway, we can look for an address for him that way. If you want."

Analía thought that this had to be a bad idea. But Shelley hadn't led her astray yet. "The police will not know?" she asked.

"Absolutely not. I'll get Ricky to show us. Want to do it tomorrow? I get out of class at 10. We can come pick you up. About 10:30?"

Analía lifted one hand, palm up, in the classic I-don't-know gesture. "I see you tomorrow," she said, and gracefully climbed out of the car.

With that settled, Shelley's thoughts returned to her own situation as she drove away from the motel. She hoped Louise was right. With few exceptions, her classmates at the community college were in pretty much the same boat she was. They nearly all worked while going to school, because it was necessary to eat and pay rent while expanding their minds. Few people in her graduating class had the money to go off to full-time college. It was much cheaper to live with family and eat at home. They could all take a few classes here, a few there, hanging onto the hope of a four-year degree in six or eight years. The finish line might creep away into the future, but they all counted on it being a true finish line.

What would come after was less clear. By the time most people received their six-year four-year degrees, they had built up seniority in their "college jobs." They managed the restaurant instead of waiting tables, they oversaw production teams in the few remaining factories rather than working the assembly lines. An entry-level job in their degree area was often a step back financially, assuming such a job was available in this small Appalachian town, where the spouses and children they had acquired during their long college years were settled into their own jobs and schools. The excitement of graduation faded into frustration at the job market or veered into a tearful move away to a larger city. Some gave up and stayed in their college jobs, bitterly complaining that all they got for their degree was a big pile of debt.

Still every year the promise of college played its siren song to the graduating class of the high school. Guidance counselors and teachers dangled going to college in front of those students whose performance suggested they were deserving of the good life. Those who hadn't been to college, like Louise, spoke as if it were a golden boat that left the port just as they were distracted by marriage or ailing parents, as if getting on that boat could have carried them away from all the troubles and worries of the human condition. Shelley's stellar high school performance had left no doubt in anyone's mind that she would go to college, and she had signed up at the community college the semester after graduation to get everyone off her back and because she didn't know what else to do.

Everyone was proud of her, but she knew it was a cowardly move. She couldn't tell people that she did not want to be evicted from this town. Refusing to enroll would have been announcing that she would work at the convenience store for the rest of her life. Registering for classes was supposed to be an escape plan, a way to run away from the possible futures arrayed in front of her in the mountains. But it was escaping in the dark: she just took off running in the direction they pointed her, not wanting to leave what was behind her, and with no idea what she was headed toward. Even the people who regretted missing the boat, like Louise, could only tell her vaguely: "Big things."

6
Abandoned Nests

"How the hell can she not know anything about her own brother?" demanded Ricky the next morning, sliding his seat back and forth in the car. "What kind of family is this?"

"For the love of god, Ricky, he's been 2000 miles away for three years. You want her to keep track of his bowel movements?"

"Fine," he said in a bored voice. He settled with the seat laid back in napping position, crossing his arms behind his head and gazing out the window. "If this guy's got any sense, he moved somewhere else about five minutes after the police wrote his address down."

"Ugh, probably. But it's a shot. Do you have something better to do today?"

"Than hang out at the courthouse?" His slid his eyes toward her. "Yeah," he muttered, but didn't specify.

They pulled into the motel parking lot. Analía was standing under the portico at the door.

"That's her," said Shelley.

"That's her?" asked Ricky. His seat popped fully upright. Shelley had noticed that customers often stared at Analía, torn between their upset at having to deal with a "foreigner" and their appreciation of her glossy dark hair and eyes the color of grass during a dry season. Analía's smile and old-fashioned manners

never wavered as she completed their transactions and sent them on their way. Ricky looked just as contentedly befuddled as the customers when they left the gas station.

He hopped out and held the front door open as Analía approached the car. She smiled and got in and he closed the door delicately. He maneuvered into the back seat and sat with his hands folded in his lap.

"This is my cousin, Ricky." Shelley shot a smirk over the back seat but kept it from her voice. "This is Analía." Analía crossed her right hand over herself to reach around the seat and take Ricky's hand in a gentle shake. He beamed at the touch.

"I hope we can find out something about your brother," he said, then sat tongue-tied all the way to the courthouse, grinning like a very polite monkey.

He leaped to get Analía's door again at the courthouse. Shelley shook her head at him over the top of the car, but he didn't see it as he solicitously directed Analía toward the building, which was not hidden by any trees or other obstacles. Shelley trailed after the two of them, and considered whether she should wait at the car like a good chauffeur. At least when he opened the courthouse door for Analía, he remembered to keep it open for her.

At security they made him take off his belt, and Shelley saw Analía look away quickly, blinking. *Jeez,* she thought, *maybe I should let them have their own private elevator so they can make out. Bet that would get the police's attention.*

Ricky was making the most of his role as knowledgeable leader, reassuring Analía that their search would be done at a public computer and no one would be the wiser. Shelley almost felt bad for him when he sat down at the terminal and hesitated. She noticed an instruction sheet lying on the table and slid it under his hand. He gave her a grateful glance. Analía carefully spelled out "Jaime" and "Cuevas" and "Alvarado" while he wrote diligently on some scrap paper. Ricky put the pen down and squared himself to the keyboard as if he were about to perform surgery.

Soon he said, "Looks like he got two tickets. One for driving without a license and one for...driving without a license. They got two different addresses on them." He copied the addresses onto the scrap paper.

"Do they have dates?" interrupted Shelley. He clicked a few more times. "Make sure you put each date with the right address," said Shelley. He rolled his eyes. Ricky folded the paper in two and stood up. He held it out to Analía, who felt a shimmer as she took it from his hand. She wasn't sure if it was from touching him or from thinking that this might be the first real clue about Jaime. Ricky felt the same shimmer but was sure of the cause.

Back in the car, Analía sat with her head bowed toward the paper open in her hand. August 9, 6 Emma Lane. March 19, 138 Brougham Road. Jaime had come home to these houses, walked in their doors, and filled them with the scents of pork and chiles cooking. He had stepped out of the bathrooms after showering, the steam billowing with his cologne, and fallen asleep in these houses, maybe to dream of Aguascalientes. She read the addresses over and over until she felt the car stop.

They all peered out the windshield at the house and its shell of aluminum siding that had seen better years.

"What are we going to do?" asked Ricky. "Just knock on the door?"

"I guess so," said Shelley. "At least we're prepared for whoever answers. Whether they speak Spanish or English, one of us can explain what we're doing." She turned to Analía. "You ready?"

They piled out of the car and crossed the dirt yard. A few steps led them to a bowed porch. Empty beer cans lined the railing. Ricky knocked.

After several minutes of scuffling inside, a man of about

thirty answered, sporting no shirt but a gallery of tattoos. Shelley tried to make them out while Ricky stepped forward to talk.

"Hey, how you doin'?" He held out a hand like a politician at a church dinner.

"I don't want to buy nothin', including Jesus," said the man, not unkindly.

"That's alright, we ain't got nothin' worth sellin'," said Ricky quickly. "We just need a little help. We're looking for a guy who used to live here. A Mexican guy named Jaime, you have any idea about him? Last we heard of him was several months ago."

"Several months? That's a while. He owe you money or something?"

"No, no, we don't have any problem with him. He's, ah, well, he's kind of family. We're worried about him."

The man noticed Analía for the first time. He didn't look her up and down, but he stared at her face longer than was polite. He looked away before he started talking again, as if he couldn't do both at once.

"Naw, I've only lived here a couple months. I don't know anything about him. He your family?" he asked, lifting his chin toward Analía. She nodded.

"Sorry. Hope you find him. Maybe ask the neighbors. They're Mexican." He pointed across the street and they all looked. In the dusty yard of a similar house, a small boy was propelling his bicycle over a ramp made of cinder blocks and plywood.

"Okay, thanks," said Shelley and Ricky together. The three of them clattered off the porch and crossed the street.

"This one's all yours, I think," Ricky said graciously to Analía. She called out to the boy in a melodious jingle of Spanish. His head jerked up and he looked over his handlebars at her. Analía spoke again, and the boy got off his bike and ran toward the house. There were pots of tomatoes growing in the corners of this porch, their vines wound around chains of wire coat hangers that went all the way to nails stuck in the crossbeams of the ceiling. Analía went slowly after him, giving him time to announce her presence.

Shelley and Ricky waited at the edge of the yard. "I see you've changed your tune," said Shelley quietly. Ricky tilted his head away, but not so much that he couldn't watch Analía all the way to the door of the house.

"Hello, hello? I guess you want to help now, don't you?" Shelley said.

Ricky turned to her and grinned. "Girl's gotta find her family, right?" He paused. "Hey, Shelley, when that girl smiles, I don't know if it's the angels singin' or the devil callin', but I hear *something*."

"Now you're a poet," muttered Shelley.

A woman opened the door of the house and came out onto the porch. She and Analía began with a few quick exchanges in questioning voices, then the woman's voice changed to a sympathetic crooning. Ricky could see the hope leaving Analía's face bit by bit. Eventually the woman reached out to Analía and hugged her. Her voice was regretful and then encouraging. Analía came down the steps and went straight to the car without speaking. Shelley followed and stood beside the car with Analía, Ricky trailing awkwardly.

"It's okay, Analía, we still have another address," said Shelley. "And we can go to the Western Union office where he sent money from." Analía put her arm through Shelley's for a moment and withdrew it. Ricky marveled that he could be jealous of such a fleeting intimacy.

In the car Analía said, "She said she knew Jaime and he was a good boy." Shelley and Ricky waited for more information, but Analía shook her head. "She didn't know where he went from here, or where he worked. She said he was never home, so she thought he had more than one job." She looked morose. Each tiny proof of

Jaime's existence just cemented his absence.

The second address turned out to be a trailer park. At the entrance was a wooden sign that looked handmade, with flowers and leaves encircling raised letters painted pink and yellow. As they pulled in, a smaller sign similar to the first stood sentinel at a Y intersection, its arrows declaring the left to be Emma Lane and the right to be Emma Road.

"Somebody's daughter must be named Emma," said Shelley.

"Be easier for the mailman if they'd had another kid," said Ricky, hoping to lighten Analía's mood.

Number 6 Emma Lane was surrounded by a collection of the most durable automobiles in America. Neither minor collisions nor windshield cracks nor the absence of nonessential parts like bumpers had stayed these vehicles from service. Ricky maneuvered to park on the only remaining empty grass and they all traipsed to the door, barely fitting on the landing at the top of a short staircase. Ricky and Shelley tried to look innocuous as Analía chatted with the man who opened the door. Then the man turned and disappeared back into the darkness of the trailer, leaving the door open. Analía said quietly, "Someone here knew my brother." A younger man appeared next, spoke with Analía, and disappeared again.

He reappeared with a small stack of mail. Analía took it and thanked him. She sighed as she turned from the door. No one knew where Jaime had gone, or where his money had come from.

7
Going to the Authorities

Sophia leaned back into a crocheted afghan on the couch, and gazed at the carved wooden toys on the table in front of her. Dr. Bead's waiting room in a turn-of-the-century house-turned-office resembled a grandmother's living room, or maybe a small museum of Appalachian crafts. In Boston the medical centers had generic blond furniture and nylon carpet tiles. Sophia folded her hands on her stomach and focused on her breathing, but couldn't keep from tapping one thumb rapidly on the opposite knuckles. At every visit to the doctor, she expected confrontation, or at least condescension.

The doctor himself came out of a door that probably once led to a parlor. He crossed the room and held out a hand, grabbing her other arm as they shook. At her last visit they had reminisced about Boston, where he had practiced many years before coming to the South. Dr. Bead held open the door to the examining room and watched her pass. He knew she had been fighting off weight gain, but his patients liked him better if he only weighed them every few visits.

"How have you been feeling?" he said to her back as he followed her into the room.

"Better," she said. "I still feel tired most of the time, but once I get moving, I'm able to forget about it. It's less debilitating." Now that she was completely free of prescription medications, she was afraid to tell the doctor what she had replaced them with, afraid of being dismissed again, this time for ignorant superstitions.

"Chronic fatigue syndrome can be mysterious," the doctor allowed. Some doctors refused to even call it medical, insisting that its sufferers belonged in the offices of psychiatrists instead. Patients pored over studies reporting differences in metabolism, heart rates, and brain waves during sleep, though none of these tied directly to the symptoms they reported. "Generally we recommend that you stick with anything that gives you relief. You feel that exercise is helping?"

"It could be, I suppose." She squirmed a little in her chair. "I think it might be something else, though." The doctor lifted his eyebrows.

"I've been taking something over-the-counter. I don't know if you'll approve..." She twisted her hands together a bit, glancing away at the map of internal organs on the back of the door. "I heard that people take ginseng for general purposes, and it's not supposed to have any negative side effects." She rushed ahead. "I'm not on anything else now, so it can't interact —"

The doctor cut her off. "That's just fine, Sophia. I'm not going to get on you for taking ginseng. It has no worrisome effects." Keys rattled as he made a note in his laptop. "Are you getting it from a reputable source?"

"Oh yes, at the EarthGoods store." Buoyed by this acceptance of her new health plan, she considered maybe it could be improved. "You know, it's not cheap, and my insurance doesn't cover it. Is there a prescription version that they might cover?"

The doctor laughed gently. "No, the insurance companies see it as nonmedical. If you feel it's making a difference," he shrugged, "I'm technically unable to recommend herbal treatments. But I can say I don't think it will hurt." Sophia felt her shoulders relax and a sense of possibility wash over her. After the usual probing and poking, she left the doctor's office freshly confirmed in her belief in ginseng. She walked out into a late summer day dotted with distant clouds. The parking lot was a wide open dance floor ready for her next moves. It was Thursday again.

Shortly before seven, Sophia and Gale joined the huddle of people waiting outside the door of the gymnasium. They watched the band members carrying equipment around the building to a side door.

Ricky, loaded with his guitar and a bundle of cords, pretended to himself that he was thinking about Jaime as he crossed the out-of-bounds line painted on the floor. He knew it was Analía motivating his thoughts. In his short years of romancing women, he had bought the obligatory flowers and chocolate. He had given up his coat at late-season football games. He had provided rides to work on winter mornings. He had dedicated songs at dances; once he'd even written an entire song enumerating and exaggerating the winsome qualities of his intended. But locating a missing person who didn't even speak English would be a new level in the trials of courtship.

He frowned as he dropped the cords on the edge of the stage and leaped up in a practiced move.

"What's goin' on?" asked the fiddle player.

"Thinkin' about chasin' women," Ricky growled, still deep in thought.

"If chasin' women makes you look like that," the fiddle player said, "you're doin' it wrong."

In a short time Ricky and the other players had everything rigged and were squawking their way toward being in tune. They argued amiably about the playlist for the evening. Early-arriving dancers stood around in small groups and taught each other moves, sometimes with one person clapping a rhythm for them. At one point the drummer picked up the clapped rhythm with a few light taps and everyone laughed. The taps ricocheted over the dancers' heads in the huge space, but instead of feeling lonely, they enjoyed the elbow room before the floor filled up.

Sophia smiled briefly at the others standing around outside and commented loudly to Gale, "I wonder how I can find out who's in charge of this." No one in line offered any insight. While they stood around, Sophia studied the situation. There was the band, obviously. She couldn't see any other formal activity happening. There was no doorman, no emcee – the band members took turns giving instructions and making jokes between the dances. *Cleanup*, she thought, *somebody's got to clean up and lock the door*. She zoomed in on a man standing to her left and opened brightly, "It's wonderful that we all get to do this. Who is it that makes it possible?"

"Them boys, I guess," grinned the man. "Wouldn't be much of a dance without them playin'. They've got some real talent."

"Of course!" she agreed. "They are the heart of it, aren't they?"

"And the good Lord that gave us ears and feet," the woman at his side smiled.

Sophia forced a polite smile and turned away. She couldn't stand the way everyone here assumed everyone else followed the same god. She did not want to get drawn into one of those conversations where her only options were to lie or upset some provincial Sunday school teacher.

A table near the door caught her eye. A man sat behind it and a few dancers crowded around, passing cash to the man, which the man flattened between his palms and placed in a Tupperware container on the table. He must be in charge of *something*, she thought, so she sidled to the table as the others were leaving.

"Are you collecting entrance fees?" she asked.

"Oh, goodness no," the man laughed. "We're taking up a collection for Willie Blankenship. He's got the stomach cancer, you see, and they didn't have any insurance. Him and his wife never did have any kids, so they need a lot of help." He gestured at a homemade placard at the end of the table. It held a picture of a thin pale man sitting in a wheelchair, an IV bag and pole at his side. A woman stood on his other side, leaning into the picture with one arm around the man.

"Oh." Sophia said, a little taken aback. She felt the unspoken request and fumbled in her pockets. "I'm sorry, I don't usually bring my purse into the dance."

"That's all right," the man said. "That's just fine. Maybe next week. I figure he'll still have the cancer then." Resignation, not sarcasm, in his voice.

"Do you happen to know who organizes these dances? You know, is there a director or something?"

The man looked perplexed. "No, there isn't any kind of a director. I guess the band just comes and plays and everybody comes and dances."

"Oh," she said again. "I was just wondering how it gets cleaned up afterwards, who turns out the lights and everything." *Someone in charge would delegate such tasks*, she thought, *but maybe such tangible details were all anyone else noticed.*

"Oh, well, if you want to help clean up, just stick around at the end. Some others'll stick around to help you. We don't make much mess. I guess it's like at home, last one out hits the light switch."

"And locks the door, I suppose."

"Sure."

Sophia tried to think of what else the person in charge would do.

"What if there were a fight or a medical emergency?" she asked.

"A fight!" The man started to laugh but then looked mildly

annoyed. "Everybody's havin' too much fun to fight," he said and turned his gaze toward the dance floor. When Sophia continued looking at him, expecting an answer, he leaned to the side and pointed around her hip to a tall man with a crew cut and a nose like an eagle's beak. The man was spinning around the floor with a woman half his height. "That's Ed Snowfield," the man at the table said. "He's a sheriff's deputy, and I reckon if there's a problem he'll take care of it. He knows CPR, too." He softened and asked jovially, "You give up on cleanin' and now you're goin' to start a fight?"

She laughed. "No, no, of course not." As she moved back to the dance floor Gale appeared and grabbed her arm.

"You're not dancing much," she teased. "It doesn't count as a workout unless you actually move."

Sophia let herself be pulled. "I just don't understand it, Gale. Nobody has a clue how this is put together."

"Sophia," Gail said impatiently. "Look around. We're in the *high school gymnasium*. Why don't you ask the principal? Now dance."

In the daytime the high school looked like every other high school in rural America: a campus of low-slung red brick buildings, snaked through by parking lots and bus lanes, backed by a football field surrounded by a pea gravel track. The visitor parking spaces were marked near the main door. Even though Sophia hadn't attended such a school, walking up the concrete sidewalk gave her flashbacks. The architecture of education was consistent in the rows and rows of classrooms that trailed off the entrance, either horizontally or vertically, in the unadorned metal poles supporting the portico at the entry, in the echoing linoleum-floored hallways that greeted her when she opened the front door. In the way the office was never obvious inside. She had to stand there, a new kid on the first day of school, wondering which way to go, expecting a threat in some form, either from bullies or school personnel with questions about why she was here. She had no choice but to wander a bit, until her unfamiliar face triggered someone to investigate.

But no curious personnel appeared. She continued along a cinder block hallway until she finally came to a glass-paneled door, through which she could see a woman at a computer. She opened the door and walked partway inside.

"Hello?" she said in her most professional voice. "I'm looking for the principal."

The woman at the computer looked up. "I'll try to find him for you." She went behind a room divider and made a phone call that Sophia couldn't hear. She came out and said, "He'll be here soon." There were neither extra chairs nor a coffeemaker in the room, so she didn't offer Sophia either. Sophia stood awkwardly near the door, her purse hanging from her hands clasped together in front of her.

In a few minutes she heard slow steady footsteps coming down the hall, and soon a man opened the door and entered. In his late fifties, he looked like an ex-athlete who continued to run, or maybe swim. He moved gracefully but not fast, and looked at home in his suit with a tie in the same color scheme that Sophia had seen on the sign when she entered the school. He examined Sophia for a moment and said, "I'm very sorry, ma'am, I don't recognize you. Are you one of my parents?"

The question boggled Sophia until she realized what he meant. "Oh, no," she jumped in to say. "I don't have any children in the school system. But I live in the community and I have a concern, or maybe an opportunity, for the school."

Parents looking for the principal rarely made the trip to the school to express their overwhelming satisfaction with school programs. Non-parents were usually salespeople. The principal kept a pleasant face and suggested they go to his office to talk. He led Sophia out a different door, around a corner, and through another glass-paneled door. Here the school secretary sat behind her desk and computer, as she had for twenty-two years, creating reports and guarding a first aid kit. As they walked past her desk, the principal reached out and briefly touched a small statue of a Spartan warrior, the school mascot, on the desk. The secretary observed the brief touch and interpreted its double meaning as always. The principal was asking for strength, and requesting that the secretary interrupt the meeting soon.

Before they were seated, the principal introduced himself and Sophia did the same. "So how can I help you?" he asked. He hadn't forgotten that she "had a concern," but he wanted to lead the conversation to a definable task that he could complete or not complete, and keep this short. He gestured to the chair facing the desk.

"I've been coming to the Thursday night dances," Sophia began as she sat down, "and they're just wonderful. I wanted to speak to whoever organizes them, but no one knows who it is." The guest chair gave her a view of the wall behind the principal. It was plastered with certificates, but she realized they were all black-and-white copies, and they all had different names on them. They were students' certificates, for spelling bees and math contests and quiz bowls, and some of the dates on them were almost thirty years old.

"I'm glad to hear you're enjoying yourself," the principal said from his chair. "Of course that's not formally a school program. We just let the community use the space."

Sophia nodded. "That's what I understand. Do you know if the band has a manager, or someone that kind of runs things?"

"Well, you know what they say about musicians," he smiled conspiratorily. "I don't think they like too many rules or regulations.

One or the other of them calls me if there's something they need, or something I need to know."

"Hmm," said Sophia. She did not want to be too aggressive, but no one seemed to take any of this very seriously, an informal horde of people stomping around a high school gymnasium at night with no one in charge. "I guess I was thinking that since it happens on school grounds, that you'd be the ultimate person in charge of it."

The principal laughed. "Oh no, not at all. I'm not much of a dancer, I hardly even go. I stop by once in a while. Most of those boys in the band, and the dancers, went to this school, so I know them. I like to catch up on what people have been doing since high school. But I'm certainly not in charge."

Sophia decided it was time to push a little. "Are the dances covered by the school insurance policy? People bring all sorts of homemade refreshments, and you never know if those are safe." She smiled and made an offhand gesture. "I'm sorry, I used to be in the insurance business and these things come to my attention."

The principal was unfazed. "I don't think there's much risk with sodas and homemade cookies. It's not that different from a bake sale, which we still have every so often."

"Is the school board as comfortable with the informal arrangement as you are?" she asked.

The principal lifted his chin a touch and smiled with his lips closed. "Of course they are," he said. "Several of them are regular dancers. I'm sure if they had any issues with what's happening, we'd already know about it."

"What if someone got hurt?"

"People do get hurt from time to time," the principal said as if he were reporting the weather. "But it's usually their own fault. Somebody twists an ankle every once in a while, but that's a risk of dancing. People know that, they don't need to blame anybody for it." A thought occurred. "Did you get hurt?"

"Oh no, nothing like that. I'm just worried about the kids, and the school itself. These dances are such a wonderful expression of mountain culture, I would hate to see them marred by any sort of problem." She looked at him for a moment. "That is my only concern. I do love them, as I said, and I wouldn't want anything to happen to ruin them."

"Well, ma'am, I don't think you need to worry about that. If a problem arose, people would take care of it. They've been dancing together a long time. Part of that same culture you mentioned is looking after each other." He said this in a fatherly, reassuring way, yet it felt to Sophia like a warning.

The principal was wondering why the secretary hadn't knocked on the door yet. He did not like people sniffing around his school talking about insurance and danger. He stood up. "Thank you for your appreciation of the dancing, and for your concerns. I'm sure everything will be just fine." He came around the desk and Sophia recognized her dismissal. She stood, heard one of her knees give a small pop, and was ushered out the door while she was trying to think of something else to say.

Sophia trundled along the concrete walkway again to her vehicle in the visitor space, feeling unsatisfied. The principal might be able to ignore her, but a quick check of the county's website had a school board meeting coming up soon on the calendar. *They* would understand the risk involved. Sophia knew that all it took was one litigious person to turn these happy-go-lucky social events into a storm of lawsuits and blame-throwing. She'd seen it enough times. People were content to go about their lives, jumping on their trampolines and letting their dogs run free, until one day the predictable happened. Her former colleagues had their own version of an old joke: "It's all fun and games until somebody files a claim."

8
The People's Supper

Louise let both Shelley and Analía off of work on Saturday if they promised to go to the church supper. That was a fair trade, so they parked in a grass lot and approached the long row of picnic tables in the yard beside the church.

"Shelley Morgan!" announced a woman with a weatherproof helmet of frizzy gray hair near the first table. "Where have you been?"

Shelley made an appropriately penitent face. "Just busy with school and work, Ms. Brown. This is my friend Analía. She's from Mexico," she said, knowing that should be a sufficient distraction from her own absence at church.

It was. The woman zeroed in on a new face as surely as a cat would follow a toy on a string. "Is that right? Well, now, honey, you can try genuine North Carolina food. That's my casserole right there, I raised those zucchini in my own garden." She pointed at a flat dish with a layer of browned bread crumbs on top. Having advertised her cooking by the dirt it grew in, she handed Analía a paper plate and directed her to the table jammed with mismatched dishes adorned with masking tape name labels. "You just get you a spoonful of everything, see what you like. Don't be shy." She handed Shelley another plate, without instructions. Shelley surveyed the corn, beans, ham, and chicken, looking for her favorite, mashed potatoes.

Across the yard, a group of men stood with their plates, shuffling napkins and plastic silverware from one hand to the other as they chewed.   George pulled at a fried chicken leg with his teeth while nodding along with another man's football commentary.   The commentator watched Analía filling her plate.   He paused in his tale of a fourth down to ask George, "Who's that Mexican?"

George glanced at Analía and raised an eyebrow at the man. He flung the stripped leg bone into the weeds at the edge of the parking lot.   It went a little further than it needed to.   "She just started working for my wife, down at the store.   Louise says she's doing a good job."   The commentator locked eyes with George for a second, and continued his history of a failed kick.

Analía balanced her plate and trailed Shelley through the knots of people, stopping to be hailed with updates on the choir, an apple festival, a canned food drive.

"They have many...projects?" Analía said, unsure of the word.

"Oh, yeah."   Shelley led her to the lawn chairs set on a bed of needles under a tall pine tree.   "Louise spends all her free time at church activities.   Nobody goes hungry or bored if Louise knows about it."   They occupied themselves with managing cups and plates and no table.

"You were supposed to wait for me," Ricky complained to Shelley when he got there.   "The food's half gone."

"Please," Shelley shrugged.   "They'll have leftovers 'til Tuesday."   Ricky sat down next to her and leaned forward over his plate.   She saw him glance at Analía several times.   She could feel him trying to choose from the conversation starters he would have thought of in the truck on the way over -- most likely music or hunting.   He surprised her.

"So what do you see different between here and Mexico?" he asked Analía.   Shelley didn't even hear the answer; she stared at

Ricky. She got up and went to get more food.

When no one could eat any more, Ricky devoted himself to impressing Analía with his performance in a pick-up football game starring church members from the senior choir all the way down to the kindergarten bible study group. He tackled the bible students by hoisting them off the ground and tickling them until they screamed. Everyone lost track of the score.

Analía allowed herself an occasional glance at Ricky while she explained the differences between football and *futbol* to Shelley.

"Wait, you play a whole game and if no one scores, you just quit?" Shelley marveled. "Both teams just say, 'oh well' and go home?"

"Unless it is a championship. It is very hard to get a goal." Sometimes there was a robotic touch to Analía's English, as she pronounced each word carefully, which separated the words from their context and lent them a foreboding tone.

"And players can't go in and out?"

"Can go out but if they leave, finished."

"Let me get this right. Once there's a substitution, that first player is not allowed back in that game? Just that game, right?"

"Of course."

"So you might have to just run and run the whole time?" Analía nodded. "And there's no stopping the clock?"

Analía shook her head. "They rest at half. Fifteen minutes." She waved at Ricky, who was cheering for the organist, who had achieved a touchdown by ignoring the choir director's touch-tag.

"They do all that running around and nobody wins or loses?"

"Is what happens sometimes."

Everyone says Mexicans work hard, thought Shelley. *I guess if their idea of fun is running their asses off for ninety minutes for nothing, no wonder they'll work so hard for money.* She felt a little lazy for complaining about work and school. They watched the football game until it was too dark to see, then helped clean up the tables. Shelley dropped Analía back at her motel, and drove off worrying about the expense of Analía staying in a motel all these nights.

9
Good Medicine

A small metal bell on the door jingled as they entered.

"I've never even been in here," Shelley said.

"No? You never are sick?" asked Analía.

"Aw, it's not that. There aren't too many of these little pharmacies left," said Shelley. "I guess everyone goes to WalMart or CVS now. This place is so cute and old-fashioned. I bet Sue's been here." The wooden floors creaked under their steps. Bright red tape on the floor and a handmade sign warned them to Watch Your Step as they navigated a change in the floor height.

"There it is, in the back," said Analía. Next to the pharmacy counter was a gold and black Western Union sign. They moved through the aisles and Shelley noticed that the products on the shelves actually carried price stickers.

"What can I do for you?" asked the man at the Western Union counter, who wore a pharmacist's coat.

Analía and Shelley looked at each other. Shelley moved closer to the counter.

"We need your help, but it's probably against the rules," she started.

"Well, at least you're honest," the man smiled. "What is it that you need?"

Shelley gestured toward Analía. "Her brother used to come

here all the time to send money to Mexico," she explained. "Now she can't find him. He's just gone. We don't know if something happened to him. We're trying to find out if you have any addresses for him, or anything else that could help us. He used to come here every single week for three years."

"Every single week for three years? Sounds like a good customer."

"That's right. And now something might have happened to him. You should help us."

"I don't know if I'll be able to tell you anything, you know. What was his name?" Shelley told him.

"Jaime Cuevas Alvarado? You know, I do remember him. He was in here every single Saturday morning for a long time." The man shook his head. "I'm sorry to hear he's disappeared. He seemed like a nice kid." Analía blanched at the word disappeared. She had explained to Shelley that that was a meaningful word in Latin America, it meant "disappeared on purpose by someone, probably dead." Shelley had insisted that it was more innocuous here, but Analía still reacted every time someone chose that particular word.

"So can you help us? Can you look in your records and see if you have any addresses, or phone numbers, or anything else to help us track him down?"

The man grimaced. "You know, I'm not supposed to do that. With the money we handle here, we have some of the same laws that banks do."

Shelley nodded but didn't move. They all three stood there for several seconds looking at each other across the counter, the friendliest standoff in history. Shelley had an idea. "How about you look at your paperwork, and we'll tell you the addresses we have for him, and you just tell us if they're the same ones?"

The man didn't answer but he went to a filing cabinet and dug around. He came back with a thick folder and opened it at the counter. "What have you got?"

Analía pulled out the slip of paper from the day at the courthouse and handed it to Shelley. Shelley read the addresses and Analía recited the disconnected phone number that she knew by heart. "Are those the same ones?" asked Shelley.

The man flipped through the folder. "Yeah, we've got those same ones," he confirmed.

Shelley understood an incremental approach to a problem. She asked, "Do you have any different ones?" The man peered at her over the top of the folder.

The phone rang in the pharmacy.

The man looked at Shelley again over the top of the folder, then laid the open folder on the counter and went to answer the phone. Shelley glanced around the store, then reached and turned the folder to face herself and Analía. She grabbed a pen from the counter and scribbled on her hand. She heard the man say "You have a good day now" into the phone and she pushed the folder back to its approximate original spot.

The man returned to the counter, glancing at the folder. "You know, I do remember one day that boy was in here and he said something about working for a timber company. He didn't say which one."

"Did he say anything else? About his job, or anything else?" asked Shelley.

The man thought for a moment, "Can't remember anything else. We just talked about it being dangerous work." The man shrugged. "Sorry I can't be more help."

Shelley graced him with her best smile. "You've helped a lot. Thank you so much."

As they walked away, Analía asked, "What is a timber company?" Shelley explained that timber was trees. Analía nodded thoughtfully. "Do you think he got hurt with the tree company?"

Shelley shook her head. "We need to check with the hospitals. I didn't think of that before." She sighed. "They have privacy rules, too."

When they got outside, Analía turned to Shelley and asked, "What was in the folder?"

"Another phone number. Jackpot!"

Analía wasn't so sure. "Let's try the number," she suggested as they got into the car. A strong breeze was blowing and it slammed her door shut, almost catching her leg. Shelley dialed the number and handed the phone to Analía when someone said, "*¿Bueno?*" Analía spoke for a few moments, but Shelley could tell by her voice that she wasn't getting any good news.

"We'll have more ideas, okay?" Shelley said when Analía hung up. Analía nodded. A few minutes went by.

"You didn't have to give him money?" asked Analía.

"Who? The man at the store?" Analía nodded. "We didn't buy anything...?"

"For helping us when he wasn't supposed to."

Shelley's head pulled back on her shoulders. "You mean *bribe* him? Jesus, no, that's illegal." She shook her head. "He was just trying to help."

10
Return to the Scenes

The next day while Shelley was at the gas station, Analía sat alone on an orange plastic bench in a bus stop half a block from the Western Union. Inside there was a person who had seen Jaime every single week of his time in the U.S., and he had helped for no other reason than that he could. She set her eyes on the sidewalk in front of the door, where Jaime's feet had passed twice a week. She wanted to feel where he had gone from here.

She looked around. A glass shop. A bike store. An interstate interchange. A photography studio. In the blocks behind everything were gently run-down houses, built in a time when each house was considered individually, each shape, style, and layout lovingly envisioned over hand-drawn blueprints by its future owner and his family. The houses looked comfortable to Analía, painted in wild color schemes, each with its own porch bedecked in signs of its current residents' lives – bicycles, guitars, plants in pots, towels or clothes thrown over the railings. How had Jaime chosen this place? It must have been convenient, somehow. These streets carried his footprints, the brick walls along them had echoed his voice, maybe even his laughter. But the asphalt and bricks were silent, offering no clues, no whispers.

Down the block she spotted a sign that read "Llantería Gomez" on a cinder block building. Analía sprang from the bench and marched toward the building, then realized she shouldn't appear too threateningly determined. She dodged grease spots in the parking lot, feeling in her bag for Jaime's photo.

"Buenos dias!" rang out as she entered. "Se descompusó su coche?" *Did your car break down?* Someone had seen her approach on foot. She smiled.

"No, no tengo coche...." she began. *I don't have a car. I am looking for someone...* Soon all the mechanics and the customers on hand gathered around Analía, passing Jaime's photo around with black oil-stained hands as she breathlessly hoped it wouldn't get dropped or damaged. She repeated the story she had repeated in restaurants, she answered the questions she had answered at construction sites. She accepted the sympathies she had accepted in laundrymats. These were Hondurans, not even her countrymen, but they knew about being alone far from home. They told her there was a *tienda,* a store, down the street.

She was walking in the direction they pointed when a pickup truck half a block behind her gunned its motor. The rippling engine noise echoed off the old brick buildings along the street. As the truck passed, its driver leaned out and shouted, "Go home, amigo!"

Analía jumped, but the truck kept moving. "Working on that, *pendejo,*" she said to the rusty Toyota-emblazoned tailgate. Though it was far weaker than at home, the sunlight seemed harsher now. She walked a little faster.

The cashier in the tienda was an older woman, so tiny that she could barely reach all the way across the counter. She listened to Analía's story, looked at the picture, and gestured for her to follow. Analía's heart sped up and she froze for a moment. She followed the woman, static tension in her body, holding her hands together like a child in a store, trying not to knock over the clue that might be about to emerge.

But the woman only went to the food counter on the other

side of the store. She demanded a bowl of soup and a Jarrito from the girl behind the counter, and led Analía to one of the tables in the front. She waved a hand for Analía to sit, and she did. The woman put the soup and the drink in front of Analía and gestured again. Analía thanked her and began to eat. The soup tasted like home.

The woman studied Analía's cloth bag, embroidered with cobalt blue birds and a riot of flowers. "Aguascalientes?" she asked. Analía nodded. To those who could recognize them, the patterns of ribbons, flowers, and other details were as distinct as state flags.

The woman nodded, too. "I did see that boy, from time to time," she said. "Never knew his name. He was a gentleman. He must have lived nearby."

Analía thought he might have simply stopped by on his way to the Western Union. But at least it had to be the closest Western Union to his home. Or his job.

"I know you must be tired," said the woman. "But you are doing the right thing," she said. Analía nodded. "This is a hard job, *mija,*" the woman continued. "You will have to find him by his face, won't you?" She thought a moment. "It's the only way."

"I have American friends helping me," said Analía. "They try everything, the internet and the courthouse, but we never find the right information." She delicately slurped a spoonful of soup. The older woman nodded. Neither of them needed to tell the other what they knew: that Jaime could have been working under a different name, or using a different birthdate. That the police had his correct name when they gave him tickets only meant that he hadn't lost his Mexican ID's. It didn't mean he used them everywhere.

The woman looked at Analía, trying to decide whether to say what came next.

"This is a fairly safe place," she began. "Certain places in the U.S. you hear about people...chasing immigrants, gangs of people, hurting them." She caught Analía's eyes for a moment and looked off across the store. The Toyota tailgate drove away again in Analía's mind. "But here, mostly they just have small fights sometimes, usually over a girl or a job. You know, normal fights. Do you think your brother...?"

Analía shook her head. "I don't think so. Jaime...He was not a coward. But he stayed away from fights. He was...like a smart horse who won't come when his owner is mad. He knew how to hide until things calmed down."

"Maybe that's what he's doing now," said the woman.

"But for nearly a year? I haven't found anyone who is mad at him or knows of any problems he had," lamented Analía.

"You just keep looking," said the woman. "If you plant enough corn, it will rain."

Analía already operated on that theory. Every day that she was free of the convenience store, she felt compelled to make use of the time, even when she had no leads to follow. She remembered that she had told everyone in every Mexican restaurant to look for her at the motel where she had begun her stay in the U.S. The same red-haired man was working the front desk when she returned. He recognized the woman he had watched discreetly for a week.

Analía smiled at the familiar face, one of the strangers that had made her time here a little more comfortable.

"Hey, I haven't seen you around for a while. You find a place to stay?" he asked.

"Yes – well, I got a job, and now I stay with a friend from the job." Shelley had officially been elevated to friend since she had convinced Sue to let Analía stay in the spare room.

"Havin' any luck with your brother?" he asked cheerfully.

She shook her head. "I was wondering if anyone came here

with a message for me?" she asked.

His eyes dropped to the counter. "Sorry." He wanted to have something to tell her, or brilliant advice that would solve her problem and make him her savior. But he had no clue how to find a lost Mexican. Working the front desk in this little pit stop of a motel left plenty of free time for thinking, and the mystery of the beautiful girl with the missing brother had filled a lot of his hours without any meaningful result. And now she had returned, and he had nothing more to offer than the day she left.

"I've thought about your problem," he offered. "I don't have any good ideas," he added mournfully.

If her situation made strangers this sad, thought Analía, it must be truly hopeless. "I came to tell you I have a new phone number, if anyone comes by," she said. She gave him Sue's phone number. He watched her go again.

At Sue's house she went directly to the small guest bedroom where she slept. She sat on the bed and pulled the plastic phone card from her bag. Each report home was another small defeat, another time she had to admit she was getting nowhere. She couldn't ignore the people in Mexico waiting for her to deliver a heroic success. With each call she recounted her efforts, handed over tiny facts that she had learned. Her mother latched onto each detail as if it were another cinder block mortared deftly into a building that would grow inevitably into itself. The family's faith was complete, as hers had been at the outset. She would simply land in America, look for clues, and find Jaime. No doubt was permitted. In the small *colonia* that she had left behind, no one imagined a land full of people so anonymous that one person could be swallowed up.

But Analía had seen it. Traveling on buses had exposed her to homeless people. They ambled through their days with as much free time as people back home, ever ready for a chat, prepared to confront the unexpected with interest and humor. But no one waited for them at the end of the day. Any one of them could drop into a hole in the ground and no one would miss them. It hurt to think of Jaime here in the same way, a sole disconnected individual passing through the world with only the fleeting connections of a phone bill paid, a conversation with a cashier in a *tienda*. How did he ever sleep, she wondered, having no truly safe place, always having to be on alert for himself? She had never conceived of this before coming to America.

That solitude was for her, she knew. That exposure was so he could buy her an education that he would never have for himself. Not long after their father had taken off with another woman, leaving their mother penniless, Jaime vowed that the same would not happen to his sister. She would make her own money, carry a certificate that, while it said she was trained in some mundane field, also meant she would never answer to any man unless she chose to. Just as he had threatened the bullies with sticks on the playground when they were children, he promised to provide her with a stick she could use to defend herself for life.

She blinked and shook her head, focusing on the calling card in her hand. She dialed the 800 number, punched in a passcode, dialed the country code, pressed the special code for a cell phone, ticked off the local phone number. By the time the ringing sound played in her ear, it had already been exhausting.

"*Bueno?*" said her mother's voice. Instantly Analía was back in that concrete building, the walls bleeding off the day's heat while the sounds of evening played outside: neighbors shouting greetings upon arriving from work, children yelling while they played, food sizzling on outdoor stoves. She missed the smells as much as anything. She was a connoisseur of smoke: the bitter odors of people burning green weeds ripped from the yard, any number of food smells, the scent of wood fires in the cool months for a bit of extra heat, even the incenselike fragrance of *palo santo,* the sacred stick, kindled to bless a home or an event.

"*Hola mamí, soy yo,*" she began. She claimed that she was fine, that all was well. She recounted the latest assistance from the Americans who had adopted her cause. Her mother was impressed as always, and confident that Jaime was just around the corner. Señora Alvarado announced that certain saints would bless the helpful Americans. Analía's aunts in the background called out good wishes and optimism, their voices crossing and mingling over the line.

Analía wished she were as sure of her imminent success as everyone in Mexico. Apparently they reasoned that Jaime had effectively defended his mother and sister since he was twelve, therefore it was impossible that he would come to harm as a grown man. They skipped over the detail that it was now *she* who would have to be a hero. Her search drew reinforcement from the strength of the one she searched for. Jaime had never failed them, therefore he would not fail to be located.

11
Committee of Guardians

The building that hosted the school board meetings squatted under a cluster of trees in its parking lot. One level of brick was accented by aluminum-framed windows and a Smokers' Outpost by the door. Sophia left her car by a pole under a flickering light and pasted on a smile as she entered. The feeling in her stomach might have been her old friend, or just nerves. The front door opened into a large meeting room with several metal folding tables clustered in the center to form a larger surface. Nearly all the chairs around the tables were already filled with board members chatting in undertones. Sophia found a seat next to a sturdily built woman in a dark blue suit. She hung her jacket over the chair and sat down.

The woman introduced herself as a community programs director at a local bank. Sophia explained that she was here about the dance program at the high school. The woman looked puzzled, but that was part of Sophia's plan. After her mysterious announcement, she turned and focused on the "Agenda" page on the table in front of her. Out of the corner of her eye she spotted the principal she had met with, who was trying to get her attention, but she kept her eyes on the page. She realized she had made a tactical error with the principal, beginning with concerns about insurance, and she didn't plan to repeat it. This time she would be in full flattery mode.

Sophia listened to committee reports on budgets, sports

funding, graduation rates and college entrance statistics. These last two sounded so much lower than the same numbers she had read in the paper in Boston. Several people in the room looked familiar, and she figured they were from the Thursday night dances.

Eventually the meeting worked its way to New Business, and Sophia waited while a parent protested the candy machines that newly graced the halls of the high school. Then it was her turn.

"Good evening everyone, I'll try not to take too much of your time. I'm Sophia. I'm new to this area but I know several of your faces." She nodded at the dancers. "I see that some of you enjoy the same dances at the high school that I do." One of the dancers couldn't help but acknowledge her with a nod and then looked away.

"The dance program is what brought me here tonight. I enjoy it so much, I'd love to see more done with it."

People glanced around, meeting each other's eyes briefly, then looking uncertainly at Sophia. The Board secretary glanced around the room and leaned forward.

"Well, you know, those dances are not a school program, they just use the space."

The principal found his voice. "Yes, I believe I explained that to you recently," he said.

"Oh, yes, you were very helpful," Sophia gushed. "I certainly don't want to step on any toes. I just think a great opportunity is being wasted. I served on the board of a small art museum where I lived before. I'd love to develop the program, and since the school hosts the events, the school system would naturally want to know what's happening."

"I'm confused," said the principal. "Are you saying you want to promote the band? Have you talked to the band about this?"

"Oh, no, I don't mean promote the band specifically, more the event itself, the way everyone comes together. The zeitgeist. The traditional music itself, it's a piece of culture that isn't widely known."

The bank programs director adjusted herself in her chair. "I think everyone is aware of bluegrass," she said. "Entire record companies…"

"You want to publicize the dances?" asked a man with a grey cowlick, who Sophia was sure she'd seen at the dances. "We've been doing it for years, probably everyone who wants to come already knows about it. Or has been dragged there by his wife." He winked at another board member and a few others laughed.

Sophia wasn't ready to give up. "You know there are foundations that try to preserve traditional cultures, we might be able to get some grant money." She expected that to be a clincher.

"What would we do with the grant money?" asked the bank programs director.

"Oh, I don't know, maybe the band could participate in Appalachian music festivals. Maybe put on exhibitions," suggested Sophia. "We have some great dancers among us." The circle of tables seemed to expand. Sophia had a perception that every body in the room leaned away half an inch in unison. Or did the floor sink a bit into the earth, nestling these people away from attention? They looked away from her, at each other.

The committee reports she had listened to a few minutes ago came back to her. "How about a scholarship fund? Maybe help with the college entrance statistics." She paused, clutching at ideas. "Maybe we could offer workshops, invite corporate leaders to visit here, teach them to dance, get them to donate."

The board members continued to look around at one another. Finally the man who made the joke about being dragged to the dances by wives spoke up again.

"We haven't done too well with corporate leaders coming in," he said. "They like us to build them infrastructure that's expensive to maintain, then they move on to Mexico. We're their last resort in the U.S. for cheap labor."

"But they wouldn't be building factories, just enjoying a visit to a potential place to put their charitable contributions."

"We're not at the top of people's lists for public relations projects," said the bank programs manager.

"You know we have an existing community scholarship fund," said the principal. "You could get involved in fundraising for that." He nodded encouragingly at Sophia. "That would be very helpful."

"Of course, I would love to." Sophia had been in a few meetings before. "How could we tie that to the music?" she asked with energy, turning his redirection back on him. He was silent.

The bank programs manager spoke up again. "I think you should talk to the band about your ideas," she said firmly.

Sophia nodded as if that were the obvious thing to do. "I thought I'd start a little higher up. I'm not sure which of them is in charge, so I came here, since the school system supports them by providing space."

The secretary seized the moment. "And that's really all we do," she declared. "If it's the music you're interested in, you should talk to the musicians." She turned away from Sophia and picked up her agenda. The rest of the Board followed her lead, and Sophia could not find another inroad for the rest of the meeting.

She sat there and didn't think much about whatever the board discussed next. She wanted so badly to have more people see the worth of what happened at the dances. So many different kinds of people came to dance, from so many walks of life, probably of varying political persuasions and even conflicting values, but they all enjoyed each other and were happy together once a week. The dance was a secular church of acceptance and cardio; the sermon given through music had held a community together for generations. Sophia couldn't bear to risk leaving something so beautiful to chance.

The dance was too precious to leave it dependent on nothing more than the continued goodwill of unorganized people.

12
Absentees

The first clue was the empty parking lot. Sophia always tried to arrive early to get a good space, but tonight as she circled to the back of the high school, she faced a vacant gravel expanse. Then she noticed there were no lights on in the gym, and the doors, usually propped open, were shut tight. She checked the clock on the dashboard. Had she missed daylight savings time? Since she'd quit working, she'd once made it to Tuesday before the time change came to her attention, but today was Thursday, and the change was weeks away, anyway.

Her heart jumped as she wondered if the school had canceled the dances after her warnings about the risks. Had she scared off the very thing she wanted to preserve? She hadn't meant to do that, only to get things straightened out and done properly. Could her warnings have caused such an overcorrection? Sophia took herself very seriously and so she imagined others did, too.

She was on the phone with Gale, debating what to do, when an old blue truck rounded the corner of the building. A fluffy-haired woman and a man whose belly exceeded his pants eased out of the truck. They brushed off their clothes and looked around the empty lot. They saw Sophia, and their instinct to greet others kicked in. They spoke a moment between themselves and then set off in her direction together. The woman called out.

"How are you this evening?" She came to about ten feet from Sophia's vehicle and stopped.

"I'm fine. I'm wondering where everybody is," said Sophia. "I'll call you back," she said into the phone and tapped the screen. The woman looked at the closed doors and nodded slightly.

"It's after seven," she said. "I guess somebody canceled the party and forgot to tell us," she said. She took a few more steps in Sophia's direction, the man tagging along behind her. She looked uncomfortable, but addressing the puzzle of the closed doors did require company. "I just don't know where everybody would be."

The man edged up next to her. "Maybe the band is sick," he offered.

She shook her head. "Shelley would have said something. George, can you call someone? See if anybody's heard anything." The man obediently pulled a cell phone from his pocket and poked at it. The woman turned back to Sophia.

"I'm sorry," she said. "I've seen you around but I don't know your name. I'm Louise Dillingham and this is my husband George." George nodded, holding the phone against his face.

Sophia introduced herself and recognition showed in Louise's eyes. She looked at Sophia for a moment before speaking. "You're the one who's on about a scholarship program."

Sophia smiled proudly. "Yes, that's me. But it's not just about scholarships, I want to find ways to promote the whole dance program," she said.

Louise nodded. "That's what I heard. You know it's not an official program, right? Just something we do."

"Of course," said Sophia. "I just want to make it better."

Louise and Sophia stood in the parking lot in silence as the sky grew a bit darker. George put the phone in his pocket and mumbled something close to his wife's ear. She blinked.

"Oh my God, you're right," she said. "That's where everybody is. We are pure idiots for forgetting. Lord, we're not dressed for that. We've got to get over there. Oh, we are going to look like somebody's country cousins." They started to bustle off, but Sophia stepped in their way.

"What's going on?" she asked.

"Oh, honey, there's no dance tonight. The band is playing at a wedding. They'll be back next week, same time as usual!" Louise and her husband scurried back the way they had come before Sophia could say another word.

Sophia stood alone in the empty darkening lot with no one to complain to, at least until she called Gale back. She felt tricked. Everyone who she had danced with for the last several months had known about tonight's schedule. Everyone except herself. Admittedly she had hardly chatted with anyone but Gale until she began working on the scholarship program. Didn't people realize others were affected by their unannounced change in plans? No one had ever mentioned an email list, or even an old-fashioned phone tree. No one would admit to any sort of organization whatsoever. Yet they all knew not to show up one random night. She didn't expect to be invited to the wedding. Who had a wedding on a Thursday? But it proved her right. This was a perfect example of the kind of glitch that happened in these casual situations. This kind of irregularity would never support a scholarship program, or grow to receive any sort of recognition. Sophia got back in her SUV determined to prevent this from happening again.

She had not figured out how to do that by the time her phone rang Saturday morning. She was eating breakfast, at one perfect place setting at her antique farm table, with her good china and a cloth napkin. She placed herself where she had a view into the great room and its walls covered with paintings she had collected over her years at the museum. Canvases of all sizes had taken her weeks to arrange. Every rectangle represented an artist in whom she saw a special gift, or who had shared a singular insight with her, or who had gifted her with a treasured compliment or an inside joke. She had wrapped each one lovingly herself and carted them away from the city to be her stand-ins for the creative sages who had kept her from despair while she withstood doctors and quarterly reports.

Sophia had read somewhere, and believed it, that every day counted and every meal should be honored. With time on her hands, there was no reason not to take care of herself. Order in her home helped avoid the stress that exacerbated her symptoms. Phone interruptions were not in the restful-environment plan, but her annoyance quickly dissipated when the bank programs director announced herself over the line.

"I'm intrigued by this scholarship idea," she said.

"That's wonderful!" interrupted Sophia.

"...perhaps we could talk to the band about a small admission fee, and add that to the scholastic achievement fund." Joanna went on. She explained that the small fund gave merit-based awards to graduating seniors.

"Well, since they're using the school facility, I don't see how they could object," Sophia said. She hesitated. "Wouldn't it be more meaningful if it were its own fund?"

"More meaningful?"

"I'm just thinking that if we are hoping to draw attention to mountain music traditions, wouldn't it give more emphasis if it's a separate fund?"

"Ah, well, perhaps. Of course that involves quite a bit of structure, new bank accounts, and so on. I'm not sure it's necessary to go through all that. We could certainly do a press release to the newspaper announcing that the band and the dancers held a fundraiser and have made such and such contribution to the fund."

"Well, sure, of course," allowed Sophia. "Of course the

dancers are not organized either, I'm not sure *who* we would say held the fundraiser. The Thursday night dancers? Joanna, I don't know how to tell you this, but nobody even showed up last week. It seems there was a wedding, and everyone went there. There was no notice or anything.   I agree with you, this is going to require a lot more structure. Maybe we need to form a committee."

At the other end of the line, Joanna squeezed her eyes shut for a second, seeing an image of her own plate full of fried chicken and pecan pie at the reception in the Jamesons' barn. The usual dancing crowd had barely fit, and some guests ended up dancing on the hard dirt outside the barn door.

Joanna willed herself to smile, the way she always did when she was about to disagree with someone. It warmed her voice so as not to offend as she clarified, "I was saying that I think the amount of structure needed to create a new fund could be inefficient. We might be making a lot of busywork for one event."

"Oh, I hope it isn't just one event," gushed Sophia. "I'd love for it to be an ongoing scholarship, maybe awarded every year. We could hold a publicity event to award the scholarship, and bring attention to the band and the dancers who support it at the award event."

Joanna was silent. "Sophia, have you talked to the band about this? Do they want to do this?"

"Well, I tried," Sophia sounded defensive. "At the dance I kept asking who was in charge, but no one knew. They don't even have a manager. That's how I ended up talking with the school board. But it's about more than the band, it's the way everyone comes together. The band is important, obviously, but it's the whole community that makes the event."

"Then I guess you need to talk to the whole community," said Joanna.

Sophia slumped in her chair in front of her napkin and good

china. "How am I supposed to talk to the whole community?" she asked defensively. She realized that by now she had probably touched every hand in town, twirling her way through stars and rings and posies. But she hardly knew anyone's name. "I can't get a handle on where to start. Should I just put out a coffee can on a table like the man with cancer?" *Willie!* she thought. *I know his name.*

Joanna laughed gently. "That might work better than you think," she said. They said goodbye without committing to anything.

Sophia sat with her coffee and tried to think of an inroad. Getting anything done in this town was like hiking through a briar patch. From a distance the dense mounds appeared green and soft, welcoming. Up close there were no sturdy gates, no massive logs felled across the path, but passage was impossible. Every thrashing push forward was resisted by a thousand tiny tugs from hidden thorns that raked across any exposed sliver of herself. The shallow cuts went unnoticed until she got in a hot shower. But she felt them.

She folded her napkin and brushed a few wrinkles out of the batik-printed tablecloth, wondering what to do with her day. Once the dishes were in the dishwasher, she usually took her assortment of vitamins. She squeezed the last drops of the ginseng extract out of the dropper from the old-fashioned brown bottle, and along with the drops came a purpose for her morning.

She wheeled her SUV into the parking lot of the natural food store, glancing at the outdoor tables populated by people drinking herbal tea and eating crusty granola bars. Behind them, above and beyond the roof of the store, wispy clouds floated past a few low peaks. Sophia paused to absorb the scene: she lived in a vacation brochure photograph. Before she opened the car door, she sent out a prayer of gratefulness to no specific addressee.

Inside the front entrance, apples and mangoes shone up at her from racks designed to look like timeworn barrels, and a line of spouts that looked like frozen drink dispensers offered quinoa and barley. She took a few minutes to roam the store. Perky young people in brown shirts offered assistance, but she declined it. Having dragged herself out of the house, she wanted to stay a little longer among the people and the pomegranates.

Ginseng was on aisle twelve, not far from the aspirin, another ancient cure processed and packaged in sterile bottles. Sophia scanned the prices on the shelves below the various ginseng formulations. There were liquids, pills, powders. She sighed. Each formula recommended a different dosage, each package therefore contained a different number of days' worth of ginseng. Finding the least expensive product was a daunting math problem. And there was quality to consider. She figured that anything that grew all alone out in the woods had to be organic, but only certain packages flaunted that status. She reached for one, then dropped her hand. This would be so much easier if the FDA would manage this for her, certifying the potency and purity of a prescription that she could count on. Then the insurance would cover it, too.

Sophia's budget was in better shape than most people's in this town. When she left her job in Boston, she brought with her a retirement fund and investment accounts that threw off enough income to cover a simple life, the kind she wanted to have here. Her financial advisor had made it clear to her that Boston was impossible without a job, but the lower cost of living in the mountains made the difference between having to work or not. Thankfully she did not have a partner, or children, or even a cat anymore, to support in addition to herself. Doctor bills up north had chewed up funds as they tried to locate the source of the malaise that accompanied her. Quitting those antidepressants when she came to the mountains freed up some money, but she still knew that every expenditure put her a little closer to another stint in cubicleland. The longer she could hang on to what she had, the longer she might be able to enjoy these days of peace.

But it was the ginseng that brought this peace, the ginseng that staved off the heaviness in her body. It wasn't a necessity in the sense of food and shelter, but she did not want to return to the state she was in when she dragged herself to North Carolina. Those days were frightening, when she had to force herself through her days, when she looked in the mirror and saw a woman who rarely smiled or bothered to fix her hair. Sophia was not sure how she got out of that place, therefore she wasn't sure what might put her back there. Ginseng was a lifeline that she was not ready to let go of. She chose a pack of organic capsules and carried them to the front of the store. She could skip the fancy coffee for a few mornings.

The little cardboard package fit into the console between the seats as she drove away. She felt better with it there, the opposite of a worry stone in her pocket. Months ago, a man at her yoga class had suggested ginseng, and at first she dismissed the idea, but she had finally tried it out of desperation. As she had woken up every morning to sunrises over the mountains, it began to make sense to her that the earth might know something the doctors and laboratories didn't. She wondered if maybe her initial attraction to the mountains came from deep inner knowledge of what she needed. Maybe something old and wise in her body had recognized the remedy waiting in the half-lit valleys, even before someone named it for her. Now she had what she needed right here in her plastic cupholder, shrink-wrapped in daily doses.

13
Temptations

Analía and Shelley guarded an empty store on a Tuesday afternoon. Crinkly plastic packages in every shape and color were silent and still on their shelves, waiting to be chosen. The only sounds were the hum from the refrigerators and the alternating squirting of glass cleaner from two bottles as the girls wiped down the front wall of windows, working their way toward each other from opposite ends. They finished the doors side by side and walked behind the counter.

"Boy, we haven't done that in months," said Shelley, taking the squirt bottle from Analía and plunking it with her own and the paper towels on a shelf under the register. "I swear it's several shades brighter in here. Now you can see all the dirt *inside*."

Analía smiled. "Tomorrow."

"Oooh, let's not plan too far ahead," said Shelley. "Don't want to spoil Louise."

"*Oye,* Shelley, I wanted to tell you." Shelley looked alert. "I don't know how to thank you for your help. You are spending a lot of time with me, and probably you want to be together with your own friends."

Shelley glanced away at the shelves before she answered. "Oh, well, I don't have a lot of time to see friends, anyway, between work and school...especially this time of year, Sue keeps a garden and that takes work."

"Do you miss your friends from high school?" Analía asked.

Shelley nodded unconvincingly. "Sure." Analía seemed to be expecting more. "You know how it is, after high school. People leave for college, a few people get married, everybody kind of goes their separate ways. You aren't stuck in the lunchroom together every day any more. If your friends don't start college, too," she shrugged. "It feels different." She was ashamed to tell Analía how conversations with her high school friends had changed. Every time she related events from school, she sounded to herself like she was bragging, and every time her friends spoke, she saw them hold their lives up to a yardstick and try to stretch them another inch.

"The people in your college classes, they are not the same people?"

"Hmm, not many. A lot of them come from other towns, we're the only community college for about an hour in any direction. So I don't know a lot of them. Anyway, they have jobs, too. We don't have a lot of time for hanging out, except family stuff sometimes. I guess Ricky's been my best friend for a while now."

Analía nodded again. That sounded familiar. Between birthdays and baptisms at home, most of her free time was spent in ever-changing clusters of extended family.

Shelley cocked her head. "I guess you're sort of my first college friend," she grinned. "Do you miss being in school?"

"Some. I miss everything. But I know it will be there when I go home. Now I am occupied with understanding this place. What are you studying at college?"

"I'm just starting, so I have to take a little of everything. I'm planning to major in botany," she said offhandedly, as if it didn't matter nearly as much as it did.

"What do you do with that degree?" asked Analía.

Shelley wasn't sure. She didn't know any botanists, the newspaper never had any "help wanted" ads for botanists. None of her family or neighbors had ever mentioned calling the botanist, the way they called the plumber or the large animal veterinarian. They did call in advisers from the Extension Service sometimes, about caterpillars in the apples or spots on the tomato leaves. Generally the answer was "Spray it with such and such." Shelley could not fathom a career telling people which toxic chemical to spray on which plant, roaming the county recommending pesticide bombs day after day. That sounded as dead-end as selling beer at the convenience store. At least beer wasn't poisonous, except in large amounts, and only to the person drinking it.

"I guess I'll figure that out in college," Shelley said. Analía frowned at this vague plan for making a living.

"Why do you like plants?"

"Huh," said Shelley. "No one's asked me that." She poked a button on the cash register, which responded with a ping. "Well...they're everywhere, and they're different everywhere. There are thousands of different ones, and each one has secrets. Some can hurt you, some can help you, some can do both if you treat them different ways, or use different parts. Every single square foot of earth has a slightly different combination. Everybody gets so excited about seeing animals, wanting to protect animals, but where do animals live? Not in the parking deck, not at the gas station. You want to see an animal, you look for the green places. People think plants are boring because they just sit there, but they're the home of all the animals. They used to be the home of the people, too." She surprised herself. "They still are, if people would remember. I guess I like living with the plants, like the animals do. Plants are like...our house, but alive."

"You sound like my grandmother," said Analía.

"She liked plants?"

"She was a *curandera*," said Analía. "She knew how to use plants for medicine."

"Oh," said Shelley. "My grandmother did that some, too. When I had chicken pox or poison ivy she would make this brown stuff and put it on me. It smelled awful." Her grandmother had hinted of other medicines as well. One day when Shelley was in the living room, her grandmother in the kitchen had pounded the counter with her fist and muttered that if her son hadn't taken *so many damned pills*, he could have kept the car on the road *that day*.

Analía asked, "Did it work?"

Shelley shrugged and smiled faintly, dropping the subject of her grandmother. "I guess so, here I am alive and well." She paused. "Plants heal places, too. You know, if you have a forest fire, or you leave a parking lot alone, especially if it's just gravel, after a while, plants come up, like magic out of nowhere. It's not, of course, but it feels like it. You didn't do anything, but here come the weeds. Animals might run through there at night, but if people have ruined a place, and then left it alone, it's the plants that show up and *stay* to turn it back into a liveable place." Analía was listening intently, and Shelley felt a little embarrassed, but she finished the thought. "I guess plants build the world. Or maybe they're like…the housekeepers in a motel. You know, they creep in, you don't see them coming, and they take care of things while you're not looking."

Shelley felt a little sheepish after such a long speech and she needed to turn the attention away from herself. "Hey, what about you? What are you studying?"

"Oh, business administration." Analía smiled.

"What kind of business?"

"Any business. How to control expenses, how to know if you make a profit. I want to work in a business that makes something people need, so I can always have a job."

"Yeah," Shelley agreed, nodding, those prickles of doubt in

the back of her mind again, wondering how a botanist gets a job.

"You owe me one," Shelley said into Ricky's ear as he hugged her when she and Analía arrived during a break in the dancing. Ricky wasn't listening. He could smell Analía from three feet away. She was flowery and complex, with an afternote that simply said "woman." The scent made him think of church, and something he'd never do *in* a church. He was still sorting this out in his head as he performed the now-familiar delicate handshake with Analía. This time she pulled on his hand, leaned in, and made tiny loud kisses on each of his cheeks, which turned as red as the fruit punch someone had brought for the refreshment table.

"Well, you've made him a happy boy," commented Shelley.

"Is not polite here?" asked Analía.

Shelley and Ricky spoke up together, "Oh, yes, it's fine." "It's better than fine," continued Ricky, desperate that she not be scared off this wonderful practice. Analía looked satisfied.

"How long is this break?" Shelley asked Ricky.

"It's almost over. Big crowd tonight." He looked around at the people milling in the gym. "Some woman's here telling everybody she wants to start a scholarship fund for dancing, or something. Maybe you can find out what it's about."

"I never heard of anybody going to college on a dancing scholarship." Shelley mumbled. "I mean, unless it's art school."

Ricky turned back to Analía. He hesitated. "Would you like to dance?" he asked shyly.

"Of course." She leaned toward him. "There's no music," she not-quite-whispered.

He took her hand for a second, as if sealing the deal. "In a minute! I'll tell them to play one where they don't need me. I'll be right back." He rushed off across the wooden floor.

"Never seen him act quite like that," Shelley observed. "I'm going to find out about this scholarship." She waved across the room to Louise and George, who were chatting with another couple, and made her way toward them.

"Hey, Louise, hey George, how's it going?"

"It's nice to get her out of that gas station once in a while," George laughed. The music started up around them, and people surged toward the floor. "Let's sit this one out," said George, and Louise nodded.

"Ricky said that woman is here again talking about a dancing scholarship?" Shelley said.

"I don't think it's a dancing scholarship exactly. Something about wanting to make a scholarship fund out of the dances, I think."

"How is that supposed to work?"

"Not sure, honey. You could ask her, she's around here, she's got on a red shirt with ruffles and black pants." After a few minutes George and Louise went back to dancing, and Shelley watched Ricky and Analía weaving around the floor. As in all the dances, a couple didn't so much dance with each other as spin from partner to partner, so she figured Ricky was going to need another strategy. Pretty soon she saw what it was. After the first song, the drummer announced a couples' dance, and the people on the floor sorted themselves into pairs. Ricky grinned broadly over Analía's shoulder at Shelley. She shook her head at him and started looking around for the woman in the red ruffled shirt.

She found her poised in one of the chairs lined up near the door, sitting sideways on the edge of the seat, talking energetically to a couple seated next to her. Shelley thought the couple owned a burger place downtown, but she wasn't sure. She sat down a few chairs away, trying to look tired and nonchalant. She was spying for Ricky, but also for herself. Her ears had learned to perk up at the word scholarship.

"...it's a way to do something good and a have a good time, too," Sophia was saying.

The man regarded her skeptically but he was trying to be polite. "Well, no doubt we're having a good time," he agreed. "I don't think anybody's thinking about school or money while we're here, is the thing." He paused and glanced around the gym. "'Round here, thinking about money will usually ruin a good time." Just to be sure she understood, he added, "You know, we're usually a little short in that department."

"Sure, of course," conceded Sophia. "Money's a challenge for everyone. That's why it's so important for the young people, who might not have the resources to fulfill their potential. I know the community wants to support its young people."

The woman tightened her lips a little. "Of course we support our young people," she said coolly. "Just about everyone here has young'uns, who might *all* want to go to college someday."

"But what about supporting those with the most potential?" Sophia continued. "Maybe not everyone can go to college...but the community could come together and support those with the most ability."

"So you want to cherry-pick the kids," said the man. "You want the best and brightest, right?"

"Right!" Sophia agreed. She blinked, feeling she had been led astray.

Shelley realized it at the same moment. She herself had been labeled "best and brightest" more than once, and always took the compliment modestly. Now she saw what it meant. It meant grabbing at the few opportunities that existed, and then what happened to the rest of her classmates? They struggled harder to get B's than she did to get A's, but she knew that when every one of them sat down with the guidance counselor, they all had the same dreams of a non-dead-end job and a future where they didn't fall asleep every night worried about paying the bills. In Sophia's plan, a few lucky ones got that. The rest stayed on the tree to rot, exactly like cherries that got left behind because they had a spot, or had been nicked by birds.

The man and the woman rose. "Good luck with your program," the man said as he turned away.

"But it's not *my* program..." Sophia mumbled. "It's for the community..." She looked at her lap and sighed.

Shelley's eyes followed the couple, and she nearly rose as well. But she thought, *what the hell...*

"What kind of scholarship program is it?" she asked.

Sophia saw in front of her a person of an appropriate age to possibly receive a scholarship. She studied her for a moment. "Well, it isn't, yet. But wouldn't it be wonderful if there were funds available so you could go to college?"

"I *am* going to college," offered Shelley.

"Oh, I didn't realize! That's wonderful," Sophia gushed. "Where do you go?"

"Cinderton Tech," Shelley said.

Sophia's face fell slightly. "Oh, the community college," she said. "Well, that's great. Have you thought of transferring to a regular school?"

"The community college isn't regular?" asked Shelley.

"Oh, I didn't mean that," Sophia backtracked. "I just mean, wouldn't you prefer to have a quality education?"

"I thought I was getting one," Shelley said.

"Of course," Sophia gushed. How was it that no matter how hard she tried, she always ended up offending these people? "But wouldn't you like to go to a school with, oh, I don't know, a complete lab with all the latest equipment, and professors who've done groundbreaking research? You'd learn so much more, you'd come out so much further ahead..." she wheedled.

Shelley had looked away during this speech. There it was again, people laying temptation in front of her, never realizing that the glowing descriptions of a promised land only insulted the land where they now stood.

Sophia tried to turn back to her mission. "I know it can be hard for people to pay to go away to college. That's why we want to rally the energy behind these dances to develop a scholarship fund for Appalachian students."

"Rally the energy?" Shelley asked.

"You know, inspire people to give. While they're having such a good time."

"So where's the money come from?"

"Well, from the community."

"Um, what community?"

"*This* community, the dancers."

"The people dancing? You mean, get the people who come out to dance to put up money for scholarships, that's what you're talking about? I thought you had somebody who wanted to put up money." She nearly rose again, but she was starting to feel angry, like someone had dangled a cookie in front of her and then handed her a recipe and told her to go bake her own. "So you want to grab people while they're havin' fun and bug them for money? My cousin Tim does that all the time, to round up cash for beer runs at parties." She rose and strode off.

Sophia was unfazed. "There could be sponsors!" she called after Shelley. Shelley's shoulders dropped and she turned around.

"What?"

"Sponsors. Companies with money could sponsor the dances, and the money could go to a fund..."

"Why would people sponsor something that's already happening?" asked Shelley. She'd heard of fundraising runs, and she knew that car parts companies sponsored Nascar. "There's no money involved here. The guys play for free, people bring snacks, and it's at the school." She spread her hands to show they were empty. "See? No money here." It felt a little traitorous to mention the band's arrangements to this woman.

"But it's an event people enjoy." Sophia coaxed. "It's an opportunity. What happens here has value."

"It's not for sale." Shelley turned and walked away. Sophia watched her cross the room and speak to a young Latina woman. Sophia hoped the conversation was polite.

Shelley and Analía sat on the edge of the stage, kicking their heels against the metal struts that held up the platform, as the band packed up their instruments.

"So did you have fun?" Shelley asked. "What do you think of our dancing?"

"Was very fun," Analía nodded with enthusiasm. "Ricky is a good dancer." Shelley raised her eyebrows. Analía grinned. "Is easy dancing."

"Easy!" Shelley snorted. "Most people don't say that their first day at it. You're a great dancer. I guess everybody in Mexico is a good dancer, right?" Analía shook her head. "I mean, I know, not *everybody*. But you start when you're small, right?"

"Every party has dancing. But it is not a special skill. You just listen to the music."

"Sure," Shelley nodded. She glanced around the empty floor, still seeing the people whirling and stomping. "So what you're saying is, people that are bad dancers, what they have is a listening problem, not a dancing problem?"

Analía started to speak, but Ricky jumped off the stage next to them, his shoes hitting the floor with a slap. He put his guitar case next to Shelley and used both hands to gesture.

"What does a scholarship fund have to do with bluegrass?" he asked. "I mean, don't get me wrong, nobody's against scholarships. Hell, you could use a scholarship, I know, but I don't see the connection. Why would people who just come out to dance and have fun want to pay for a scholarship fund?"

Shelley leaned away slightly. "She said something about companies sponsoring the dances." She swung her feet again to keep things casual.

"Like sponsoring the band?" Ricky pondered. "We haven't never been trying to grow really... And then we'd just give the money to the scholarship fund anyway? Sounds a little...crooked."

"I don't know, I don't understand it either. I told her it was like Tim, you know how he always tries to get the drunkest people to chip in for a beer run? I guess she figures people havin' fun will empty their pockets."

"I don't want to ask people for money," Ricky said. He held up one hand in a "stop" gesture.

"Relax, she can't make you," Shelley waved him off. "Let's go." She slid off the stage.

Analía asked, "What about the people asking for money at the table?"

"That's for sick people," Ricky told her patiently. Out of the corner of her eye Shelley saw him put an arm around Analía's waist. "It don't have anything to do with the music."

14
Morning:
Coffee, God, Advanced Communication

The baptism dresses hanging in the tienda had reminded Analía that there might be a greater source of assistance than even Shelley's energy. And now she knew where the Catholic church was. She announced her plans at dinner on Saturday, over ham and green beans. Sue had stocked up on hot sauce, and accepted it with grace when Analía used it to christen every meal.

"Can I go with you?" Shelley proposed. "I've never been to a Catholic church." Ricky kicked her under the table. Shelley knew he was working on Sunday and would be unable to go. Analía stared at her a moment and agreed to bring her along.

"That reminds me," began Shelley. She turned to Sue. "We need to know if Jaime ever went to the hospital. Doesn't your friend Blanche work at the hospital?"

Sue looked uncomfortable. Tabasco sauce on Virginia ham, and now this. "Well, sure she does, Shelley. But you know they have rules."

"Of course they do," Shelley confirmed. "But we're not asking if he has AIDS. She doesn't have to tell us anything, just let us know if there's a clue where to look for him."

"I don't know, Shelley."

"Just explain it to her. Just tell her he doesn't have any other family here, and he might need help. We don't even care why he was in the hospital. All she has to do is look in the computer, and then she can decide what to tell us." Sue avoided looking at Analía, who was silent during this exchange.

"I'll see what I can do," she said. Shelley held her gaze a few more moments, counting this as an agreement, but not requiring a commitment.

"Okay," she said. "If she's willing to do it, she's going to need to understand about his name. She has to look it up both ways, under Cuevas and Alvarado." Shelley had picked this up watching Analía asking others about Jaime. "I'll write it down for you." Sue sighed, long and slow.

Shelley never got up early unless it was for work or class, but the adventure of Spanish mass helped overcome the fall-chilly air outside the covers. She stumbled toward the scent of coffee and found the kitchen warm and steamy.

"I make Mexican coffee," Analía informed her apologetically.

"What's that?"

"You will see." She paused. "Thank you for coming with me. It is too early to go on a date with Ricky."

"It is way early." She wriggled her shoulders in a lazy version of a morning stretch and tried to open her eyes all the way. "I don't know what you are talking about. You can't have a date in the morning?" She scowled. "Did you and Ricky start dating?"

Analía blushed. "In Mexico if a young man and a young woman show up in church together, it means they are a couple. It is too early for that."

"Oh," said Shelley. It was too early to interrogate Analía, who sounded like she had plans for Ricky. Shelley rubbed her face.

She was not ready to deal with this at this hour. First, it was none of her business. Second, as much as she liked Analía, and loved her cousin, this did not seem like a good match. Wouldn't Analía be leaving after she found her brother? Was Ricky ready for the kind of entanglement Analía might be plotting? Didn't they get married in Mexico at puberty, the way people joked about people in the mountains doing? She took a deep breath and sat down, not looking at Analía.

Analía put a cup on the table and Shelley swigged the powerful black syrup.

"Holy Jesus," she said. She stirred the coffee and the grounds in the bottom swirled to the top. "Did you put the ground coffee right in the cup?"

Analía smiled. "In the pot." She pointed to the saucepot on the stove. "That's how we do it."

"And you just drink it like that?" Shelley sputtered and picked a few coffee grounds from her tongue.

Analía almost laughed. "Yes. But you don't have to drink the coffee powders." She took the cup from Shelley's hand and set it on the table. "Let it—what do you call it? Like be quiet? Sit'll down?"

"Settle down?" said Shelley. "You mean let it settle?"

"I think. Let it sittle down in the bottom, and drink the top."

"But you can't mix the sugar and milk in, it stirs up the grounds," Shelley complained, pausing with the sugar spoon in her hand. She sighed and dosed the dark liquid with double sugar and a couple ounces of milk. She sat with her head in her hands and watched particles spin on the surface of the coffee. "This coffee takes patience," she said with resignation.

"Is good for you," Analía confirmed.

Shelley studied the coffee like a science project. "With the grounds in the bottom, I won't be able to drink all of it."

"Only if you are a real man." Analía bumped her chest with

her fist and Shelley wondered if Analía counted Ricky as a "real man."

"I couldn't find the Catholic church before," commented Analía as they parked the car. "This is the hour for the Spanish mass."

Eleven-foot-high arched wooden doors were propped open to the sunshine, and they joined the line entering. They passed through an alcove into the church proper, covered by a dome that absorbed all the sound from below.

"This is so beautiful," Shelley whispered. Analía entered, but instead of sitting, she looked around and located the priest. She approached him and greeted him in English. He answered in Spanish. They spoke a while. Analía, glowing, turned back to Shelley. "He is going to make an announcement," she said quietly. "We will wait to see if anyone knew Jaime."

The mass began, and when everyone in the pews shifted their butts forward and slid off the seats, Shelley nearly giggled at the ingeniously crafted kneeling pads that dropped down on hinges from the back of the pew in front of her. She had been under the impression that the whole point of kneeling was to feel the pain of lowering oneself before a higher power. *None of that suffering foolishness here,* she thought. *God has blessed us with upholstery.*

She arranged her face into a semblance of piety and focused on the murmuring of the serious petitioning going on around her. Vowels and consonants that had been familiar friends since kindergarten turned on her, bobbing and weaving past her ears, unintelligible. She couldn't tell where one word ended and another began. She glanced over at Analía. Suddenly a few syllables coalesced into "pardon." She latched onto that and found that if she brought Latin plant names into her mind, they drew in other words, orphans adopted from the air.

After one more *señor* and another *espiritu,* the priest gestured in Analía's direction as he spoke, and the entire congregation turned to examine Analía and Shelley, seated in the back. Shelley squirmed while Analía gazed around at people with her usual calm.

They placed themselves near the door, where the exiting crowd would pass right by them. Shelley tried to channel her Girl Scout cookie days, where she looked hopefully at passersby without assaulting them, trying to make them stop without being aggressive.

Many people spoke with Analía, and as usual the conversation was a mystery to Shelley. Analía accepted their good wishes with grace.

"Bless you, and I hope your family can be reunited," said one woman to Analía in Spanish.

"You are a good sister to come so far," said another.

"The Lord will give you the guidance you need," said another.

Analía was polite to every one of them. After each condolence she turned brightly to the next person in line. After a while there was a slight drop in her shoulders after each one, and a smile renewed with effort for the next person. She began to look tired, and the people passing grew more and more attentive, offering more and more nurturing pats. Eventually she hardly smiled at all, but she stayed in her spot until every single person had left the church. To Shelley it looked like a sad, downward-spiraling version of a receiving line at a wedding.

"I am not getting any closer," said Analía on the way home from church.

Shelley squinted out the windshield. To God? To Ricky? But she knew that wasn't what Analía meant.

"You mean about Jaime, right?"

"Of course."

Shelley drove another mile, taking the curves slowly so she could think. "Well, let's see. That's not exactly true. We know he got two tickets, so we found where he *used* to live. We found where he sent the money from. It sure would be helpful to figure out where he worked. Hey, what about his cell phone? They can track people by their cell phones, you know."

"His phone has not worked since right after he stopped sending money."

"But we only need to know where he *used* to go. Tell me that number again."

Caught up in her search with Shelley, Analía had stopped calling Jaime's old phone every morning. The number was no longer pinned in her mind. She pulled her wallet from her bag and unfolded the tiny slip of paper from behind her *matricula*. She read the number to Shelley, who tapped it into her own phone and listened to the recorded message that Analía had heard so many times.

"This is a TMobile number," Shelley said. "Their office is open on Sunday afternoons. Let's go." Analía shrugged.

The office was located in a small plaza between a pizza place and a Chinese restaurant. Shelley parked under the sign with the big pink T.

But Tmobile had a lot of privacy rules. Analía played the desperate family line, she flirted as hard as she could. Shelley angled about customer service, and displayed impressive pushiness. TMobile countered with an assistant manager and then a full manager. Forty-five minutes later it was clear that nothing short of a court order would get them any information about Jaime or his phone. And that order would only come after a missing persons report.

As they crossed the parking lot, Shelley asked Analía again.

"Why don't you want to make a police report? That's the only way we can get more help to look for him."

"No!" Shelley was surprised that the even-keeled Analía could be so forceful. But she knew how to escalate, too.

"Analía! Why are you so afraid of the police? Do you think Jaime was selling drugs or something?"

Analía stopped walking and stood completely still on the asphalt in the sun. "How can you say that?" It was the closest to angry Shelley had ever seen her.

"I'm sorry, Analía, I know he's your brother. I know he's a good person. I just don't understand why we can't go to the police. They have resources that we don't. That's what you *do* when someone's missing. I don't mean anything bad by it, I just don't understand."

Analía shifted the strap of her bag on her shoulder. "Can we just go in the car?" She sounded defeated.

They sat in the car and Analía began speaking again. "I don't know what to say to you, Shelley. I am afraid you will not help me anymore. But there is something I need to tell you. Jaime did not sell drugs."

"Okay, that's good," Shelley said. Then she thought better of it. It might be even worse.

"Remember I told you it took me eight months to get permission to come here?" Shelley nodded. "Well, my brother was not very patient. He tried to get a visa but he couldn't. He just came with a coyote."

Shelley sat behind the wheel without turning on the engine. She knew that there were lots of immigrants in the U.S. who had snuck in without papers. She had vague memories of news stories about it, some with people angrily insisting that they all be sent home, others saying they contributed to the economy. She hadn't thought about it much. One thing she knew for sure, they were great customers at the gas station.

"Do you mean he is illegal?" she asked Analía.

Analía let her eyes roam the parking lot. She hadn't been here long enough, and had been far too busy, to develop a political position about the i-word. But she couldn't see a difference between the people who waited for visas and the ones who didn't, except the ones who didn't were more desperate. "He did not have a visa to come here," she said. "Look, Shelley, it's not that simple," she continued. "I got a visa in eight months, but that doesn't usually happen. I had to lie, okay? I am investigating American business methods." She smirked, an expression she had learned from Shelley.

"What?" Shelley asked.

Analía pursed her lips and half-laughed. "For school. I make a report about the gas store," she said. "How you keep the customers happy, how you arrange the products." She paused. "A gas store is very complex when you write it in business language," she grinned. "Very sophisticated."

Shelley shook her head. "Oh my god, so you've been studying us?" Analía flipped her hands as if to push all that away. "Huh, two birds," said Shelley.

"Two birds?"

"It's a saying, to kill two birds with one stone. It means accomplishing two things at once. Looking for Jaime and getting school credit, at the same time."

"Is the only way," shrugged Analía. "No one would let me come here just to find my brother. They don't care about that."

"That seems mean," Shelley said vaguely. She was still thinking about how Analía in her tranquil way was so sure of her direction that she sidestepped obstacles as gracefully as the dancers steered around each other in the gym.

"Well, if you write about us, you better not use our real names," Shelley said. They both chuckled. "So what does that mean?"

"It means we cannot ask the police to look for him."

"What would they do? Would they put him in jail?"

"For a while. Then they would send him home." In a way it didn't sound so bad to Shelley, since getting him back home was exactly what Analía was trying to accomplish. But she wouldn't want to be responsible for getting one of her family members stuck in jail, either, even "for a while."

"Okay," she said finally. "I guess we're on our own." *Still*, she thought to herself.

"So you will still help me?" asked Analía.

"Of course," said Shelley. "Hey, I told you, my cousins break the law, too, sometimes, hunting. And look at that road there -- everybody out here is speeding. And half of 'em probably aren't even late for anything important." She plugged her phone into the car's speakers. "I guess it's like Ricky trying to pay the bills with illegal 'sang. Sometimes you just can't get by inside the law."

15
Collecting

On her day off, Shelley wound her car around the one-lane curves in Pisgah National Forest, looking for the turnoff to the trail that dipped into a particular valley she knew. She was here on assignment, a field project for class. She thought about Sophia's pitch for "quality" education. When she told people she was a college student, why did some people say, "oh," after she specified *community* college, as if it weren't a real college, as if she didn't work her ass off studying in between customers at the gas station? She did everything those professors asked for, and often more. Wasn't it their job to ask her to do the right things? Wasn't botany botany? Weren't the families and species the same, didn't the chemical reactions happen the same whether you learned them at Harvard or BFE University? Did some schools call themselves the "Ivy League" because *only they* knew certain top-secret facts about photosynthesis? Maybe the education was more powerful because it came from further away, like the ginseng being swapped across the globe.

When she got out of the car in the woods, Shelley knew that the slam of the car door would be the last sound of the man-made world that she would hear for a while. She thought of a jail cell door slamming, locking the rattling, cacophonous gluttony of modernity in the car. She could hit the lock, slam the door, and stroll off into the woods leaving it contained. The thump of the car door was her reset button.

After her parents were gone, she overheard the phrase "alone in the world" a few times when no one thought she was listening. Out here, walking through a crowd of hundred-year-old tree trunks, amid the gossip of squirrels and the work songs of crickets, she was relieved to be alone with the world. She could scrub off the film of pity under droplets of leaf-broken sun. There were no expectations to form herself to: she didn't have to be sad *or* strong. She could be a creature among creatures, navigate by sniffing and hearing, choose a soft spot to rest by the same criteria a deer would.

Google Earth had ruined the woods for her for a while. She had grown up with the wild, at least in her imagination and her neighborhood, being bigger than the inhabited land, a bounty you could never outstrip or fully know. Woods were unpredictable and required a certain combination of fatalism and action. If a forest wasn't big enough to potentially get lost and die, it didn't count as a forest: it was just a nice green neighborhood. *Woods* challenged you and forced you to respect them, to make your own *Hansel and Gretel-*style bread-crumb trail using particular rocks, certain curves in streams, notable trees.

But once you'd seen the land in a satellite photo, you couldn't fool yourself anymore: your unknown quickly bounced up against someone else's known. Rather than being a vast surrounding in which humans huddled together here and there in pods, carefully tending each other, the unknown was now itself surrounded by known, a fugitive finally backed into a corner with SWAT officers on every side. The forest shrank every year as the roads and clearings swept through the valleys and crept up the mountainsides.

There was no place left to lose yourself, unless you were already so lost to begin with that any little green patch would take you outside yourself. Ancient hunters had learned the ways of animals to hunt them; now Shelley needed skill and cunning to *avoid* running into humanity, to stick to the ridges and scope out the corridors.

Still she relied on those shrinking strips of green on Google Earth to have secrets tucked away. Shelley hoped that, like those people who lined their walls with lead to keep out the radio waves, the woods had hunkered down and buried some treasures. She wrangled her way into corners and copses, hoping that somewhere underneath the satellite overseers there might still be an untouched place. Come to think of it, this might be "why botany?" For so long humans had stripped off the earth's coverings without knowing that in this leaf, in this root, were substances that could do more for their health than the hospitals and pharmacies they built on the cleared land. From the mountain bikers who shredded rain-wet trails to the hikers who scrambled along chattering and poking the ground with their unnecessary sticks, sometimes Shelley hated every last one of the people who never stopped to look at a single one of the individual leaves that, one by one, made up the entire place they claimed to love so much.

But none of those people were here today.

She set her backpack, now empty of books, on the hood of the car and rifled through the contents. Cell phone, notebook, a pen, the plant list, chapstick, Diet Coke, and peanuts. She was supposed to photograph each plant and its general location, to prove she'd been there. She knew lots of people in class would just get together and pick someone to take a lot of pictures from different angles, but she wanted to find every plant on her own.

Ten plants, all woodland natives, some with medicinal value, some simply unusual. No trees this time, no bushes, just small specimens that would be sprinkled over the forest floor. A few were gimmes, plants you couldn't miss on any walk in the woods if you knew what you were looking at. Others had to be sleuthed out by knowledge of their likely microhabitats, and the teacher would count any nine of the ten as an A. Her favorite on the list was bloodroot, a white flower named for the bright red latex-like substance in its roots. In the spring it blossomed white flowers about an inch in diameter, but now in the fall its distinctive leaves took more effort to spot.

Shelley ambled down a trail. Her head swung from side to side as she scanned the ground on both sides of the trail. There was little sound except her own soft footsteps and various birds. Squirrels rustled occasionally – they were such fast animals that they had no fear of alerting predators to their presence. Or maybe they just weren't that bright, Shelley thought.

Wild ginger was the easiest, as it grew all over the place and didn't mind being trampled on. She clicked a photo only inches from the path and flamboyantly crossed it off the list. Poison ivy was on this list; the professor was just giving that one away. Anyone who lived in the mountains had better be able to spot poison ivy by the time they were five years old. She crossed that off, too, and continued along, reciting the list to herself.

Ginseng wasn't on the list, but that didn't stop it from poking its five-leaved head above the black and red soil of mingled clay and leaf rot. Shelley noticed several patches, and finally she stopped to examine one that seemed particularly healthy. Several large old plants stood next to 10-inch high specimens, whose leaves shaded smaller sprouts with only one or two sets of leaves.

"You've been here a while," Shelley mumbled to it, or herself. "I guess you like this spot," she concluded, thinking of those families that moved into a holler and then kept adding on to the house when the kids grew up, until five generations lived in a compound. She noticed that the smaller plants had migrated downhill from the older ones, the seeds having been carried by gravity to their adult lives within a snake's-length of where they began. The sudden drumming of a woodpecker over Shelley's head startled her, and she stood up straight, then wandered on through the woods.

One challenge on the list was trailing arbutus. North America had only one species, whose tiny pale pink spring blossoms smelled so lovely that it was illegal to pick them in some places. As with bloodroot, finding the leaves on their vines inches from the ground was harder without the flowers to grab one's eye. But it had only taken one whiff in the spring to cement the plant's particular look in Shelley's mind, and she found it sprawling daintily under a mountain laurel.

She had two plants left when she heard a woman's voice.

"Hey there." Coming upon someone else in the woods was always an unwelcome interruption, and she often sensed they felt the same way.

"Hey," she called out in a noncommittal tone. The woman marched toward her.

"How are you doin'?" the woman asked, and Shelley correctly interpreted it as a polite form of, *What are you doing?*

"I'm good," she answered. "I'm doin' my homework. I'm taking a plant class, and we're supposed to find all these plants in the woods." She waved her notebook in the woman's general direction.

"Huh," said the woman. "Are you lost?" she asked.

"Uh, I don't think so," Shelley said. She knew what this question meant, too. "I started out in Pisgah, but I might've wandered out. Am I on your land?"

"Well, it's my daddy's land," the woman said. "I saw you from the house." She pointed down the hill, to a tiny structure barely visible in the trees. The woman must have spotted Shelley's red fleece, or she would never have seen her from that house.

"Oh wow, there is a house down there. I must've got turned around." Shelley looked around. "This trail comes right through here."

"That's alright, it's my great-granddaddy's trail. It went into Pisgah before it was Pisgah. My daddy still walks around up there about every month."

"Oh. Well, sorry, I can go back that way, I guess."

"Well, you're not hurting anything. It's a pretty day for walking. You findin' all your plants?" The woman looked at Shelley's backpack.

"Most of 'em. I'm not picking anything, I'm just supposed to take pictures and write down what other plants were growing around each plant, whether it was in the shade, if the ground was wet, stuff like that."

"Boy, they didn't make me do anything like that in school," the woman said.

"This is for a class at Cinderton Tech," Shelley said.

"Oh? Well, good for you, honey," the woman said. She paused for a moment, then pointed further down the trail. "You just keep at it, then. There's wet spots down that way, I see Jack-in-the-Pulpits down there. You'll come to a gate if you go far enough. Make sure that gate stays closed, okay? We've got a few cattle in here."

"Oh yeah, absolutely. Thank you," Shelley smiled broadly. The woman set off back down the hill. *Finally*, Shelley thought as she moved down the trail, *someone who appreciates community college.*

On Thursday Shelley zipped along Willard Stuart Road, the back way to Sue's house from the gas station. She looked over at Analía in the passenger seat, and thought about her conversation with Sue earlier that day while Analía was still at the store.

"Blanche couldn't find anything about that girl's brother," Sue reported, shaking her head.

"Did she try all the versions of his name?" Shelley nitpicked.

"Ye-es, Shelley." Sue's tone was mildly corrective. "Isn't that good news?" she asked.

Shelley wrinkled her brow. "I guess so," she said. "Although it doesn't help us find him."

Sue looked like she knew something she wasn't saying. "I have to admit, Shelley, this seems like a wild goose chase to me," Sue said gently. "He's been gone a pretty good while, right? Don't you think he would have contacted somebody if he wanted to?" She didn't say, *if he could.*

Shelley sighed. "Well, kind of," she said. "But she needs to know."

Sue grimaced. "Look, Shelley, he's what – eighteen, nineteen? That's young. Maybe he just got sick of having to support everybody. Maybe he decided he liked the American lifestyle and he wanted to spend that money on himself. You know, it's all new to him."

Shelley glared at her. "After three years? No kind of person who sends money home every week for three years is going to just walk away one day. Just 'cause he's in America doesn't mean he forgot where he came from."

"I know, Shelley, I know." Sue felt rebuked. "Maybe I'm just frustrated, too. That girl calls home every few days, and I can hear her crying afterward sometimes. She's a nice girl, and I don't see why she has to be responsible for fixing this all by herself."

"How do you know he's not somewhere crying over her? And she's not by herself, me and Ricky are helping."

"I just want to make sure you're not getting distracted from the things you need to be doing for yourself. Have you even touched your college application?" Sue didn't wait for answer, just sighed and turned back to the sink. Shelley had put her hands on her hips, found nothing ready to say, and left to pick up Analía for the dance.

Now she had to explain this to Analía.

"So, Analía, my aunt said that her friend at the hospital

couldn't find Jaime in their system." She tried Sue's angle. "That's good news, right?"

Analía was quiet. "It's good he didn't get hurt or anything," she allowed. She sighed loudly. "Unless he had a fake ID for work and something happened to him under the other name."

"Christ," said Shelley. If a person died in the hospital under a fake name, no one would have a clue. They probably didn't take pictures of people who died. Suddenly finding Jaime seemed more impossible than ever. She felt childish for thinking that she and Analía could do this. Shelley wondered again if going to the police was their only hope, but she also wondered how hard the police would look.

Analía thought of the stories she heard in Mexico about people getting lost in the desert at the border, or bodies being found that could never be identified. Matching missing people to found bodies was a gruesome puzzle that often left police and families with permanently unanswered questions. Who knew the same thing could happen *after* they were safely on this side?

That night the whining fiddle melodies rang through the trees all the way beyond the pea gravel track. The band ripped through piece after piece of fast-tempo music almost without pausing. Every heartbeat in the gymnasium was elevated, every smile glistened through sweat. "I think they're trying to kill us old timers," one gray-haired man joked to the thirty-something woman he was pivoting backwards around. He wiped his face on his sleeve, unable to access his handkerchief and keep his hands connected to his partner.

Finally the band called a break. Ricky laid his guitar down and hopped off the stage. As he headed toward the drink table, the high school principal slid in alongside him and dropped an arm over his shoulder. Ricky smiled and held out a hand. They shook warmly.

"How's it been going?" the principal asked. "Kind of miss you around the school."

"Not too bad, I'm working at O'Hare Plumbing," Ricky said. "You keepin' the kids in line?"

"I try." The principal grinned. "Heard you got in some trouble over ginseng," he said in a fatherly way.

Ricky shrugged. "Yeah, you know, just tryin' to keep up with the bills. We can't always get a permit in the lottery, even if me and Tim and Shelley and Sue all put in for it. And then I gotta get off work when the season hits, same time as everybody else is tryin' to get off work." This long after graduation, he still felt an urge to defend his misbehavior to this man. Ginseng hunting permits were so desirable that the Wildlife Commission had resorted to random selection to hand out permits, which caused whole families to make applications, even people who wouldn't recognize ginseng if it colonized their flowerbed. If they drew a permit, these unenlightened recipients were viewed with a mix of envy for their luck and disgust that such luck had befallen the unprepared. Their only hope to redeem themselves was to share the permit by taking someone with them and splitting the earnings. They would be accompanied into the woods by a less-lucky but more knowledgeable brother or cousin, who would point out plants and supervise their extraction.

The principal nodded.

"You remember my cousin Shelley?" Ricky said. "She's going to the community college. They say it's cheap for college, but it's still a lot of money."

"I heard she was attending there. Shelley was always a fireball, and smart. She'll go a long way if she sticks to it."

Ricky was quiet for a few steps. "I reckon that's exactly what she's afraid of, goin' a long way. She's thinkin' about transferrin' to State, but she don't wanna leave home." He glanced into the principal's eyes and looked away. "I think she's afraid she won't never come back." He grimaced. "I worry about that, too."

The principal nodded again, several times. "Shelley always seemed to know what she was about." His eyes roamed over the dancers for a moment, leaving a polite pause. "It's none of my business, but you might have to let her make up her own mind."

"She can't, Mr. Williams." It came out with such urgency that the principal's gaze jumped back to Ricky. "I mean, she knows what she wants, but she can't figure out how to get it, or if it's gettable." He cleared his throat and looked at the ground. "I don't know what to think, seeing her like that. Shelley was always smarter than me, and stubborn, too, and I always figured she'd just keep right on going to whatever she wanted, you know, like it was easy for her. Nothin' ever stopped her before, she was a little bit of my hero. She had somethin' I don't. But now she's...stalled out. If Shelley don't know what to do next, I sure as hell don't." He inhaled sharply. "Sorry, man, didn't mean to drag down the party. You want to get a drink?"

"Sure, sure." They walked on toward the hallway. After a few minutes the principal said, "I think you can trust Shelley. Give her time." Ricky nodded as if this was good advice, but he wondered, *Time to...leave?* Shelley felt more like a sister than a cousin, and he guessed it would be wrong to want to keep her hanging around here. Women took a lot of sacrifice, no matter how they were related to you.

Mr. Williams paused to let the subject fade. The he asked, "Have you met this woman who's wanting to start a scholarship fund?" Ricky pulled back a bit, but he had an old habit of respecting this man.

"Yeah, she's all up in arms about it."

"She's been coming to school board meetings, wanting to 'promote' the band, all kinds of ideas. We can't get rid of her."

"I know the feelin'," said Ricky. "She's got all sorts of ideas involving the band, but I don't think she's ever talked to any of us. I keep hearin' about her from different people."

"Yeah," allowed the principal. "Her style can wear you down, it's like getting pecked to death by chickens. I hate to do this to you," he said. "But do you think maybe we could do a scholarship night, just to get her out of our hair?"

"I don't know. What do you mean, a scholarship night?"

"Nothing too complicated. Maybe just put out collection bowls, maybe the band could ask people to contribute?"

"I'll have to ask," Ricky stalled. "It's not just up to me."

"Of course, of course, Ricky. I don't want you all to be uncomfortable. Maybe you could just ask the rest of the band to help us get this woman settled down so she can move on to something else."

"I'll let you know," Ricky said as they picked up cups of lemonade.

"I appreciate it, Ricky," said the principal, and he moved on to another part of the crowd.

Ricky carried his lemonade out to the parking lot, where he poked around in his truck as if he were looking for a spare pick. He stood behind the open driver's side door and looked up at clouds glowing in the sky, the varying densities of vapor backlit by the moon behind them. An image came to him of himself and Tim tearing out the poison ivy vines along the back fence every summer. They would each put on a couple layers of old clothes that they could throw away afterward, and go to the fence with several big garbage bags. You couldn't compost poison ivy; it would grow right up in the compost pile. They would tear out every scrap of leaf and vine that they could, careful never to scratch an eye or ear while working.

Afterward they would undress on the porch, topping the last garbage bag with their tainted clothes. They would shower and drop into the porch chairs, feeling a good day's work was done. Knowing they would have to make the same battle again the next year, and every year after that. The ivy's roots would never let go; they would never stop trying to greedily suck what they needed from the ground. They would wind themselves in deeper and deeper to steal the nourishment from the other plants. Every spring the ivy would stretch out its leaves again at the first hint of warmth, soaking up the sunlight before it could reach the more delicate plants. Left alone, it could take down mature trees in only a few years. The only way to manage poison ivy was vigilance and stubbornness. It could never be defeated, only beaten back from time to time. All summer they watched it grow, knowing the next skirmish was just around the corner.

After the dancers left the gym, the fiddle player propped the side door open and lit a cigarette. He enjoyed the idea of smoking in school, although he also brought one of the fans stored in the corner of the gym and turned it on facing the door to blow the smoke out. He grinned at Jack the drummer and started disassembling the amp system.

Ricky sighed to himself and asked, "Have y'all heard about that woman with the idea about scholarships?"

The fiddle player nodded and spoke through the cigarette tucked in one corner of his mouth. "Yeah," he said. "I heard she's all excited about our music, but I don't see what one's got to do with the other."

"Well, I reckon she does," Ricky said. "See, her idea is to try to collect scholarship money at the dances," he began.

"So why don't she just ask people for money?" said Jack offhandedly as he hoisted three instrument cases at once. "Why's she keep talking about it, why don't she just do it?" He shrugged.

"Well," Ricky drew out the word. "I guess she wants it to be more official." He looked around at the skeptical band members. "See, Mr. Williams came by tonight and asked if we could kind of make a fuss about it, you know, a special event." Consternation showed on their faces. Like Ricky, they had spent their high school years being mildly, respectfully afraid of Mr. Williams, wanting to be on his good side but wary of him finding out everything they were up to at school. He'd always been fair when he caught them at the kind of extracurricular activities that weren't photographed for the yearbook, therefore they listened to him most of the time.

"What's that mean, exactly?" asked Jack.

"I don't know," Ricky admitted. "But, you know, the money would go to kids from our school, so that'd be a good thing. It could be our way of paying the school back."

"Payin' it back for what?" The fiddle player looked indignant.

"Teachin' your ass to read and write," quipped Jack. "I don't know if you ever got the math part."

"Very funny." The fiddle player rolled his eyes. "Whatever. If y'all want to do it, it's all right with me."

Ricky scanned the other members' faces. Consensus was reached by a combination of shrugs and eyes dropping to the floor. "It's just one night, no big deal," he said. After a pause, he finished, "I'll tell Mr. Williams it's okay."

16
So Close

Saturday morning, Sophia's phone brought good news again. That woman from the bank might actually share her commitment to the needs of the students, although Joanne had been clear that Sophia would be "allowed" to hold a scholarship night for one week, and that no one could be required to contribute. Sophia was appropriately grateful and hung up the phone.

"They act like they're giving *me* this great opportunity, when it's the other way around," she muttered to herself, shaking her head. But never mind. She was in. With very little time to prepare – her permission was for this week's dance, a few days away. The rapid turn-around hinted at sabotage, but she wouldn't expect these people to plan that far ahead. She would need Gale's help.

Her resentment faded as she began to plan how to pull in donations at the dance. As she strategized ways to sell the idea of children fulfilling their potential, she began to feel as if she was accomplishing something. She *did* feel grateful for the chance to apply her old skills. The weakness and apathy of her first months here had left her feeling useless, and now she had a way to combat that. Sending multiple children to college would be a sort of legacy, she thought. Every dollar she could raise for scholarships would be her own little push forward for progress.

All that pushing would take energy. A flutter of nausea

appeared just from imagining it. She still wasn't quite satisfied with that other source of vitality in her life, her ginseng supply. If the processed pills and capsules had changed her life this much, the real thing might create even more wellbeing. Maybe she could go all-natural without relying on a manufacturer, she thought to herself.

After she designed posters for the scholarship fundraiser, she printed herself a map of the local farmers' markets. No point in paying for someone to process and bottle it, when the websites all said you could just eat a little piece every morning. No extra chemicals, no questionable sources. No middlemen, just a personal relationship with someone whose livelihood depended directly on customers such as herself. An authentic relationship, unmitigated by wholesalers and marketing agencies. The kind of relationship she wanted with these mountains that were the source of her healing.

Her first stop was in the lower parking lot of the Chamber of Commerce. The farmers' makeshift wooden stalls stood almost in the shadow of the three-story glass-and-brick Chamber building. It made her think of a homeless man selling oranges in front of a Walmart. Or else the farmers persisted in their age-old ways in spite of the corporate box braced against the highway. Or maybe the whole scene demonstrated an inclusive approach, with each approach to business counterbalancing the other. Sophia couldn't make up her mind what to think: the poor farmers holding out against modernity were romantic, but the juxtaposition of two forms of capitalism was fetchingly diverse.

Whatever it was, no one had any ginseng. "Too early," said one vendor, his gruff tone matching his bristly gray mustache. She was about to ask if she should come back later when he clarified, "Most people dig it in the fall, then it has to dry."

Of course. She had read that. She cruised the rest of the stalls. The produce selection was less exotic than at the EarthGoods store, and less polished. She reminded herself, *this is all locally grown;*

it's only what's in season here. Shopping here would still require a trip to the other store to create a full meal, unless she got creative.

In the last stall of the fifth farmers' market, she passed a handsome young man standing behind a rack of tomatoes and strawberries, placed in a checkerboard of alternating bins so that their tonal reds and different size fruits reminded her of the patchwork quilts hung on the walls of the school gymnasium.

"So artful!" she exclaimed.

He smiled. "Delicious, too. How many pounds would you like?" She smiled back, wanting to reward the skill behind this presentation.

"I suppose I can use a basket of tomatoes," she said. He lifted one and tucked it into a paper bag, leaving a hole in the pattern. He handed Sophia the bag while deftly drawing another basket from behind the rack. The basket went into the hole, and the quiltwork was restored as if nothing had happened.

"Four dollars," he requested.

She paid him and started to walk away with her bag when she spotted sad-looking roots in a box on the ground. Afraid to hope, she asked, "Is that ginger?"

"Oh no, that's ginseng," he said. "Four dollars an ounce or fifty dollars a pound." He replaced a sign that had fallen off the box.

This was a remarkable price, therefore Sophia was skeptical. "I thought it was hard to find at this time of year," she commented, now an expert.

"Well, you can find it if you know what you're looking for," he shrugged. "But we can always find ours," he grinned. "That's grown 'sang."

"It's what?" Sophia asked.

"It's grown," he repeated.

"Do you mean it's fully grown?" she asked. "I know you're not supposed to harvest it when it's small. Is that what you mean?"

The young man grinned. "No ma'am, I mean we planted it. In a garden? That's why it's cheaper."

"You grew it yourself from seeds?" Sophia asked.

"For six years," he confirmed with a slow nod that conveyed the patience involved.

"And that makes it *cheaper*?" Sophia was mystified. Any product that took that kind of work cost *more* in the real world. These people's sense of business was truly backward.

The young man was not about to denigrate his product to a potential customer. "It's great ginseng, one hundred percent organic," he explained. "It's dried slow in a smoke shed, the way you dry tobacco?" He flinched to himself, concerned that mentioning the evil plant that previously supported generations of Carolinians might ruin his sales pitch. "You ever take it?"

"Oh, yes," said Sophia. "Every day. That is a very good price," she admitted.

"How much would you like?" the young man repeated.

She smiled at him. "Well, I've got plenty right now," she said. "But I'll remember you."

The young man watched her go off with her bag of tomatoes and remembered the temptation he felt every time he set up his stall. He often considered making a new sign and leaving off the word "grown," knowing that at this market frequented by tourists he could triple his price on the ginseng. But he also knew the other farmers would talk about him behind his back and stop helping him load and unload. Passing off farmed ginseng for wild was a serious breach.

Ginseng's mystique came partly from the fact that the roots often grew with a main trunk and offshoots to the sides. At proper harvesting age, it might have formed four offshoots, two upper and two lower, making it look like a small headless human form. Or a body with the stem and leaves sprouting from where the head would be. On a naked plant, out of the dirt, the proliferation of greenery looked like ideas sprouting, like a human whose imagination was blooming out of proportion. The oversized spirit of the plant blossomed far beyond the body trapped in the dirt.

Traditional botanical medicine held that curative plants resembled the problem or the part of the body that they would heal. Thus the entire human body represented in ginseng suggested that it was a panacea that would support all functions of the body, a tonic to provide overall strength and resilience.

Efforts to cultivate ginseng were mixed in both method and result, and applied a blend of mythology and farm science. Ginseng plants would wilt in full sun, preferring to develop their magic half-concealed under the protective arms of deciduous hardwoods. They tucked themselves into the cooler north sides of ridges, often near streams, where the water trilled past the plants unfazed by its own symbolic baggage of cleanliness, fertility, and the preciousness of the unrepeatable moment in the hurtling passage of time.

Damp and shade exposed ginseng to another threat, a fungus similar to tomato blight. Just as a soft couch and the gentle blue light of a television could lure a person into an immobilizing depression, the moist dirt and the filtered light of the forest floor could create the conditions for floating spores to settle in and suck the life from the ginseng leaves. Cultivating the plants required finding the sweet spot between sunburned and moldy.

After all that work, if the grower was successful in producing a few pounds of dried roots, cultivated ginseng was not as valued as wild. People who had taken ginseng for years were snobbish about it, refusing to drop good money on "grown" ginseng. Sellers and buyers at the market spoke of wild ginseng the way other people spoke of German cars, French wine, Italian shoes. It was indisputably better, an entire universe of quality contained in a single word: wild.

No lengthier explanation existed. Plenty of scientists had deconstructed both wild and cultivated ginseng and listed every single chemical component. Differences had been found, variations in the amounts and proportions of ginsenosides, the active ingredients, similar to the way certain strains of broccoli have more iron, or certain strains of carrots more vitamin A. But ginsenosides came in several forms, which behaved differently in different studies, and refused to be linked cleanly to specific biological effects. They played hide-and-seek with the test tubes and blood studies, operating sometimes like steroids, sometimes like antioxidants.

There were other explanations for the difference. Cultivated roots, not fighting for nutrients, hardly ever shot off the side roots that made them look like tiny people. Thus their carrot-like shapes, pointy torsos with no limbs, could not suggest their healing properties to humans. Wild ginseng, not coddled with precise watering schedules and maybe even fertilizer, grew more slowly. According to some, it therefore drew into itself more healing power from the earth over the longer time period.

If the young farmer had put out his misleading sign, buyers in the know would have seen right through him. But Sophia left the market still in awe that spending years to cultivate a product could make it *less* valuable.

17
Scholarship Night

"FOR THE SCHOLARSHIP FUND" read a hand-lettered sign that someone had put on the table. The sloppiness of it annoyed Sophia the minute she walked into the gym. "We're not collecting for the latest sick neighbor," she mumbled to herself. Thank goodness Gale lent her a tablecloth and a basket of flowers. Sophia had designed and printed up a standing card that read, "The Future is Built on Tradition." She replaced the hand-lettered sign and the Tupperware bowl with her standing card and a shiny new cash box. She hung her posters off the front edge of the table. She folded the old sign and put it under the bowl on the shelf above the coat rack while no one was looking.

She and Gale would man the table, since no one else volunteered. Sophia pasted on a smile and waited. The band warmed up in the gymnasium, the random drumbeats and fiddle riffs uncomfortably loud. She found two folding chairs and settled in one, hoping Gale would arrive soon.

The first couple in the door gushed over the idea, but did not put anything in the cash box. The next people looked startled, and asked all sorts of questions, and didn't put anything in the box. Sophia consoled herself that she was raising public awareness. Gale showed up and did not let a single person go by without telling them about the scholarship fund.

"Boy, this is getting to be the place to ask for money," said George to another man as they passed through the vestibule. "You can't hardly get in the door," he half-joked.

Both men looked back at the table and the women by door, their brows wrinkled. "I guess it's alright," said the other man. "Gonna need a longer table so they can line up all the collection boxes," he laughed and clapped George on the back. They turned away and joined the rest of the dancers.

Joanna from the bank appeared at the door. Sophia was relieved to see someone who understood what she was trying to do. "Oh, thank you for coming," she greeted Joanna.

Joanna pushed her ten-dollar bill into the cash box. "How's it going, ladies?" she asked. Gale and Sophia glanced at each other.

"It's slow so far," Sophia said. "But we're still optimistic," she smiled enthusiastically.

Joanna winked. "I'm sure the scholarship fund will do better than my dancing," she said. "I'm not much of a dancer."

"Don't worry," Sophia gushed. "They'll show you what to do before each dance."

"That might not do it," Joanna laughed and moved into the crowd. She was quickly spotted by Mr. Williams.

"Hey lady," he shook her hand warmly. "You think we'll have any luck tonight?" They chatted about the fund and the next year's graduating class. Another man approached; new people at the dance were an automatic attraction.

"We don't see you here often," he smiled at Joanna, and dropped an arm around her shoulder. She shook his hand.

"Well, you know someone's gotta haul all the money to the bank," she offered.

He smiled and nodded. "Sure, sure. Do you think there'll be much?" he asked. "I don't think folks carry much money to go dancing."

"Every little bit helps," she said.

"You get a little dancing in, too, while you're here, okay?" Joanna nodded. After the men wandered away, a thin woman approached.

"You're from the bank, right?" she asked timidly. Joanna nodded. "You probably don't know me. My husband's sick and we usually put out a box on the front table. I just wanted to let you know I'm not putting it out tonight. I don't want to interfere with the scholarship fund."

Joann did know who she was, even if she didn't know her face. "Oh, Ms. Blankenship, don't you worry about that. You just do whatever you normally do. We don't want to interfere either."

The woman glanced toward the table overseen by Sophia. "Well," she hesitated. "I don't think one week will make a big difference. I just wanted to let you know, the floor's yours tonight. I hope the kids get a lot of money for school." She forced a smile and walked away.

On stage, Jack stepped up to the mike. "Okay everybody, we're going to get you moving in a minute. But we wanna let you know about the collection box at the door. Mr. Williams asked us to put that box back there, that money's going into the scholarship fund that Coach Hedridge started before he retired. So, if your pockets are weighin' ya down tonight –" he grinned and a few people tittered – "lighten 'em up back there at that box!"

During the next few dances several people wandered back to the door and left money in the box while Sophia fumed quietly to Gale that she herself had not been mentioned in the announcement, but the man who had fought her idea had been. Shelley and Analía stayed among the bodies on the dance floor, spinning and weaving and passing each other periodically, ignoring the box at the door and the people around it.

"It's almost as if they're offended that we're asking them to direct part of their resources to education," Sophia complained. "They don't want to take responsibility for their own future." She jiggled the cash box and listened to the rustling made by the paper inside. "I know this is not a wealthy community, but look at all the pickup trucks and fishing boats. There's money available. I just hate it that these kids don't get to see that they have more options in the world. I want to do something for them. Their parents are satisfied for them to just follow in their footsteps."

"It's a matter of priorities," said Gale. "They have to learn to see the value of what we're trying to do. And they need to contribute to it so they are invested in it."

The couple who owned the burger joint took a break outside, cooling off in the fall evening. A white van with a satellite antenna pulled in. Two men got out, and reached back into the van for camera equipment.

"Is that the news?" the man asked his wife.

"Sure looks like it," she said worriedly. "What happened?" They rushed back inside, but everything looked normal. Most of the crowd was dancing. A few people milled around the bathrooms and the refreshment table. Sophia and Gale sat at their cash box, looking a bit worn. The couple scanned the room and then backed into a corner as the news crew came through the door.

"That ain't the local news," the man said. They stayed away from the newspeople, watching as the reporters roamed the room, chatting with whoever they could grab. Someone directed them to Sophia, who welcomed them, flushed with excitement. They began filming the dance itself, but as people noticed the cameras, steps were missed. Hands that were supposed to catch passed each other like high-fives gone wrong. Heads turned the wrong way as everyone looked around to see what was being filmed. The fractal spinning of two hundred people devolved into turbulence.

"Goddammit," muttered Ricky to Jack, and they kept

playing. They finished the song as the camera crew reassured Sophia that there was no problem, they only needed a few seconds of dancing for the story. People drifted on the dance floor, some awkwardly going through the steps, others not even making a pretense and just getting in the way.

"Break!" announced Jack curtly at the end of the song. Shelley stood on her toes in the crowd, looking for Analía. She wanted a drink, but she didn't want to go near the refreshment table and the women sitting with their sign. She located Analía and waved to her. They sat on the edge of the bleachers and faced away from the cameraman.

"That woman doesn't know when to quit," complained Shelley.

"You need money for school, no?"

Shelley glared at her a moment.

"I'm out of school already, I don't qualify for that scholarship," Shelley said. "But that's not the point. She's not making any money, just rearranging the money that's already here." She risked a glance around the gymnasium. "She thinks people are too stupid to know what to do with their own money. I *do* need money for school, but if everybody in here put in a week's grocery money it wouldn't cover one semester. She's not even from here," Shelley said dismissively, then looked quickly at Analía. "Nothing personal."

"She is from where?" asked Analía.

"Don't know. Up north." Shelley had paid attention in geography, too. "Hey, I wonder if she's from as far away as you in actual miles? She could be, I think. Anyway, she might as well have gone to Mexico if she wanted to be someplace different. She could learn salsa dancing and bug somebody else."

"*Oye*, don't put her to me," Analía laughed and put up her hands. "I didn't do anything." She looked over her shoulder, laughing. "Mexico already had people telling us what to do. Is why we had the revolution!"

Shelley watched the people moving around the gym as if they were magnets and the reporters had opposite poles. "I might need to hear how you did that," she said.

"You have the heart of a chicken," Analía said fondly. Shelley stared at her, her mouth open.

"What's that supposed to mean? How do you figure?"

"You want to protect everything and everyone."

"How's that being a chicken? How's that being scared?"

"I didn't say you were scared. You are like the mama chicken protecting her babies. That's what we say in Mexico: *corazon de pollo.*"

Shelley blinked a few times and then erupted in laughter. "Oh my god, that's hilarious! Here we say that's being a mama *bear!*"

Analía didn't see what was so funny. "Of course, is the same. You are a mama bear. Trying to protect everything."

Shelley was still grinning. "Here, being a chicken is being a coward. I thought you said I have the heart of a coward." She leaned back on the stage and clapped her hands. "Ah, that was funny! I'm Shelley the chickenhearted! That's pretty good." She wished Ricky was there to hear this. *Speaking of which…*

"By the way, you and Ricky will be on your own this weekend," she said, watching Analía's face. "You think you'll be alright?" she asked with a straight face.

"What? Of course, we will be fine," Analía reminded Shelley of a kid reassuring his mom that he would be *fine* alone after school, wouldn't touch any knives, would keep the door locked, would *never* skateboard off the shed roof. "Where will you be?" she asked.

"My advisor at Cinderton Tech says I should visit colleges. She organized it," Shelley said, wrinkling her brow. "My old principal gave me a gift card for gas…I didn't know you could visit college *socially.*" She kicked her legs against the wooden bench of the bleacher below. "I guess I'm supposed to see what I might be getting into. I'm not sure what I'm supposed to do there."

"It is far?" asked Analía.

"About four hours driving. I'm leaving first thing in the morning. I'm supposed to sit in on classes tomorrow."

When Jack called a break, all five band members scooted out a side door near the stage and gathered outside near the trash cans.

"We're the whole reason them newspeople is here," said Jack. "Shouldn't you make a statement or something?" he asked Ricky as he blew cigarette smoke in a lazy whorl.

"I'll make a statement all right," Ricky threatened. He punched Jack lightly on the shoulder. "Take it easy, man, it's money for people to go to school. I guess that woman wants attention, but money's money."

"Don't reckon we'll see any of it," commented the drummer. The others scowled mildly at him. He backpedaled. "I'm not complainin', it's just weird that this whole thing couldn't happen if we didn't play, and now she's going on TV, and we're hidin' out back smokin'."

"You want to go on TV?" asked Jack. "Go on in there," he grinned, challenging the drummer.

"Hell, no," the drummer laughed. "They'll ask me questions and I won't know what to say. I'll look like a damn fool. You go." He nodded back at Jack. It reminded Ricky of summers when they all stood at the top of the cliffs over Lake Fontana and dared each other to jump off. Sometimes one of them did. This brave soul would be the subject of conversation for days, a warrior who took on gravity and could relive his triumph while installing bathroom sinks.

When the reporters' van pulled around the building and its taillights went down the lane toward the road, they went back inside and started playing without any announcement, letting the music pull the dancers back into formation.

The next evening phones rang all across town, in sheet metal trailers, in houses covered in brittle eighty-year-old asbestos siding, and in others faced with inch-thick synthetic stone panels that would never see twenty years.

"They had an interview with that Sophia woman," said the man who ran the burger joint to his wife. "Made it sound like she was responsible for the whole darn thing," he marveled.

His wife was in the kitchen cooking anything but hamburgers. She came around the corner with a wooden spoon dripping in her hand. She listened to the TV for a few moments.

"Who does she think she is?" she asked no one in particular. "There must be two hundred people at that dance every week, and who knows how many must have put money in that box. I wonder if she put anything in there? Give credit where credit's due!" She shook the spoon at the image onscreen. She stomped back to the kitchen and her husband followed her.

"Why does she have to go stirring things up?" she demanded, poking at the pot on the stove.

"You know, honey, stirring is how you make good things." He nodded toward the pot, hoping to calm her.

She shot him a look. "You have to know when – and what – to stir." She yanked open a cabinet. "You don't stir pudding, Lloyd. It ruins it." Lloyd slunk back to his den.

"My brother saw us on the news in Raleigh!" reported a startled auto mechanic to the woman ringing up his groceries at the supermarket.

"Yeah, my daughter-in-law in Kernersville did, too. I didn't know all you had to do to get famous was donate five bucks to a school fund. I been giving to the FFA since I was in it, and they never put me on TV," the woman laughed.

"They said they raised enough money to double the scholarship fund for next year," the man elaborated.

"Well, good for them," the woman confirmed. "That was nice of everybody to pony up. Real nice."

No one called Mr. Williams, but he watched the news, too. He was glad for any attention for the school or the scholarship fund, but he suspected this would mean more contact with Sophia and her plans and warnings. He knew that creating more scholarship money should make him happy, but it didn't, somehow.

"It was an excellent start," Sophia said to Gale on the phone.

"I know! So many people walked by and ignored us, I couldn't believe how much we ended up with. Around here that should be enough to make one of those giant checks and take a picture with it!" Gale joked.

"Maybe next time," Sophia laughed. She paused. "That woman from the bank was very complimentary, but I haven't heard a word from the principal. I know he was opposed to the whole idea, but we've produced money and publicity for the scholarship program. He could at least say thank you."

"He'll get on board," Gale assured her. "He'll have to, if you keep raising money like that."

"Assuming I have the energy," Sophia noted. "I never know when I'll have another attack of that nausea."

"Isn't the ginseng still working?"

"Oh yes, so far. But every time I buy it, I wonder. Should I keep taking the same brand? Would another brand be better? Or worse? Would raw be better? There are so many different formulas, I feel great now but how do I know I'm taking the best one?"

"I'd stick with the same one. Why mess with success?"

"Sure...but I've been thinking. Wouldn't it make sense to get it straight from the woods? Couldn't I find it myself? If people with a high school education – or less – can find it, it can't be that hard."

"You mean collect your own, out in the woods?"

"Why not?"

"Do you know how to find it? Do you know what it looks like? What if you get the wrong plant and poison yourself?"

"I don't know, I don't know," Sophia laughed again. "But I'm a smart woman. I can figure this out."

"Are you sure you should bother with this? I'm going to Costa Rica next month, why don't you come with me? Just buy your ginseng at the store and come have fun. It's a mindfulness retreat, yoga and smoothies in the Central American *sierra*," she wheedled.

"I need to learn to be mindful here at home," Sophia said. "And I have a lot going on. Maybe something will come of this scholarship fund."

When they hung up, Sophia turned her newfound momentum to solving her medical situation. There was no reason she couldn't claw all the way up the supply chain and get her own medicine. Another internet search provided dozens of images of it, its leaves, its berries, its tiny flowers, its magical roots. She printed out pictures in color, made notes: shade, north-facing slopes, near oaks and poplars. Now she had to identify not one plant but *three*. She would have to buy a compass.

She sat staring at the computer. What would she do, just drive out to the nearest woods? She figured she could *find* it in the national forest, but she thought she might have heard that hunting ginseng on public land was illegal. She was sure some of those people at the dance had lots of land where ginseng probably grew, but she hadn't made the kind of friends who she could ask to allow her to hunt on their land. After studying the pictures, she was itching to go out and look for it, but she couldn't plan the search any further than her own front door. She pushed all the printed pictures to one side of her desk and leaned back in her chair to think.

When she first started as an insurance adjuster she rode along with a police officer as a training exercise. Something about understanding how the police investigate accidents. Could a person do a ride-along with a forest ranger? To her happy surprise, YouTube had videos of just such a thing. After a series of phone calls and some awkward conversations, she was officially scheduled to accompany a Wildlife Preservation Officer on a patrol of Pisgah National Forest. She could hardly wait.

18
A Trip to Town

Shelley remembered Interstate 40 mostly from trips to the beach. It was seven hours across the state to the coast, almost directly east as the land got flatter and the road got straighter. People called the eastern part of the state "down east," and in spite of the various dips and climbs of the highway, it did feel like going downhill. That would make going home *up*hill, supposedly the harder part of any journey. Yet coming back west always seemed to go faster, as if the mountains were drawing her in.

Miles and miles of green passed, interspersed with exits dotted with gas stations and fast food restaurants. She zoomed past Morganton, and thought of Bob Mackey, the ex-Forest Ranger, out there working in a furniture warehouse. Winston-Salem was the first big city, where the highway was decorated with more concrete than trees. Greensboro was the same, then Durham, where billboards alerted drivers to the famous baseball team.

When she took the exit for the university, Shelley went on high alert. In this environment, she needed every scrap of her sense of direction. She recited every left, every right to herself after she took them, hoping to cement the asphalt trail in her memory. She hated to be on a spot on the earth without knowing its relation to home. She needed to know her way around without the GPS, because in the woods the signal didn't always reach.

Armed with the map she had printed back home, Shelley found the Admissions building and a parking space marked "Visitor." She dug through her bag for paperwork with the name of the person she was supposed to meet, took a deep breath, and got out of the car. When she shut the door, she felt like a turtle who had stepped out of his shell.

The woman in the Admissions office greeted her like an arriving diplomat, and they headed out for a walking tour of the campus.

"What are you looking for in a school?" asked the Admissions Officer.

Shelley was surprised by the question. First everyone was pushing her to attend "regular" college, now she was expected to evaluate it like a used car?

"Uh, I want to get the best education I can?" Shelley suggested.

The woman nodded enthusiastically. "Academics," she confirmed. "Our professors are very respected in their fields. They publish frequently—" she winked at Shelley, "—we keep that pressure on them. Everyone's got to produce new knowledge regularly."

Shelley was not sure what that meant, but didn't see any reason to let on. She nodded, and was nearly silent through the rest of the tour as she heard about lab equipment, independent student research, and professional journals. She formed a mental list of things to look up later.

The Admissions Officer led her to the science building, another stately red brick structure. She went straight to the classroom, relieved to have a place here where she wouldn't be on display, where she could just sit and observe.

She sat in the back and hoped the professor wouldn't notice her. As the class filled up, she studied the paperwork given to her by the Admissions Office, trying to be inconspicuous. She needn't have worried, as over a hundred students filed into the auditorium-style room.

When a tall thin man in a plaid shirt came in and put a leather bag on the desk in the front of the room, she relaxed. Here she knew what to expect, and more importantly, what to do. She was prepared to be an absorbed audience. This was the show she came for. She wondered what would happen here in this college that was supposed to be so fundamentally different from all the "school" she had sat through so far.

It was similar at first. Then she began to notice that it moved a little faster. When a half hour had gone by, she realized they had covered what felt like a few days' worth of material. She realized no one around her was passing notes, or making jokes. She started looking at each student, one by one. Nine out of ten were diligently making notes. *Damn,* she thought, *when two or three weeks' worth of this shows up on a test, that's going to be one hell of a test.* It was scary, but thrilling, too. She wondered how she would do on a test like that.

She relaxed into her invisibility, but at the end of class she heard her name being called.

"Where's Shelley Morgan?" the professor waved an arm over the class. She cleared her throat and raised an arm.

"There you are. Ms. Morgan is a visiting prospective student. If you see her around, be sure to tell her who your favorite professors are," he grinned at the class. Several students tittered dutifully. "Can I see you a moment after class, Ms. Morgan?" the professor asked. She nodded. "Don't worry, you're not in trouble yet," he smiled.

The class filed out and Shelley went down the steps to the well. The professor sat on the desk and smiled at her. "How's your visit going?"

"Great," she said. She wasn't sure what else to report.

"I heard you're a potential botany major. I was wondering if you want to accompany a field group tomorrow, see what that's like," he offered. "A seminar group is heading out to Duke Forest to look at some specimens." She nodded. "We'll meet in Bryson Hall parking lot at 8:00 a.m. sharp."

Immediately after class Shelley was back on tourist duty. The student volunteer assigned to guide her through the weekend shifted from foot to foot in the hall and accosted Shelley only a few feet from the door. Becky introduced herself and dragged Shelley to dinner. The cafeteria was a different world from the high school cafeteria. Shelley had never seen so much food except maybe at Golden Corral. All you can eat, every meal, every day. In between descriptions of the band that would be playing later and the Fall Festival that Shelley would miss the following weekend, Becky explained the "freshman fifteen" to her.

"You're kind of quiet," Becky observed, applying the empirical skills she was learning in her science curriculum.

Shelley recognized the demand for her to speak up. "Oh, well, I'm supposed to be checking things out, so I guess I'm doing that."

"Don't you have any questions?" Becky asked. "What do you want to see on campus?"

"Um. I went to a class earlier, and I'm staying in the dorms tonight..." Shelley began. That seemed to cover it: where she would live and the classes she would attend. "I found plenty of food already," she attempted a joke.

"What about the student center?" asked Becky. "Do you want to see the football stadium?"

"Sure," Shelley figured she should look at whatever they wanted to show her. She wasn't planning to rack up thousands of dollars of debt to watch football games.

"How many schools are you looking at?" Becky asked on the way to the student center.

"So far just this one," Shelley had a feeling that wasn't the right answer.

"Just *one?*" Becky was incredulous. "How will you know if you'll like it?"

Shelley risked a question. "So how are schools different?"

Becky looked shocked. "Well, lots of ways. Better dorm rooms, or better parties. Don't you want to make sure you'll be happy living here?"

Living here, thought Shelley.

Evening involved a tour of campus social life. Becky appeared to know someone in every clique on campus, so Shelley attended a meeting of a campus environmental group, heard a mediocre band, and played drinking games at a dorm party. She met students who reported that their parents were Divisional Controller, Risk Management Analyst, and Director of Operations. She had even less idea how one would apply for these jobs than how to get a job as a botanist.

Shelley was finally dropped at a dorm room where she gratefully realized she would be the only occupant. She sat on the bed enjoying her first moment of privacy since she got out of the car. She hadn't known college would be so...*involved.* All these people who didn't know her from Adam were so friendly, it reminded her of church. No matter who you were, or where you were, if you went to a church, people would be friendly to you. They would be interested in a stranger, and ask you all about yourself. The community college staff seemed more like bureaucrats at the DMV. She supposed this was a church, in a way. The Church of Education. The Church of Your Future, maybe.

But so much busier than a church. People strode quickly to class, quickly to the cafeteria, quickly to the student center. They moved so fast, you could imagine them suddenly running out to catch a pass, or maybe you expected an abrupt abracadabra and a magic result. They talked of their futures that way, as if things just automatically happened in the expected way. Shelley imagined a rollercoaster, with people hollering along the tracks to a predetermined destination. She was a stray dandelion puff floating through the amusement park while the roller cars screamed past.

Shelley got up early Saturday, and after another round at the fatten-you-up buffet, she found the group for the field outing milling around a battered green van in a parking lot. Duffle bags and backpacks littered the gravel, along with metal cases and other equipment, some of which was familiar to Shelley from classes at home. The professor was there in a floppy brown hat. She counted six other people.

"I'm sorry, I didn't think to ask if you had gear for a trip like this," the professor greeted her.

Shelley looked around at the mess in the parking lot. "It's just one day, right?"

"Just the morning. We'll be back around 2 or 3."

"I think I have what I need, except for, you know, research equipment."

"We've got that covered," he winked. A student had appeared at his side, glancing over Shelley's tennis shoes, T-shirt, and the flannel shirt tied around her waist. She had a backpack with her usual peanuts and chapstick.

"You sure?" asked the student, who turned out to be a teaching assistant. "Do you have lunch?"

"I had a lot of breakfast," Shelley replied. "I have snacks."

The professor smiled generously. "Let's get going."

On the ride to the woods Shelley listened to the students talking about campus activities until one of them turned to her.

"So where are you from?"

"Suncross."

"Where's that?"

"Outside of Cinderton?" He still looked blank.

"West of Charlotte?" she tried again.

"Oh," he said, still looking confused. "I'm from Pennsylvania."

She laughed. "Western North Carolina, in the mountains."

A girl with short hair with blue streaks spoke up. "We went there last year on a field trip, to Celo. It was so beautiful."

Shelley nodded. The girl continued, "Do you kayak?"

Shelley shrugged. "I've never done it. I don't really have time." She added helpfully, "We used to float down the river on inner tubes a lot when I was a kid."

The girl drew her brows together. "Inner tubes? What do you mean?"

"From tractor trailer tires. They're huge. You can tie them together and make a raft."

More of the group was listening. The young man from Pennsylvania asked, "Aren't they dirty?"

Shelley shrugged. "You can wash them." She thought it was time to change the subject. "So is there ginseng where we're going today?"

All heads turned toward the front, where the assistant was driving and the professor was in the front seat. "It's not impossible," the professor answered. "It can be farmed here, but it's unlikely that we'll find any wild ginseng in these woods."

Another student turned to her. "Do you hunt ginseng?" he asked excitedly.

She shook her head. "My grandpa and my cousins."

"Like *American Outlaw?*" asked the girl with blue-streaked hair.

Shelley sighed. "I don't know, I haven't seen it," she lied. She gazed blankly at the girl, waiting for her attention to move along. It did, and Shelley did not start any more conversations. She had watched a few episodes with Sue, Ricky, and Tim. Ricky and Tim picked it to pieces, triumphantly counting inaccuracies and guffawing when the ginseng hunters misrepresented certain details of ginseng hunting to the audience. Sue got more and more agitated until she finally got up and went to the kitchen. "This is so fake," she would yell at no one in particular. "That damn show makes us out to be idiots." Shelley wondered whether after five or six semesters here, she would start to believe everything she saw on TV.

When the group piled out of the van in Duke Forest, laughing and calling to each other and tossing bags around the parking lot, Shelley knew they wouldn't see any animals today. She stepped out lightly with her backpack in place and stood quietly off to one side.

"Okay, folks, we're going to catalog sections of forest floor today." The professor handed out clipboards with checklists and maps. He assigned the students to various spots: a hillside, atop a small ridge, by the creek. He nodded at Shelley, "If you want to check for *panax q*, you'll want to be with the creek group." She nodded and followed the two other students.

Shelley said nothing as the girl with blue hair and another

student hauled their gear into the woods and trekked the path to the creek. As they walked side by side on the trail, Shelly named to herself the plants they crushed, making a miniature eulogy for these plants that died for science. The girls marked off a two-by-two foot square by the water and peered at it, holding their clipboards. Shelley peered at the square as well, and eavesdropped as they identified a few plants she hadn't seen in the mountains. She wished she had a notebook, but she recited their names to herself. After half an hour both students stood up and stuck their pens in the clipboards.

"Alright," said the girl with blue hair. "I guess we've done these woods." She headed back up the path. Shelley and the other girl looked at each other and followed. Shelley realized she hadn't even thought to check for fish in the creek. She glanced longingly at the woods along the trail, feeling that this was a spectacularly uninspired walk in the woods.

Shelley stayed on the edges of the group as they slowly re-gathered at the van and listened to instructions from the professor on what to do with their findings. She handed in her clipboard and, regretfully, its map. As much as she hated Google Earth, she loved maps. They felt sacred in her hands – the rustling paper, the colors and symbols of a place, set down so it wouldn't be lost. They were a form of the land that she could hold in her hands, clutch to her chest, or fold and carry as a powerful talisman in her backpack. She had only seen a relief map once, where the land could be read like Braille, her fingers feeling the mountains and ridges.

But maps scared her, too: the ones she had seen on the walls at the county planning office when she went with Sue to pay the property taxes. In those maps, every holler was laid bare and stuck with pins like butterflies in a museum. Maps could be like a photograph of a loved one, so that when the person wasn't near you, you could pull them out and point to a mark or a scar and say, "that's where such-and-such happened." But they were also like driver's license photos or mugshots: they could be used against you.

That was the danger with recorded wisdom. With however much love knowledge was set down, it could be picked up again as a weapon. Keeping this map would mean she had some intention to return, and right now, she would not commit to that.

Even tired, the group was noisy as they crawled out of the van at a gas station on the way back to campus. Shelley followed them into the store and wandered around, comparing the layout to the one she knew so well. She tried to guess what Analía might say about the "product arrangement" and "point-of-sale marketing."

Shelley chose snacks and waited to pay behind the other students. She watched the woman behind the cash register as she made change and bagged items, saying nothing more to the students than the necessary numbers. Her face was only a few years more worn than those of the students, and no books cluttered her space behind the counter.

Relieved to return to campus, Shelley joined in her fieldmates' claims that they needed showers, and went back to her room. She had been invited to several parties, but she didn't want to answer any more questions about herself. She ducked the girls in the room next door, and scooted out of the building and toward the far side of campus. There were trees in the distance.

She wended her way through the buildings toward the trees. Passing the last building, she sighed as she rounded the corner and saw in front of her a path through an unmown field. She wondered for a moment if this field was part of the campus, if she was allowed to go there. She looked around, didn't see anyone, and decided she didn't care. There was no one there to complain. Once she got far enough into the woods, no one could see her anyway.

Before the woods there was a pond, hidden in a dip in the field. As she looked over the water, a few bird sounds came to her attention. She resisted the urge to throw herself into the tall grass and roll around, settling for sitting in a dry spot at the edge of the water.

After a few minutes of watching air bubbles surface here and there, indicating frogs or fish, she became curious again about the woods. A little pinprick in her head suggested there might be different wildflowers in there. She knew she shouldn't expect ginseng here, but she might as well prove it.

But she didn't make it to the woods. She took what looked like the less-traveled path around the lake, and started to smell something odd. Passing a stand of overgrown azaleas, she found where a paved road joined the path, obviously used to bring garbage to the six dumpsters arrayed inside a "U" of azalea bushes.

"Huh," she said to herself. Before she could think of any deeper meaning to this, a grey-brown shape waddled from between two of the dumpsters. The raccoon looked up at her, pausing with one foot in mid-air.

She blinked. She held still. They stared at each other for several seconds. The raccoon waddled back around the next dumpster. She waited, planning to sneak closer and peer around the dumpster. But she made it only two steps before the raccoon emerged again and headed toward the tall grass, followed by two others, in diminishing sizes. They ceded her the dumpsters. "Don't worry, it's all yours," she laughed to herself.

Running into the raccoons restored her energy. She felt ready for another round on campus, and decided to check out the library. She could hear noise in the distance on campus but the paths near the library were empty and as quiet as the pond had been.

Like the cafeteria, the library held a spread the likes of which she had never seen. She saw dark areas that she assumed were closed, but they weren't marked off, so she wandered in and found light switches with timers. *So many books you can't afford to light them all at once,* she thought, happy about the energy-saving gadgets. She wandered past categories so specific it was hard to imagine an entire shelf on them, until she realized that "Botany" was an entire room, bigger than Sue's house. Maybe this was why they covered so much so fast in class. It reminded her of when she arrived at the field in back of campus, as if there were things to discover here.

She picked a row and wandered down it, reading titles. *Vascular Plant Families; Cryptogamic Botany; Soil, Hydrologic and Site Parameters in Wetland Restoration; Catalog of Toxic Plants.* She closed her eyes and reached for a book. *Pollination Biology,* the cover announced. She opened it and flipped through a few pages with photos of flowers she'd never heard of, much less seen. She leaned on a carrel at the end of the row and looked at a section on leaf structures over the life cycle. She'd seen similar drawings in her own textbooks, but these drawings went on for pages and pages. There were gloriously long latin labels for every tiny bit of a plant, every intricate step in a plant's life set down as intimately as knowing the freckles on a lover's arm.

She skimmed the book for a while, then left it on the carrel table and went back to the shelves. She found an odd-shaped brown paperback called *Earth Manual: How to Work on Wild Land Without Taming It.* Next to it was a tan book with old-fashioned botanical drawings on the cover, *Sustainable Woodland Medicinals.* She carried both of them back to the carrel, and for a while this corner of the library was silent except for the brushing of pages against each other, the ghosts of trees whispering their secrets.

The lights clicked off. *Is that a sign?* she wondered to herself. She would take it as one. It had been a long day. She scribbled down the title and author of *Woodland Medicinals.*

She looked at the clock on her phone. 11:00 p.m. *Wow,* she thought as she left the library and glanced at the sign on the door. *A library open 'til midnight on a Saturday. That's something.*

At breakfast on Sunday she couldn't wait to tell someone about the raccoons. She scanned the room for anyone she recognized from the field outing, but saw no one. There was that woman from the Admissions office.

After pleasantries, Shelley assured the woman that she had "explored the campus." "Very thoroughly," she nodded. "I even found that pond in the back."

"Oh yes, that's land that was donated to the University. Now we have room for long-term expansion, when we need it." The woman smiled optimistically.

Shelley was not thrilled to picture the pond and woods turning into more red brick buildings. "Couldn't the science classes use it, you know, for field work?" she suggested hopefully.

"Oh, I don't think there's much back there," the woman replied. "Nothing special enough to learn much from."

They're just college students, thought Shelley. *Nobody's splitting atoms.* "I saw some raccoons," she said, careful to fill her voice with enthusiasm, not contradiction.

The woman laughed. "Those things. The staff leave the dumpster doors open and those pests just have a picnic. Has the weekend helped you make a decision?"

"It's a lot to think about," Shelley said cautiously.

The Admissions officer nodded. Like the school board members in Cinderton, she was aware that students from far-flung rural areas dropped out of college at rates that resembled those of minority students. "The decision to transfer should be weighed carefully," she intoned, looking at her coffee.

Shelley wasn't sure which way she was being nudged.

After breakfast Shelley decided she had worn out her welcome, or vice versa, and headed for the highway. The whole time she was there, it was always in the back of her mind that this was a *visit*. When she was a kid, her grandparents would make a trip to town every month for staples like flour and tractor parts. It was an event, with lists written and good clothes donned. Somewhere in town during the day her grandfather would get tired, and sneak off behind a building to smoke a cigarette and have some "peace and quiet." She sensed that all day he was mildly on edge, alert, waiting to relax when they crossed the river on the way back home. She tried to imagine a four-year trip to town. Four years on edge.

Four autumns of not watching the first tips of gold land on the treetops of the mountain across from Sue's house. Four winters of not smelling the icy cold on people's coats when they came stomping into the gas station looking for hot chocolate. Jobs would be gotten and lost, the band would learn and play new songs, and she would be away in a brick building smelling of paper and synthetic fleece.

She clearly did not belong here among the people who thought raccoons were pests. Nor in the Church of Knowledge, where they were omnivorous procyonids.

19
Alone with the Woods

Back home on Saturday, Ricky drove Analía through the fall day over smaller and smaller roads, from the interstate to the two-lane to a single lane of asphalt with ditches on either side, all the way to two lines of gravel with grass a foot high in the middle. He was so nervous he couldn't think what to say. It felt like Christmas breakfast, when all he wanted to do was tear out of his seat and dive into the presents, but first he had to finish his scrambled eggs.

Analía was thinking that in Mexico this would never be an appropriate date: the two of them alone in the woods, miles from supervision. She was far from home and far, far outside the lines.

As the roads shrank, the trees closed in tighter over them, the sun becoming only a rare twinkle. They opened the truck windows all the way, and were moving so slowly their hair barely ruffled. Here and there stray leaves tumbled down past the windows like a soft sporadic rain. Analía could hear squirrels rustling above their heads and a crow cawing behind them.

"I bring something to you?" Analía said. Ricky considered whether that was a statement or an offer, and decided he was fine with either one. Analía lifted the cloth bag she always carried off the floor and reached inside. *Statement,* he concluded.

"This is music from Mexico. A very old romantic song." She

had wasted a little of her earnings from the store on something for herself. She slid a disc into the player. Ricky remembered to say thank you.

A violin played a soaring melody with a rapid percussive sound in the background. "This is *cumbia*," said Analía after a while. "For dancing."

"I like it," said Ricky. "Is that a cowbell?" he asked.

"I don't know bell," said Analía. "You put on the cow's neck so you can hear where he is walking?"

"Cowbell," confirmed Ricky. "I'll be damned."

The truck pulled around a bend and came to an opening in the trees. A wide muddy spot beside the road revealed where many people had pulled off to look out over the valley. Ricky did the same.

"You want to see a pretty spot?" he asked. "We can go down that path over there." In a gap in the brambles surrounding the overlook, a dirt track marked by napkins and other bits of trash led around the curve of the mountain. Ricky pulled the bag containing their lunch from the truck and Analía followed him into the green shade.

They walked silently for a while, Analía stopping sometimes to look at tiny flowers dotting the woods here and there. She figured Shelley could name all of them, but that wasn't necessary for her to marvel at their variety of shapes and colors. Ricky waited patiently each time she stopped. He too was reminded of Shelley, and it occurred to him that women looking at flowers might be due to some mutual attraction between pretty things.

He was standing in the trail watching squirrels chasing each other through the treetops when the pop of a branch breaking about ten feet off the trail startled both of them. Ricky moved between Analía and the sound and peered into the woods. A bush rustled and a brown-skinned man with long black hair in a ponytail leaned out.

"Buenos días!" said Ricky, testing the words he had learned

from Analía, using the language lesson as an opportunity to stare at her lips as she pronounced things more times than he really needed.

The man glowered in their direction. He tilted his head as he considered the pair who had surprised him. He navigated the stand of pine in which he had been hiding and stepped in front of them, the annoyance in his expression pairing threateningly with the well-polished rifle at his side.

"*No soy Mexicano,*" he proclaimed in a perfect Mexican accent, which immediately evolved into a soft drawl with a slightly hypnotic rhythm. "I'm James Black Dog," he said. "I'm from Cherokee, not Mexico."

"You are *indio*?" asked Analía, intrigued.

He raised an eyebrow at her. "Just like you," he said. Analía stared at this man who could just as easily have stepped out of the Mexican *selva* as out of the Appalachian deciduous forest. She had read about "Native Americans" in world history in Mexico, how they lived on reservations cut out of the country that overtook them. In Mexico the Spaniards had approached the indigenous inhabitants differently, and now nearly everyone was a blend of *indigeno* and European, their eyes and skin colors all on a continuum from light to dark.

"I like your name," she said after a minute.

"Well," he said laconically. "The Chinese say that black dogs are the best to eat. So I guess it means I'm good to eat." He winked in Analía's direction, then grinned and clapped the scowling Ricky on the shoulder. "Just messing with you. What're ya huntin'? Havin' any luck?"

Ricky blinked and composed himself. "Not really huntin' today, just showin' her around. How about you?"

He shrugged. "I'd probably take anything I could get. I guess it's turkey season, so maybe a turkey will come along."

"Sorry if we scared them off," said Ricky. "We'll move

along."

"No problem, I was getting bored in there anyway." He glanced at the lunch bag Ricky was carrying. "Nice little spot in there for a picnic. Have a good one."

James Black Dog smiled again at Analía and took off through the trees.

"So he does not live on a reservation?" Analía asked Ricky.

"He might. There's one about forty minutes from here. He might've come over to hunt. But you know, they don't *have* to live on the reservation. He might live around here. Lot of people come off the reservation to work. It was their land first, anyway, I guess they can go wherever they want."

"Everyone moves around to work," she said. "The *indios* come off the reservation, your mom's boyfriend went to Hickory, people come from Mexico. Nobody can work at home."

He shook his head. "The grass is always greener."

"What?"

"Aw, it just means everybody thinks what they want is somewhere else." They picked their way through the leaves and tree roots in silence, until Ricky pointed out a fallen tree off to one side that was at a suitable height for sitting. He held back blackberry brambles for her to get to the log and they sat down with the lunch bag between them.

Analía watched Ricky's hands as he extracted the lunch he had brought. He usually carried beef jerky and water into the woods, but he knew that wouldn't cut it for today.

"I didn't know what you like, so this is ham, that's turkey, and this is peanut butter and jelly." He laid out his offerings and looked at her hopefully. Analía smiled.

"They all look delicious," she said, and suddenly leaned forward and kissed him on the cheek, pausing with her head near his afterward. Then she pulled back and looked away at the ground.

They settled down to eating silently, each thinking about that kiss.

Suddenly Ricky looked up from his sandwich. "Shhh," he said, lifting a hand with one finger up. Analía stopped chewing and her eyes widened. She waited but heard nothing.

"It is a bear?" she whispered. Whispering was rude in Mexico but she'd noticed no one in America minded.

Ricky held back a smile, enchanted by the way "bear" resembled "beer" in her accent. If beers jumped out of the woods at him, he'd never go home, he thought. He shook his head and whispered, "No, I thought I heard voices."

"Are talking bears more dangerous?" Analía giggled. Ricky figured that yes, talking beers could be serious trouble. His head filled with a vision of a six-pack of jolly cartoon beers roaming the woods chanting "Drink me." Analía stood up with her head cocked to one side.

"*Español!*" she said to herself, and rose from the log, pulled toward the voices.

"*Buenos días!*" she called out, and Ricky thought it sounded so much prettier than his had.

Analía scrambled through the underbrush in the direction of the voices, calling out phrases in urgent Spanish. Ricky trotted uncertainly after her, not wanting to interrupt but wanting to warn her that people this far out in the woods were not always happy about being found. People who seeded marijuana in quiet coves in the national forest were rarely friendly to strangers. Maybe Mexicans were different, he hoped. He stopped when he heard a voice replying to Analía, trying to discern its tone.

Ahead of him, Analía pushed branches aside and stepped out into a clearing among six or eight people with cloth bags hung over their shoulders. They looked startled but Ricky didn't see any weapons, if you didn't count the walking sticks and gardening shears. The women and men looked warily at each other, at Analía, at Ricky. Finally one woman addressed Analía.

"*Buen día, 'manita,*" she said. *Good day, little sister.* A few of the others nervously adjusted their cloth bags. Shears were slipped deftly into pockets amid the distraction of conversation. "*Quien es ese?*" *Who's this guy?*

Analía took Ricky's hand. "*Es mi amigo.* We are having a picnic." The people relaxed visibly. Knowing smirks passed between some of the men as Analía chatted with the women. Ricky missed the rest of the conversation as he focused on the cool, smooth hand in his. He realized Analía was protecting him in this interaction, rather than the other way around.

A few minutes later Analía turned from the group and led Ricky back toward their log. Ricky was thinking how funny it was to run into a bunch of Mexicans so far out in the woods. People came all the way from other countries and they still found their way into the deepest corners of the land. When they were far enough away not to be heard he said to Analía, "I hunted turkeys with a friend and a couple Mexican guys once. Man, they don't give up, they can go all day. They caught fish and we cooked them on rocks in a fire. But they don't take the cold too well."

She laughed gently. "We are not used to it." A few steps later, she said, "They say they are hunting gollocks. What kind of animal is that?"

Ricky thought for a moment, remembering the cloth bags and garden shears. "It's not an animal," he said. "It's a flower, galax. They sell the leaves to florists. It's pretty good money."

"Do you hunt that, too?" asked Analía.

"You know, I haven't," said Ricky. "Maybe I should. You have to have a permit for that, too."

Analía laughed gently again. "I am surprised you do not need a permit to have a picnic in the woods."

Ricky smiled. "Some places you do. Out west. So many

people want to go there, they have to get a permit. Mostly for really special places, certain mountains to climb. They give out the permits by lottery."

"So these woods are not special enough?" Analía asked.

"Huh!" Ricky snorted.

"I guess that's why that woman kept telling me they have permits," Analía said. She walked a few steps silently. "Do you think that was true?"

"Hmm…could be," said Ricky. She still hadn't let go of his hand. "The permits are pretty cheap, but they're only good for a short time, and you're supposed to pick only older stems, so the plant can keep growing."

"That's what you said about ginseng," she said.

"Yeah, that's how you do it. You have to leave something for the animals and the next year and the year after that."

"Like making a garden," said Analía.

"In a way," said Ricky. "I guess it's easier and harder than gardening at home. You don't have to mess with watering and fertilizer and weeding, the land takes care of that. But then you never really know where your plants are. You never know what you are going to find, or if you're going to find anything. Sometimes you don't find any 'sang, but you find something else." He chuckled. "Indians or galax hunters. Or a sunny little clearing or a patch of sassafras."

"How do you find it?" Analía asked, hoping there might be a clue in his answer, that finding things might be a universal matter, governed by a unifying theory.

Ricky squinted. "You have to think like ginseng a little. You know how a fisherman has to think like the fish? You have to know what the ginseng likes, where it's comfortable."

Analía nodded. *Exactly.* That universal theory had gotten her nowhere so far. But it made Ricky seem like a wise ally she could depend on. She liked that feeling. He was still talking.

"If you do find what you are looking for, it's always kind of special. Like the woods were paying attention to you that day and gave you what you needed." He walked a few more steps. "Maybe when you don't find what you were looking for, that's the woods' answer, too."

Analía squeezed his hand. "Is what is said about God. Sometimes he gives you what you ask for, sometimes he gives you something else."

20
Something to Call Home About

Analía advanced to working shifts without a supervisor. She sat in the store admiring the wooden counter that she had polished to a soft glow. The scarred wood reminded her of the furniture at home in Mexico, and the illusion was extended when a familiar brown face appeared on the other side of the counter. The young man from Emma Lane in the trailer park stood there, looking around warily.

"Can I help you?" she asked in Spanish.

"Maybe I can help you," he said uncertainly. He examined the array of candy on the counter. She waited.

"Your brother had a girlfriend. I might know where she lives," he said, and looked away.

Analía was accustomed to people covering the truth gently with their words, not shoving it out in front all naked and unarmed. "That's okay," she said. "It doesn't matter how you know."

"I don't know if she will want to see you," he said.

"It's okay," she said. "If...if she loved my brother at one time she will understand that I need to find him." Analía paused, calculating. "You understand."

"She is not always understanding," he said, and grimaced as if he'd been on the wrong end of some misunderstandings himself. "I can probably convince her."

"Please take me with you," Analía begged. "What if you ask

her and she says no? Just let me go with you." Analía smiled as convincingly as she knew how.

He nodded and swallowed. "When?"

Analía looked around desperately. She couldn't abandon the store and she couldn't let him drive away.

"Wait please," she said with some authority. It was the right amount because the man lowered his head and hesitantly wandered down one aisle. Analía grabbed her phone and tapped rapidly.

Fifteen minutes later Shelley's car squealed into the lot. "You owe me big," she said as she threw her backpack into the office. "Or else I owe you, 'cause I might've died of boredom in that class." She grabbed Analía and hugged her. "Good luck," she said, and then, "Hey, wait a minute. You don't have any idea where you're going. Is that safe?"

Analía blushed. "I called Ricky, too."

"Oh my god you are a force of nature." Shelley laughed. She turned to the man. She grabbed both his hands and thanked him floridly, then threatened a couple generations of his descendants if any harm came to Analía. Fortunately he didn't understand much after thank you.

Analía was terrified Shelley would scare him off and grateful to see Ricky's truck pull up outside. She escorted the man out the door, hanging onto his arm so he couldn't change his mind.

It was just another day at the trailer park for Nicole. Since she had lost her job at the coat hanger factory, she was staying here with her mother. Her mother tried to insist that Nicole earn her keep by helping out, but she was secretly satisfied any day she came home and found Nicole sober.

Nicole was lying with her bare feet propped on the arm of the couch while she absently mumbled an old Barney tune to herself and the pale, dark-eyed toddler arranging stuffed animals into a pyramid on the floor. She clicked listlessly through the on-screen TV guide at the same time. The rattling of the screen door startled her so that she nearly fell off the couch.

She looked up at the door. There stood Chuy, a white guy who looked vaguely familiar, and a pretty Mexican girl. *What's he up to now*, she thought. She unlocked the screen door and moved out of the way, tugging at her clothes but offering no greeting.

Chuy led the group in and went straight for the little girl, picking her up and kissing her while crooning a string of Spanish. Ricky and Analía watched him, since the sight was more appealing than Nicole's dishevelment.

Chuy put the girl down and turned to Nicole, ready to issue his challenge. But Analía as usual was ahead of the game.

"I am Analía. Your little girl is very pretty," she said, and held out a hand. Nicole eyed her suspiciously, but some deeply buried training won out and she took Analía's hand awkwardly.

"I'm Nicole," she said, making it sound like "What the hell?"

Chuy had held onto his news as long as he could. "This is Jaime's sister," he announced grandly. Nicole looked surprised for a moment before her face resettled into vague hostility.

"I am Jaime's sister," Analía said more gently. Ricky looked meaningfully at Chuy and cut his eyes to the door. Chuy gathered up the little girl and said, "We will play outside."

Analía gracefully walked to the couch and sat down as if she had been invited. She crossed her legs and sat up straight, like a guest at a proper tea party, though the only refreshment on the table beside her was a half-eaten package of snack cakes. Nicole had no idea how to eject such a person from her living room, so she sat down, too.

"I have not seen my brother for a very long time," she began.

"Chuy said you used to...know Jaime. I was wondering if you know how to find him."

Nicole didn't figure that Chuy was planning to marry her. But now she wondered if this was a way of pushing her back toward Jaime. It struck her as a pretty damn rude way of breaking up with someone, trying to throw them back to their ex. Especially when that ex had taken off without a word...and Jaime had never mentioned a sister. Maybe this was a stupid game so Chuy could stop taking care of the baby. Damnit, she thought, he had been so good about that.

Analía wondered if Nicole was ever going to say anything.

"You said your name is Anna Leah?" Nicole finally asked, as if she'd gotten the lid off a puzzle box in her brain.

"Yes," said Analía, thinking maybe she needed to go slower. Maybe speaking English wasn't enough to get through to some of these people in the U.S.

"Well, I guess that explains that," Nicole said, chewing her lip. She looked off into space for moment, then shrugged. "I ain't seen Jaime in a long time either. I guess he forgot about both of us." Her voice was cutting, and it felt like the end of the conversation, but Nicole went on.

"You know, I really loved him," she said accusingly. "He was so sweet to me. He used to say such romantic stuff. We used to talk about going to Mexico together." She paused, looking at her nails. "You don't have any idea where he is?"

"No," Analía almost whispered, then cleared her throat. "I heard he had a job with a tree company."

Nicole scoffed. "It wasn't much of a company, just a family he knew that cuts and sells wood every winter."

"Do you know them?"

"A guy named Jerry? Jimmy? Something." Nicole shrugged. "They picked him up in a blue truck and paid him in cash."

Analía sighed. She stared at the floor for a minute. Then she asked, "Do you know where they cut the wood?"

"I think they had land out in Brevard somewhere. They also cut up trees that fell on people's land, you know, when trees got hit by lightning, they would go wherever that was."

Analía wondered if this was useful. A family with a Jimmy or a Jerry who owned land in Brevard and cut up downed trees. It would be a good test of Ricky and Shelley's ties in town. How could this woman not have more to offer about Jaime?

"Do you know where he would go? Did he ever talk about any plans that he had, places he wanted to go?"

Nicole looked down now. "He had plans. *I told you.* We wanted to go to Mexico with—" She stood up abruptly, went to the door and screamed, "Chuy!"

Chuy appeared quickly with the child in his arms. He handed the toddler to Nicole, who grabbed the girl from him and slammed the door in his face.

Nicole plopped the toddler on the couch between herself and Analía.

"This here's Anna Jessica," she said. "We must've named her after you."

Ricky stood outside with Chuy staring at the door. Like Analía, he felt dragged along by the force of other people's motivations, wondering if he was going in the right direction or into more trouble. But he wasn't wasting any opportunities, either. This guy knew Jaime, and had stolen his girlfriend. That couldn't have been good for their friendship, Ricky figured. It meant Chuy owed Jaime, needed to pay him back.

"So Jaime's sister came a long way to find him," Ricky began. "She took a lot of risks. Don't you figure he'd want you to help her as much as you can?" he asked.

Chuy looked offended. "I am helping," he said.

"Yeah, it was good of you to bring her here," Ricky allowed. "Don't you know anything else that could help us find him?"

Chuy squinted into the sun setting across the roofs of the trailers. "I know he wouldn't have left his baby."

Ricky's eyes widened. "That's Jaime's kid?" He looked ready to run back inside the trailer.

Chuy nodded. "I don't want to say anything bad about Nicole," he said, and let the reasons lie however obvious they were. "But he wouldn't have abandoned that baby."

"Looks like he did," said Ricky, still processing this development.

"No way. It had to be very bad for him to leave her. He was killing himself trying to make money for Anna Jessica *and* to send to Mexico. He had two families to support, and he wouldn't have quit on either of them."

"Okay, so, what about...what was there in his life that would've made him run away?"

"Don't you think I've thought about that? We were friends, you know. I didn't have nothing to do with Nicole until he was gone for a while. I thought he'd be back. Both of us sat around here thinking of what might have happened...and we couldn't think of anyplace he'd go on purpose. He seemed happy here, like he was going to stay the rest of his life."

At that moment the thin metal door of the trailer flew open and banged against the wall. Analía came out of the trailer looking shellshocked. Her eyes scanned the yard, but there were no answers there. "We will go," she said vaguely as she walked past Ricky, climbed into the truck, and sat staring through the windshield. Ricky mumbled a thanks to Chuy and got in beside her.

"That's my niece. That's my blood," said Analía. She kept

moving her hands, smoothing the fabric of her skirt over her knees, touching the door handle, moving the fins of the air conditioning vent. She shoved her hair behind her ears. She clasped her hands together and crossed and uncrossed her feet.

If it had been Shelley, Ricky would have hugged her. Instead he sat frozen in the driver's seat, unsure whether one shy kiss in the woods gave him the right to comfort her. He felt irrelevant, or selfish, to think that a few kisses would have any effect on this ache that stretched between two countries. Not knowing what else to do, he finally started the engine, feeling that the noise was interrupting something that deserved silence.

Ricky pulled into the driveway of Sue's house and turned off the truck. Analía sat in the passenger seat, still staring out the front window. She turned to him and said quietly, "Thank you for taking me there, Ricky. I need to think about this now." She dropped her eyes and opened the truck door. "Thank you," she said again, and walked into the house. He watched her go. The natural grace of her movements was gone. She walked as if she was pushing through deep water.

Inside, Analía closed the guest room door and sat on the bed for a while, flipping the phone card around in her hands. She could keep this to herself for a while, not startle her mother. Her instinct was not to spread the panic she was feeling. But wasn't that what Jaime did? She dialed her way through the series of numbers and listened to the computerized noises.

"Tengo noticias, ma," she began after the usual greetings. *I have news.* She could hear her mother's breath quicken, and her voice was demanding as she asked what happened.

"I have not found Jaime, ma. But I found his girlfriend here,"

Analía began. As her mother began to insist that the girlfriend would know where he was, Analía continued. "Ma, Jaime had a baby with this girlfriend." She paused. "I have a niece."

The other end of the line was silent. Analía wondered if the connection had been broken, or her mother had dropped the phone.

"Ma?"

A scuffling noise over the line. "I have...a granddaughter in the United States?"

"Yes, ma." Another half-minute of silence. "I know, ma, it's a big surprise." Analía mentally scolded herself for not planning this better. "She's very pretty, ma, about two years old. Her name is Anna Jessica." Her voice broke as she thought of Nicole saying the baby was named after her.

"A baby is always a blessing," her mother pronounced firmly. "I am a grandmother."

"*Sí*, ma."

"Tell me everything about her," her mother ordered. So Analía did, including how she found Anna Jessica, Nicole, and the trailer. Her haphazard search for Jaime always made sense when she recounted it; all the pieces fell into place looking backwards.

"They did not get married?"

Analía realized she didn't know. "I don't think so."

"This mother, did she refuse to let Jaime see the baby?" her mother asked. "Is that why he ran away?" Analía was startled.

"No, ma, they were living together." She sighed. "I still don't know why he ran off."

"Why did he not tell us about this?" asked her mother.

Analía had been asking herself the same question. "I don't know, ma." They were both silent, not wanting to speak ill of the absent, but confounded by Jaime never mentioning his daughter. After a moment, Analía tried to explain Nicole, whom she felt might have something to do with Jaime's silence. "This Nicole, ma, she is…it's hard to explain. She's…not very happy."

"Of course not. Her baby's father has disappeared."

"It's more than that, ma. She's, she doesn't seem very responsible. She doesn't have a job, and she seems…I'm a little worried." Analía wondered if this was fair. After all, Nicole was caring for Anna Jessica, she had a home and food and her other grandmother providing for her. But Nicole seemed much more of a person who would abandon things than Jaime ever did.

She realized her mother was crying. "Ma?"

Her mother sniffed loudly. "I will never see my granddaughter. They will not give me permission to go there. I am just an old lady." More sniffling. "My *nuera* is a good-for-nothing." Analía was startled to realize that yes, in the customary sense that didn't concern itself with official ceremonies, the mildly appalling Nicole *was* her mother's daughter-in-law. Her own sister-in-law.

"No, no, ma, she says she *wants* to visit Mexico. But I don't know if she can do it."

"You must find a way, Analía. Bring me my granddaughter. And that *nuera* if you have to. I cannot lose any more family."

"*Mamí!* Don't talk like Jaime is gone forever! I am *trying*. I am going to find him."

"I know, *mija*. You are doing a great job. I'm sorry you have so many hard things to do. That is why God made you strong."

Analía rolled her eyes to the ceiling, which didn't make her feel any better. Now she had two people to rescue from the United States. Even if she found Jaime, she couldn't very well just grab both of them and run for the border. Jaime must have felt just this way, with a distant sibling and a child under his feet to worry about. And she had, eventually, a college education to finish, as soon as she left behind the only other man, besides Jaime, who had ever felt reliable. If there was no way to gather everything she loved in one place, running away from all of it felt like a reasonable second choice.

21
All In

Sophia's appointment with the Forest Ranger finally arrived. "I'm going ginseng hunting," she said out loud to her closet. "What should I wear?" *It's basically hiking,* she thought, so she dressed for that. She was as nervous as if the little man-shaped root she sought was an actual man she would meet on a blind date. Would he show up? Would their encounter satisfy her, or would she go home disappointed? She buzzed with anticipation as she drove to the ranger station and pulled up beside the young man standing next to a truck with the Forest Service seal on the side.

Stan pulled his clipboard from the front seat and smiled at her as she got out of the SUV. He had grown into his job since his encounter with Shelley. In just a few months he had learned to keep his boots dry and his truck out of ruts. "Good morning. Got a little paperwork to do before we get started. This is a waiver of liability," he said to Sophia. "You're agreeing that you won't hold the Forest Service responsible if you fall down out there or get bitten by a snake." He smiled wider. "That probably won't happen, but we have to be careful just in case."

Sophia smiled too. "No problem at all." She took the clipboard and signed, happy to see someone take safety and liability seriously. Stan stowed the clipboard and they got in the truck. They turned from the ranger station lot down a two-lane road that led into the forest. Small green and white signs predicted waterfalls and fishing areas ahead.

"I love these woods so much," Sophia commented. "I can breathe easier out here."

Stan nodded. "I have the best job on earth."

"How did you decide to be a ranger?" Sophia asked.

"We used to come here on vacation when I was a kid," he answered. Sophia thought to herself that he still looked like a kid. He couldn't be more than twenty-five or so. "I never wanted to leave," he continued. "My parents were not happy that I studied forestry in college," he grinned at her. "My dad is a doctor in Philadelphia, he wanted me to follow in his footsteps. But I always knew I wanted to come here."

"It's lucky that you could come here so young." Sophia regretted all the years she had spent on the gritty concrete sidewalks among the buildings that obscured the sunlight. "But your career must not impress your parents."

"Not at all," Stan said. "Nor my salary. They call it the 'mountain tax,'" he continued, "that income you give up to be here. But it's worth it." He dropped the truck into a lower gear as they turned up a gravel road. "So what do you do?"

Sophia had been unable to answer that question since she unloaded her U-Haul. "I'm sort of retired," she said. "Or taking a break. I'm having health issues."

Stan made a face of concern.

"I used to work in insurance. I started as an adjuster and worked my way into upper management." Sophia stripped her resume blurb to its bones, since it no longer applied.

"I can see why you'd want to come here." Stan smiled.

"Oh yes. I feel so much better." She was quiet. "Some things I miss, though." Stan didn't say anything, so she went on. "I used to be very active in the city...I was on a few boards. The art museum was my favorite, dealing with all those beautiful creations, talking with all the artists, that was so different from files and budgets. My heart was in that art museum. But I got sick, and I needed a new environment." She watched the blackberry bushes beside the road for a minute. "So far my life here is hiking and shopping and dancing, which sounds marvelous, but I'm at loose ends sometimes. I'm trying to fill my life with the things that are meaningful to me, you know, impress myself for once instead of everybody else." Hearing herself, she thought this speech needed a little work. She hadn't had much occasion to practice it. Gale had never needed her to explain herself.

Stan did not comment, but pointed up and out through the windshield. "There's ginseng up under this ridge," he said. "I saw it in the summer. It'll be good to check and see if it's still there." Sophia was quiet while he navigated slowly around switchbacks as the gravel lane climbed and went back downhill. He pulled off in a small patch of grass.

"So do you know what you are looking for?" asked Stan as they got out of the truck.

"Well, I've looked at a lot of pictures," Sophia said. He nodded toward the trailhead and they set off, branches enveloping them in cool shade.

"That's a start," Stan allowed. "It's pretty easy to find in Pisgah, and this is the right time of year for it. Right now the leaves will be bright yellow. On the forest floor, it's hard to miss."

"It sounds pretty," Sophia said.

"It is," Stan agreed. "If you see a big patch, it's like a gold carpet in the woods." They walked for a few minutes, Stan scanning the forest floor. He paused near a tree trunk that was almost in the path.

"Now this," he said, reaching toward the tree. "See how it has five leaves?" He twisted a piece of vine hanging from the trunk so that she could see it. She nodded at the bright red whorl of leaves about the size of an open hand. "Ginseng looks like this, except for the color. This is Virginia creeper. Of course, this is a vine, and ginseng will be freestanding on the ground." Sophia studied the plant diligently. Stan pointed at the ground. "See how it looks closer to the ground? Ginseng will look similar to that, but yellow."

"Is this a poplar tree?" Sophia asked. Stan looked up.

"No. But that is," he pointed to another tree nearby. "See how the leaves are shaped like big tulips? That's why it's called a tulip poplar." He waited for her to confirm that she saw what he saw. Sophia thought for a moment.

"If they look the same when they're green," she queried, "how can you find it in the summer?"

"Good question." Stan grabbed the whorl of leaves again. "See how all five leaves are about the same size, or evenly descending in size?" Sophia looked and nodded. "On ginseng, these two at the base will be smaller than the other three."

Sophia sighed audibly. "This is pretty detailed, isn't it?" she said, sounding a little defeated.

"Just takes practice," he said. "Let's not give up yet." He let go of the leaves and turned down the path. After a while he stopped and turned to her.

"Now what are you looking for again?"

Sophia knitted her brow. "Yellow, five leaves, close to the ground..." She looked around. Stan waited.

"I see yellow, but those are fallen leaves," she muttered to herself. Stan took a step off the path. She took the clue and looked further in that direction. "There's so much yellow," she said. Stan led her a few steps and bent down, touching some faded golden leaves.

"I believe that's what you want," he raised his eyebrows at her.

Sophia gazed down at the three worn sets of leaves poking up from the leaf litter. The leaves had holes in them where she guessed bugs had chewed them. Sure, she saw the five leaves, and the two smaller ones, but if Stan hadn't been smiling at her she would have walked right by this. She figured she had been walking past ginseng all summer.

"So that's it," she said, trying not to sound disappointed.

"That's what all the fuss is about," Stan nodded. "Do you see the other ones?" he asked.

Suddenly she *did*. With one plant in front of her as a model, her eyes locked onto several other small groups of leaves that were the same splotchy color. She stood up straighter.

"I do," she said wonderingly. "It's...all over," she said.

Stan bobbed his head and shrugged slightly. "I wouldn't say all over," he said, "but it's a decent patch. We can't pull it up, but if the soil was loose enough, you could just pull those out like a carrot. Most people dig them to avoid breaking the root."

Sophia stood still. She wished there were a soundtrack with music swelling to mark the occasion, but the woods were silent except for birds and a few leaves rustling in a breeze. These bedraggled leaves hanging limply from their stems were all that stood between her and the edge of a cliff. Out here in the dusty fall sunshine, among all the other twigs that crisscrossed over the dirt, they didn't seem enough. It was hard to see the magic in pulling up a carrot, especially when its leaves didn't look as healthy as most carrots' leaves in the produce section. It hadn't occurred to her that she was sharing her sustenance with chewing bugs.

"What kind of bugs eat the leaves?" she asked Stan.

"I'm not sure. Most bugs won't because they're bitter, but I guess something is." He shrugged.

"I want to practice finding more," she said. Stan shrugged again and started walking. Sophia followed, very slowly, trying to pick out any shade of yellow in the forest.

After a bit Stan offered, "That was pretty good luck, actually. It's hard to find a patch like that anywhere now *except* here in Pisgah, it's been so over-harvested everywhere else."

"I heard about that," Sophia mumbled, distracted. She strode along staring at the ground for a few more minutes, then finally relaxed. "Yes, I heard that's a problem," she turned her attention back to Stan. He nodded.

"I spend most of my time chasing poachers," he said. "When I don't have ride-alongs."

"It must be hard work protecting the forest from all the people who want to destroy it," commented Sophia. "I guess it takes a lot of monitoring to keep people from ruining things."

"Oh yeah, we've tried everything. We put special dye in the ground so it gets drawn up into the roots. If we find somebody with roots we think are from here, the dye makes the roots look orange under a black light. We've injected almost-microscopic stamped metal tags into the roots, then you can see them in X-rays later. But everybody is looking for easy money," Stan shook his head. "They've nearly eliminated it on private land. The deeper it is in the woods, the more they want it."

Sophia was distracted for a second by the X-rays, worried that her medicine might be carrying radiation. "Yes," agreed Sophia. "I met a young man who farms ginseng. That's the perfect solution. We farm it, and the wild ginseng will be safe."

"Nobody wants that ginseng," Stan pointed out as they headed back on the trail toward the truck. "They're superstitious about wild ginseng being better. But there's not enough to meet demand, and it's going to be extinguished if we're not careful. People with these archaic ideas resist farming beneficial plants. We did it with carrots and potatoes, it's just sentimental not to do it with ginseng."

"Then the wild ginseng could stay safe," Sophia finished for him. After a few moments she continued. "So I know I can't collect ginseng here," she said. "But I would love to find my own. Do you have any idea where I could hunt for myself?"

Stan looked skeptical. "You're going to have a hard time getting anyone to let you hunt on their land. If people have ginseng growing, they will want to collect and sell it themselves. But you can hunt it on national forest land with a permit."

"But I just want it for my own use…"

"You still need a permit. The application's pretty straightforward, but the permits are assigned by lottery," said Stan encouragingly. "You'll just have to try your luck."

After their conversation it felt wrong to Sophia to get ginseng from the national forest. And luck was a poor prescription for staying healthy. "Couldn't I pay someone to collect it on their land? You know, like those pick-your-own berry farms?"

Stan wrinkled his brow. "Well, I've never heard of anybody doing that."

"No? It sounds like a great business idea to me," Sophia was enthused.

"Maybe. But you know, berries grow in one season. Ginseng takes years." They had arrived back at the truck. Sophia opened the truck door and climbed in.

"But I can *practice* hunting it here as much as I want, right?"

"Of course. Just don't let me catch you taking any." Stan grinned at her.

"Never!" she said, smiling. She spent the ride back to her car plotting a dig-your-own-ginseng farm in her head. She itched to sit down and write a business plan.

22
Threat Level: Red

"You got another package from State," Sue announced as she handed Shelley a knife and a cutting board in the kitchen. They were canning carrots. Shelley thought it was a waste of effort, since carrots were always cheap at the store, but Sue insisted on preserving every extra vegetable from her garden. Sue gestured toward an inch-thick white envelope on the dry side of the kitchen counter. Shelley switched the knife and board to one hand and picked up the envelope, turning it over and back. She tossed it back and it flopped heavily onto a pile of fluffy orange peelings.

"That environmental science program sure burns through a lot of trees for advertising," Shelley groused.

Sue picked the envelope back up, brushed off some peels, and held it up to Shelley's face. She tapped a finger on the round green symbol now slashed through with orange. "It says right on the back that it's printed on recycled paper. What's your next excuse?" She laid the envelope back in a dry spot.

"Okay, okay, anyway it's not about *my* excuses. They have their own excuse. They won't let me in the door unless I pay for it."

Sue put her arm around Shelley's back. "Shelley honey, you've got no parents and no money. Can't you qualify for help?"

"Everybody says so," Shelley said. "Have you seen the size of the financial aid application?"

"If you want to go to real college you better get used to paperwork."

"I'm so tired of everybody calling it 'real' college. Are those imaginary A's I'm getting at the community college? Don't they count?"

"Of course they do, sweetie. You are very smart. That's why you need to get a good education. You need a degree with the right name on it so people will listen to your smart ideas."

"That's what it takes, huh?" Shelley dropped a bunch of carrots onto the cutting board and whacked the tops off in one clean chop. "So I have to leave home and spend four years somewhere else, just so people will take me seriously? Nobody who's just lived with plants their whole life could possibly know anything about them? How are farmers supposed to keep their farms going if they leave for four years? Do you know what kinds of weeds can set in in four years?" She swept the carrot tops into her hand and flung them into a plastic bowl on the back of the counter. Sue had been composting since before composting was cool. Fertilizer cost money.

"Anyway, I'm not sure I liked it there. It was such a big...city. And everyone was really nice to me, but it still felt weird. I felt like I was from Mars. Those kids are so rich, and they don't even know it. They have special *clothes* for hiking – for walking around outside! Not old clothes that you can get dirty, I mean special clothes, expensive ones. Nobody's trying to be mean, not like the obnoxious kids in high school, they just think the woods are a big adventure park." She decapitated more carrots. "It was like I had static electricity, Sue, every time I talked to somebody, they looked jolted."

Shelley put down the knife and crossed her arms, leaning on the counter. "Don't get me wrong. There's so much more to learn than I ever knew. But the rest of it is a lot to put up with just to learn stuff."

"Those people need to hear from *you*, Shelley. You know as much about the woods as they do."

"I don't think they know that."

"Well, then you need to tell them," Sue concluded. "They'll graduate and get the money and the degrees to keep coming in here and buying land, and getting on committees, and getting people to do what they want. You have to get some of that."

"Yeah…" Shelley didn't see how to argue with that. But then she did. "It's not just the money and the degrees, Sue. It's also the *balls*." She met Sue's mildly judgmental look. "Sorry. But it's true. They come in with so much *energy*. What if I end up like that? If my choices are getting stuck at the gas station or turning into that Sophia woman, I'm staying home."

"You need to do it," Sue persisted. "Make them listen to you. Even if it just slows them down. Those people see a mountain, and all they can think of is chopping down trees to make a view. They don't care about the animals that live up there, or the people that go up there. I've got nothing against the sky, but there shouldn't be sky where there used to be trees." She pushed a batch of carrots from the cutting board into boiling water, wiping the steam that collected on her arm onto her pants. "They build those houses up there, hanging off a mountain, it's like they want to cut in line and go live with God before it's their turn."

Shelley had never heard Sue talk this way. She tried to follow Sue's argument. "And, so…what I'm supposed to do about that is fill out lots of paperwork, live in a concrete box, and feel awkward for four years. And then no one listens to me anyway because I'm just a redneck. This is a great privilege, why?"

Sue had walked into the pantry while Shelley was complaining. She came out and shut the old pantry door gently and went to the counter with a box of metal jar lids. She opened the flap, and the brass-colored circles rang as they fell onto the counter among the sealing rings that were already there. A few caught the light and made signal flashes.

"You didn't go to college, Louise didn't go to college. Is your life so bad?" Shelley asked before the jar lids stopped ringing.

Sue sighed and it made her look half an inch shorter. "I wasn't smart enough. I didn't have the money, either." She looked straight at Shelley. "You have a choice."

Shelley tilted her head and her voice came out cool. "I don't think I do. If everyone tells me I *have* to go, that's not really a choice, is it?"

Sue shoved all the brass-colored rings and circles into the sink and turned on the faucet. "So that's it, Shelley? You make it sound like you're going to prison. You were there for four days. You didn't see a single thing you liked?"

Shelley remembered finding her way through the half-lit stacks and leaving the library under cover of darkness, a spy gathering intelligence from the most obvious source possible.

"I don't think it's worth it," she said, wanting to be stubborn. Sue rinsed the lids with her lips pressed tight together.

It was 7:30 on Thursday night and there was still no music. Dancers milled around the gym. Some gave up expecting music anytime soon. They pulled folding metal chairs from behind the bleachers and sprawled on them, refugees in a makeshift shelter. They plied their boredom with snacks, and the refreshments on the front table were nearly gone.

"What's going on?" Sophia asked a man in wire-rimmed glasses and a flannel shirt.

"They're waitin' for a new guitar player," the man said as if there were all the time in the world.

"Where's the regular one?" she asked. If the musicians were refusing to play as a protest to the scholarship program, that would be the last straw. She was tired of dealing with their unconventional habits, their half-assed commitment.

The man glanced at her. "Don't know," he said, and turned away. *The ability to play dumb must be passed down genetically here,* Sophia thought.

"So that's where we are now?" she muttered to Gale. "Now they just show up whenever they want? The musicians just come and go as they see fit?"

"I heard the new guy's coming from Marion," Gale said. "How far away *is* that?"

Sophia tried to find out. She dragged Gale through the complacent crowd with an air of purpose, like shelter workers trying to take surveys or do a head count. No one would talk to them about the missing band member.

"Where's that girl, the one who goes to the community college, who's always with the Latina woman? Isn't she connected to the guitarist?" Sophia was ready to kick ass, but she had forgotten to take names.

"I don't see her," Gale said. "Why don't we go powerwalk a few laps around the football field? We can get our exercise in, in case this guy doesn't show up."

"Let me run to the ladies' room first."

As she squatted in the bathroom stall, Sophia heard the door to the hallway open again. Shoes clicked on the tile floor, at least two pair.

"I heard they're getting him bonded out tomorrow," a voice said. "Poor thing, they just snatched him up in the woods, out in Pisgah. He's been sittin' in jail, missing work. Not playin' tonight is the least of his worries."

A different voice tsked. "Sue must be beside herself."

"Um-hmm." Various noises ensued and the ladies didn't speak again until they were at the sink. Sophia had barely breathed since they entered.

"All over a little ginseng," said one.

"Don't take much these days. I guess Ken might be our guitar player for a while," said the other. Sophia heard the door open and close as they left the restroom. She felt lightheaded, and sank onto the seat. The oxygen returned to her brain, fueling a shaky rage. She pulled up her pants, yanked open the stall door and strode out of the bathroom, through the placid crowd. Gale was waiting at the refreshment table.

"I'm sorry, but we have to leave right now. I cannot stay here," she said. She was over-enunciating.

Gale furrowed her brows. "Are you sick?" she asked. "Are you okay?"

Sophia shook her head and clenched her jaw.

"Okay, okay," Gale shrugged at the man who had been about to hand her a bottled water, and took Sophia's arm. "What's going on?"

Sophia pushed open the gymnasium door. When they were away from the building she spun toward Gale.

"Do you know *why* there's a new guitarist player? Do you know *where* the regular one is? In jail!" She waved her arms around. "For poaching ginseng from the National Forest! What is *wrong* with these people?" She stomped toward the parking lot. "I guess he doesn't even care that people need that ginseng for medical purposes!"

Gale saw her relaxing evening going up in smoke. "I'm sure he sells it for that, doesn't he? For extra income," Gale said. At Sophia's look, she hastily continued. "I mean, it's not *lost* if he steals it from the forest, it ends up at the bottling factory, right? It's still available…"

"The ginseng in Pisgah is not meant for that!" Sophia said. "They're trying to preserve it for everybody. That's why we have laws. It's a reserve for everybody. It's the tragedy of the commons! Like in Boston. I should know! Why don't people learn from history? Do they even study history here? That man probably skipped half his school days to go kill things in the woods." She fumbled with her keys. A few rows away, her car's alarm system produced its greeting beep, a faithful steed proclaiming its readiness for battle. "Something has to be done about this." Sophia stalked to her vehicle, not even saying goodbye. Gale cocked her head and watched her go, then sighed and went back into the gymnasium to wait for the music with the other refugees.

"I just don't see how we can have criminals involved in a scholarship program," Sophia stated as if the point were obvious. She was back in the principal's guest chair first thing Friday morning, facing the wall of student success. She had attended plenty of management seminars where they warned against repeating the same behavior and expecting a different result, but the situation had changed: a crime had been committed.

The principal let his eyes wander to the window of his office cube, through which he could see the school secretary making a sympathetic face at him.

"Ma'am, the Thursday night dances are not a scholarship program," he said. "The dances are a community event. The community donated to the scholarship program. If you are unhappy that there were, as you say, criminals present, then you could collect for the scholarship program another way. We would be very grateful for any funds that you raise. But neither I nor the school board determine who plays at the dances." He looked directly at her. "We never have, and we never will."

"Do you mean to tell me that if the band members, say, were pedophiles, that you wouldn't have a problem having them in your school?"

Years of telling adolescents not to roll their eyes made it nearly impossible for Mr. Williams to roll his own, so he didn't. The idea was so outlandish that he wanted to say, *We'll cross that bridge when we come to it*, but experience had also taught him to be wary of being quoted out of context. He hadn't come up with a non-sarcastic reply when Sophia went on, thinking his silence meant she had made a point.

"Also, do you think it's a good idea to have people who break the law serving as role models for the students here? I don't think it sends a very good message that you can go to jail and be the heroes of community events. These young men have no respect for the very land they live on, and I don't think they should be allowed to go on as objects of admiration."

The principal's mind had wandered, but confusion dragged it back. "What do you mean, about the land?"

"I mean they don't respect the land, that's why he was stealing ginseng. Plenty of people depend on ginseng for their health, and that man was removing it from public lands. They don't respect the law, or other people's needs. As the principal, you have the authority to make a rule that people with criminal records can't participate in programs on school grounds. You should do it for the safety of the students. And the reputation of this school."

"Speaking of reputations," Mr. Williams said. "I noticed you called the press."

Sophia nodded. "Of course," she said offhandedly. When the principal sat looking at her, she continued. "It was an event.

Don't you think people deserve credit for supporting the students?"

"I'm having trouble understanding why you would call attention to something that you have so many concerns about. Seems to me that you created that very pressure on our reputation that you're so worried about." He paused. "Maybe you could put your attention elsewhere."

Sophia wrinkled her brow and her voice curdled. "Are your students doing so well that you can turn away people trying to raise money for scholarships? How do you think their parents would feel about that?"

The principal took a deep breath and stood up. "Sophia, I appreciate your input, and I'm sure you'll take your concerns to the school board next, and I'll see you there. As for your suggestion to order everyone with a criminal record off these grounds, if we did that, we would lose some important staff and a good number of students, who I think will be less likely to expand their criminal records if they, oh, say, graduate from high school. Have a nice day." He circled his own desk without looking at her and continued on past the secretary. Sophia sat a few moments and then left as well. Maybe this hometown bureaucrat wouldn't listen to her, but she knew someone who might.

She hurried home, inspired. Before long her dining room table was spread with printouts and highlighter pens, her laptop open in the middle, a king among his subjects. She had notes on criminal justice procedure, ginseng sales statistics, the staff flowchart of the North Carolina Wildlife Commission. She was building an argument to be allowed to join an argument. Her stomach didn't hurt at all. She picked up her phone.

When Gale answered, she said, "I need your advice."

"Okay."

"I want to go to court," Sophia announced. "I want to be a witness to the mistreatment of our precious environment."

Not usually prone to repeating herself, Gale said, "O-kayyy."

"But I'm not sure that's the right angle. You see, I'm going to call that ranger and tell him that I want to testify in a poaching case. I know it's not going to make sense at first. I know it doesn't seem that I'm involved in the case," she explained. "But I am. All of us are."

"I guess that's true in the big-picture sense."

"They need to understand that this is not a minor case. They need to know how important ginseng is," she started.

On the other end of the line, Gale bit her lip. "Isn't that why they arrest people?"

"Of course. But it's…underwhelming for them to just declare that it's a medicinal plant. People need to see a real human being whose health is affected. The ranger says there's less and less of it every year; they need to know that this is a *medical* issue. For *human beings*. I wouldn't be just there for me, I'd be there for everybody, everybody who needs something from the forest. Maybe if that man sees who he is stealing from, it will mean something to him. If it doesn't mean something to him, it will to the judge."

"I see what you're saying," Gale said. "I guess. Can you just volunteer to testify?"

"That's what I'm not sure about. I was hoping you could help me figure out how to approach the ranger that I went on the ride-along with." Sophia neatened a stack of papers with the hand that wasn't holding the phone. "He can tell the ranger who arrested that man, and he can tell the D.A. They ought to be interested in support for their case."

"That sounds like the right networking," Gale said. "Are you sure you have the energy to mess with this?" she asked. "Won't court be pretty stressful? I mean, you've got what you need, there's still plenty of ginseng in the stores, right?"

"Sure, for now. Although it's expensive. But I can't just stand by while this is happening, just because I'm safe. I'm responsible for what I do with my privilege. It would be lazy and selfish not to try."

Gale didn't want to argue with her friend. "Well, you sound very passionate. Just tell the ranger what you told me."

Sophia squeezed her eyes shut, like a child making a wish. "I hope it works." They said goodbye. Sophia tapped the End Call spot on her screen, and kept the phone ready in her hand as she shuffled the papers on the table, looking for Stan's cell phone number.

Sue had dealt with bondsmen during Ricky's previous adventures. She drove down to the county courthouse on Friday morning, since most of their offices were located nearby. The one who had been the nicest in the past had an office in the basement of the courthouse itself, down a long sidewalk and around the corner of the old brick building, next to an entrance to the plumbing and furnace systems.

He recognized her as she entered through a wooden door whose creaking hinges served to announce guests. "Ms. Morgan," he boomed. "You're the best lookin' lady I've had in here this week." He came around his desk and shook her hand. He pointed at a chair and returned to his own, leaning forward on his arms on his desk. "That boy actin' up again?" he said sympathetically.

"He's a good boy," she began.

"I know it," the bondsmen said. "I know it for sure, Ms. Morgan. It's a little early for deer, ain't it?"

Sue shook her head. "Not deer this time. Ginseng again, and this time in Pisgah."

The bondsman's cheery expression changed. He made an "oof" sound, like getting a small punch in the stomach. "So it's gonna be federal court. They're gettin' pretty mean about that. You gonna get him a lawyer?"

"Of course. Right now I just need him out of jail."

"Right," said the bondsman, and he made a few calls. He wiped his hand over his face before he spoke to her again.

"Whoo, they got him on a $4000 bond." He let Sue react, then he added, "But I know y'all. He ain't never skipped out on nothin' before. I know that boy always takes his medicine." He scratched his stomach. "He workin' now?"

Sue nodded. "He's missed a few days, of course. I called in for him, they said they'd give him a few more days. But he needs to be making money to pay the lawyer. And everything else, of course."

"Well, you know how it works. Ten to fifteen percent cash, nonrefundable." He thought for a second. "On Ricky, I can do ten percent and a promise. He got any assets, just in case?"

Sue shook her head. "All he's got in his name is that truck."

"That'll do," said the bondsman, and turned his chair to his dusty computer.

Sue picked at the strap of her purse in her lap and cleared her throat. "The title's at the bank," she said.

The bondsman turned back and studied her for a second. "You got the cash on you?" Sue nodded. "I'm gonna need you to sign onto it, too." She nodded again, and he turned again and poked at his keyboard with two fingers.

Hours of red tape later, Ricky emerged from the back of the jail, speedwalking toward the front door. Sue followed him silently. He realized he didn't know where she parked. He looked at her. She nodded to the left and he spun in that direction. He let her catch up so she could lead him to the car.

"You have your papers with your court date, right?" she asked quietly. He scowled and nodded. Neither of them said anything else until they pulled away from the parking deck. Shelley had waited with the car, and though she was relieved to see Ricky come out of jail in one piece, she picked up on the mood and didn't say a word either. Ricky scooted down in his seat, one foot on the other knee, staring out the window. His eyes dropped to his lap.

"Sorry about the money, mom," he said. "How much they charge you?"

"Four hundred," Sue said.

Ricky shook his head and looked out the window again. "Those roots were worth twice that, dried." It took four pounds of fresh roots to dry into a pound, but their value grew faster than the water content evaporated. Now they would mildew in an evidence locker, after being subjected to X-rays and black lights. "So we're down twelve hundred from where we thought we'd be."

"Plus the impound fee for the truck." Sue squinted out the window. She sighed. "Ricky, maybe you should think about planting your own 'sang." Ricky half-sneered.

"It's not the same, mom, you know that."

"Not if you baby it, no," Sue said. "But Shelley said they talked in her class about this wildcrafting thing. Simulation or something. You just plant it, safe on your own land, and leave it alone. You can't tell the difference. We've got woods on those back two acres, behind where momma used to keep her bees." She glanced in the rearview mirror at Shelley, for confirmation. Shelley pursed her lips and nodded, once, but didn't look at Ricky. She didn't want to get trapped on either side of this argument.

"Well, mom, that's a great idea for ten years from now," Ricky said, sounding defeated. "You know what them seeds cost?" He jiggled his foot. "It's not wet enough back there, I don't think."

"So water it, once in while, just enough to keep it from dying."

"It's not the *same*, mom." His voice rose. "Plus, anybody knows it's out there, they'll steal it."

Her voice stayed quiet but there was a hint of steel in it.

"You're a fine one to talk about stealing it—"

"Don't you dare!" he boomed. "Those're supposed to be *public* woods. If all those people that live other places didn't buy up land and put up No Trespassin' signs, everybody could still hunt *out* of Pisgah. Like behind the house. You know Dad hunted 'sang up there since he was my age, until them people put that house up there. How much 'sang you think they graded over to make that big ol' driveway? Now the only way I can get up there is if their plumbing goes out. Half the land in the county is owned by companies from God knows where. They never come around, but they'll fly somebody in to take you to court if you go on their property. Which law am I supposed to break?" he asked. "Trespassin' or poachin'?"

"Maybe neither," Sue said, almost placating. "That's what I'm saying. We *have* land. It's not much, but it would be better than getting arrested all the time. You could still hunt other places, but we'd have it just in case. Like a savings account."

Ricky clenched his jaw and glared out the window. "So I just farm in my backyard like I live in the suburbs? Wear a little straw hat, put up birdfeeders?" he asked.

"You can wear any goddamned hat you want to." Sue braked harder than was necessary at a light. Ricky knew his mother only cursed about twice a year, as a substitute for raising her voice.

He still said it one more time. "It's not the same."

Sue gave up, but Shelley, wishing she wasn't in this backseat, knew what Sue wanted to say to her son. She wanted to tell him it *wasn't* the same, because it wouldn't get you arrested, or sent to jail, or cause you to lose your job, or maybe even get bitten by a rattlesnake. You couldn't fall and break an ankle five miles from your vehicle, or get shot by a careless deer hunter. You couldn't get yourself killed driving home after slipping drinks all day in the woods.

Shelley also knew what Ricky wouldn't explain, even to his

mother. The pride in remembering exactly which oak on which hillock sheltered ginseng sprigs that he saw months earlier. He could not tell her that if he got tired and sat leaning against a tree, a bobcat might slip past, close enough to make his heart pound under his coat. He could not put in words the compost and mineral taste of water from an unmarked spring, or the way the air changed when he reached the crest of a ridgeline and breezes rose up at him from both sides of a mountain at once, making him wish he had wings to rise on them.

Ricky would not name the satisfaction of wandering the woods all day, from dawn until the sun was nothing more than horizontal slants of red light in the treetops, even if he found no ginseng anywhere. He could come home empty and still be full.

It wasn't the same at all.

23
An Appearance in Court

If the security guards at the county courthouse seemed extreme, what with the removal of belts and all, it was just practice for the big leagues: the federal courthouse. A sign taped to the glass entrance door presented a list of items not to be brought inside. The obvious guns and knives were prohibited, as were chewing gum, cell phones, "controversial" clothing, and children under the age of two. Half of the people who made it up the marble steps had to go right back down to return items to their cars. A few women stood on the steps, jiggling babies.

The guards wore dark suits instead of police uniforms. They were older, more courteous, yet somehow more threatening. Shelley, waiting with Ricky in the line that snaked out the door, couldn't picture them manhandling anyone to the floor or wrestling them into handcuffs. Their implacable gentlemanly confidence suggested that instead they would simply mumble into their lapel mikes and the person would disappear in a puff of smoke, to reappear in a windowless basement cell. In Guantánamo.

After they cleared the security area she whispered to Ricky, "It's like Men in Black, retired division."

"Grandpas in Black," he returned, and Shelley let out a peal of laughter that echoed in the hall before she clapped her hand over her mouth. Her eyes followed the echoes and she noticed the ceiling painted in a complex pattern of squares and lines that reminded her of Greek keys and pinwheels. A plaque on the wall stated that the ceiling had been painted this way in 1929 as a tribute to the Cherokee tribe. Shelley thought it was odd that a government that had worked so hard to kill off the Indians would paint their buildings in tribute to them. Who could understand bureaucrats anyway? She nudged Ricky and pointed at the plaque.

Wonder what Black Dog would think of that? Ricky thought to himself. He had fallen into his usual courthouse persona, tight and grumpy. Shelley eyed him whenever he wasn't looking.

Breakfast before court had been an emotional labyrinth. Sue had announced that she was too angry to come to court, but Shelley had been around long enough to know that nothing much happened at a first appearance, and Sue knew it, too. Shelley figured Sue was mad that she knew so much about court in the first place. Ricky had pretended to be pissed at his mother, but Shelley knew that anger was what he displayed when he was scared. Tim, stabbing at his eggs, had contributed an ugly rant about the forest rangers getting a paycheck to keep others from making money. Shelley had shaken her head to herself and kept her mouth shut at the table, and she sighed now, wishing they wouldn't waste time bullshitting each other when there was a crisis at hand. She and Ricky went into the courtroom. More Cherokee patterns adorned this ceiling.

"Where the hell's my lawyer," muttered Ricky, knowing it could be a while before he got an answer. They waited among the miscreants of the day, watching the digital clock in front of the judge's bench flick the minutes away.

Ricky stood when his name was called and his lawyer requested a continuance. Neither the defense nor the government was ever ready on the first appearance. The government did not even bring in its witnesses. Common practice for the defense was to stall as much as possible, hoping the U.S. attorneys would get busy with a bigger case or simply tire of one with an old date. Many people in the courtroom lost a day at work to stand up for five seconds and get a date for their next day to miss work.

Ricky's lawyer signaled to him, and he and Shelley rose together, anxious to leave. As they filed out of the courtroom Shelley noticed a thin Latino man who had been in the courtroom earlier. Now he leaned against the wall in the hallway, watching Ricky as if he had been waiting for him. She nudged Ricky's shoulder and nodded her head toward the man. "Why's that guy staring at you?"

Ricky looked directly at the man, who looked away. Ricky studied him. "How should I know?"

"Do you know him?

"He does look familiar." Ricky waited until the man's eyes landed on him again, and he recognized something. The man had been in the group of galax hunters in the woods. He had never spoken that day, but Ricky had noticed him listening intently while Analía had spoken to the group about Jaime. Ricky glanced at Shelley and strode toward the man, his politician-at-a-church-supper smile glued on. He stopped about five feet away and gave a quick nod of hello, leaving it to the man to decide whether to speak.

The man shifted his weight from the wall to his feet almost imperceptibly and said "Hello" with the same faint twists on the vowels that Analía used. Ricky stepped a few steps closer.

"I think I remember you," he said, just loud enough for the man to hear. "You in for huntin' in Pisgah, too?" The man nodded sheepishly. "Sucks, don't it? What'd they catch you with?"

The man shook his head and waved the question off. "She find her brother?" he asked. Ricky paused, suspicious of the man's motives.

"Nah, not yet," he said. "But we're still trying."

The man came fully off the wall and stuck his hands way down in his pockets, then took them out. "Listen," he said. "I maybe hunted with her brother once."

Awareness fired in the back of Ricky's mind that this was marvelous news, but weeks of frustration jumped in front of it. "Why didn't you say anything?" he nearly shouted. "Why didn't you tell us before?"

A security guard down the hallway turned square to them and stood up very straight, glaring at them. The Latino man stepped to one side and glanced around for an escape route, but Shelley stepped into the space between him and Ricky. She turned her head to Ricky for one instant and said, "You're in the courthouse. Walk away." Ricky took a step toward the man but spun on one foot and stormed down the hall, holding his hands up and bowing slightly toward the guard. Shelley turned to the man, who miraculously had not run away in those few seconds. She blinked a few times, trying to calculate everyone's emotions at once and arrive at the right way to talk to this complete stranger who might hold the holy grail in Analía's quest. No answers came, so she chose the straightforward path.

"Thank you for telling us that. I'm glad we ran into you. You think you knew Jaime?"

The man had been raised to be courteous and helpful to women. He nodded and spoke.

"I hunted before with other people, and they had a *muchacho* with them named Jaime. He said he was from Aguascalientes and, well, maybe he looked a little bit like that girl."

Shelley struggled to contain her excitement. "Do you have any idea how to find him?" she asked.

"No." The man considered for a moment. "I know how to find the people I was hunting with that day. They knew him better than me."

"Could you take us to them?" The man looked uncertain. Now Shelley had her own surge of frustration. People should know better than to make others beg. But that wouldn't stop her. "Please? We don't want any trouble or anything. Analía just needs to know if her brother is okay."

The man nodded. "Are you finished with court?" Shelley asked. He nodded again. She whipped out her phone and called Sue to round up Analía and get her to the courthouse before he could change his mind. Ricky drifted back over and stood beside the man, shifting from one foot to the other. Shelley heard him mumble something that sounded like an apology. It was accepted in the same understated fashion that it was given.

After quick introductions on the courthouse steps, Shelley and Ricky watched Analía get in a truck with the Mexican man they had managed not to lose in the intervening twenty minutes.

"Do you think she'll be okay?" Shelley asked.

"I guess so," Ricky said. "She came here all the way from Mexico by herself, she probably won't get hurt driving across town."

"With a guy we don't even know who we met at the courthouse? Not necessarily the *best* place to meet people."

Ricky glowered at her. He still had some adrenaline to burn off. "That's nice. I was at that courthouse, too, you know." He paused. "Is that why you don't like us together? I'm not good enough for her?"

Shelley's eyes widened and she almost took a step backward. "Are you crazy? I never said I didn't like you with her. It's the other way around, sort of. Both of you are perfectly good enough for each other, in fact you're so sweet together I'm jealous, but she's leaving, isn't she? You're going to be sitting in jail heartbroken."

Ricky clenched his jaw, whirled, and strode off toward the truck. Shelley stomped after him.

"I'm sorry, Ricky," she said, louder than she wanted since he was still ahead of her and moving fast. "I'm *sorry*, but isn't it true?"

24
Over the River and Through the Woods

Analía and the man from the courthouse, Ambrosio, chatted in the truck about Mexico and family and ginseng hunting. She learned that he had come to the U.S. the same way Jaime had, at almost the same age. He told her how lucky she was to have an older brother who was so devoted to his family. With every new person who joined the search for Jaime, Analía's debt of gratitude grew larger. But it didn't weigh on her. Everyone's help was a soft pillow that she could relax into while being carried around the mountains in trucks.

After a while they pulled in the driveway of a small, neatly maintained house and walked to the front door. Analía waited while Ambrosio reintroduced himself to the man who answered the door and his wife, Cirilo and María, who remembered him from the woods. He asked about the young man they had hunted with, and explained who Analía was. The woman, upon hearing this, insisted that they come in and scurried to the kitchen to make drinks.

The man looked at Analía for a few moments and said, "He used to talk about you a lot, *'manita.*"

Analía kept wanting to demand, "Where *is* he?" but she politely listened as the couple told her everything she already knew about Jaime. After a while it finally became appropriate to ask, "So do you know where he is?"

Cirilo and María looked at each other. Analía's stomach wrenched. "We are not sure where he is," María said. She smoothed the fabric of her skirt over her lap. "The last time we saw him was last year. We were all hunting together, and the police came along. We had our *permisos*, but it was the wrong week." Analía caught her breath but the woman patted her knee and continued. "There were five of us, and Jaime ran away into the woods." She looked again at her husband. He took over.

"The police took four of us to jail. We never saw Jaime in the jail. We don't think they caught him." He looked at the floor. "We didn't see him after that."

Analía glanced at the children playing in the floor. María answered her unasked question.

"They let me out of jail after a few days to take care of the children. My husband had to stay for two months," she said.

"I'm sorry," said Analía. María waved the apology away. She thought for a few moments.

"We had our car out in the woods, so we thought maybe Jaime went back to the car, but we found out later that the police towed the car away." She paused again. "Jaime was very good in the woods. I don't think he would have gotten lost. We were hunting late in the year, when the juice is in the roots and they weigh more, but it still wasn't very cold yet. He wouldn't have been cold," she repeated firmly, ruling out that fear known to people from warmer origins. "It's not like Mexico, there's water everywhere." She patted Analía's hand. "I think he would have made it home, or, well, to his home here." Maybe she needed to believe it as much as Analía did.

"The police took the car and left him in the woods?" Analía asked.

Cirilo cleared his throat. "It is not as desolate out there as you imagine, *'manita*. There are people in the woods all the time."

"But they don't know him…" Analía began, the words of the

woman in the tienda coming back to her. The receding Toyota tailgate came back. Cirilo and María dropped their eyes.

The room was silent except for the children making "vroom" noises with toy cars. Analía bowed her head and almost whispered. "I can't be sure."

Cirilo and María looked at each other again and at Analía. They bowed their heads as well. Analía did not feel rushed, or pressed to leave. No one had any answers, but they would not push her out the door to be alone with the problem.

"Do you think you could show me where the police caught you?" Analía asked.

María frowned but then she understood. "You want to see the last place he was." Analía nodded.

"It's pretty far," Cirilo warned.

"No importa." María said. "I am going to need the car keys," she announced. Cirilo handed her the keys with a loud kiss on her cheek. She gestured at Ambrosio. "You two can watch these children?" Both men shrugged placidly, and Ambrosio settled onto the couch.

Once again Analía was driven down smaller and smaller roads, deeper and deeper into the woods. All the tree trunks, all the weedy patches, all the gravelly ditches were becoming a blur, as if she were looking in the same place every time. María drove and drove, occasionally pausing at a junction and mumbling to herself about where they had hunted on that particular day. Every muscle in Analía's body tightened as she calculated walking back along every mile they covered. She wanted to lean over and look at the odometer but it wouldn't make any difference. Finally María pulled into a grassy spot and turned off the car.

"Ooh, makes me nervous to be here!" María said as they got out of the car, shaking herself as if to ward off goosebumps. "I haven't come here since the police." Her eyes widened and she gasped, then relaxed. "*Hijole,* for a minute I thought I had my tools in the car. That would be bad if the police come." She shrugged her shoulders, glanced around, unsure. Then she crossed herself, relaxed, and set off energetically. "Okay, this way," she said. Analía followed her down yet another path into the woods.

Before long María paused at a small cove. She took a few steps, zigzagging. "*Sí,*" she said to herself, bending to touch some deep burgundy leaves with her fingers. "*Aquí está.* We were digging around here when the police came," she said, and glanced around anxiously. She cleared her throat and pointed with her chin at a gap in the trees. "They came from over there. So Jaime ran—" she thought a moment and pointed again "—that way."

They both studied the trees in that direction. Analía walked toward them as if pulled by a string, and made only a few feet of progress before she was slowed by brambles. She pushed along, but low-hanging branches and vines made it nearly impossible to move forward. She shoved her way through a few briars, pulling and slapping, not noticing the first few scratches. It wasn't long before she realized she was in something even worse than a maze: there were no corridors, no lefts, no rights, nothing but tangles in every direction. She stopped.

How could he have escaped through this? she wondered. It didn't make sense. She turned around, and where she had come from looked equally formidable. A zing of fear went through her. There was no path back to María from here. She was trapped. She breathed in and out to calm herself. She could yell when she needed to. She looked up, and saw tiny patches of sky through the canopy in every direction. Branches split and crossed above her in inscrutable patterns. *He must have hidden,* she thought. It was terrifyingly claustrophobic in here, and also safe. She closed her eyes and imagined listening to the harsh voices of police arresting people only meters away. Her heart would have been pounding, she thought.

She listened to it now, trying to hear something about Jaime.

But her heart and the woods were silent. She listened until the quiet rang in her ears, and then she yelled to María for a sound to guide her back.

Back at María's house, Cirilo announced that he and Ambrosio had had an idea during their wait. "Maybe the buyer." Analía was puzzled but María was energized by the suggestion. She jumped in to explain.

"We take our ginseng always to the same woman. Maybe she remembers Jaime, maybe she knows more about him."

"Can we go to her?"

He hesitated. "We need to call first." Analía and his wife looked at him together, the same expression on both their faces. He sighed and got up and went to the kitchen. Analía heard him shuffle around, then saw him go out the back door lifting his cell phone to his ear. A few minutes passed. María stood up and patted Analía on the knee.

"We will go now, *'manita,'*" she said, and followed her husband out the screen door, letting it thwack against the frame as she went. Analía heard intent mumbling in Spanish, from both people, then Cirilo came back in alone.

"My wife is convincing her," he said with a faintly sheepish look. María came in almost immediately, the door banging louder this time.

"Dinner time is coming. Feed those savages, okay?" she said, and waved to Analía to follow her. They left the men together again in the house.

In the truck Analía asked María, "This woman does not want to see us?"

María glanced over from her position hunched over the wheel. "Oh, no, it's not that..." she said. "This woman lives very far out in the mountains by herself. She might shoot at us if she doesn't know who's coming." She smiled to let Analía know it was a half-joke. "And this way she has more time to remember Jaime."

Analía cocked her head. "You told her what we want?" she asked. Didn't this woman know it was better to ask for things in person?

María smiled again. "This woman, she is very very old. Very old. It takes her a long time to remember anything, even her own kids sometimes." She glanced out the windshield at the sun, gauging the time left 'til dark. "But she can *smell* when somebody tries to cheat her by mixing in roots of other plants."

Instead of tracking back toward the national forest, this time María turned deeper into her own neighborhood and wound left and right through a dizzying series of turns. Analía saw progressively fewer houses along the single-lane asphalt, wondering, as she did when she was with Ricky, how anyone ever found their way home here. María paused at the entrance to a one-lane bridge, checking for a car coming the other way before proceeding.

"Do you ever get lost?" Analía asked.

"Oh yes, in the beginning," María smiled. "But these are mountains, just like in Salvador. Each one looks just a bit different, different shapes, the curves and the road banks are angled differently each place...sometimes you see a place where the turn is just so, and the trees are spread the same, and you think, *hijole*, did I go in a circle? But you didn't. Usually. We're almost there," she ended reassuringly.

"How did you ever find this woman so deep in the woods?" Analía asked.

María smiled. "Her husband used to work with my husband's uncle, a long time ago. He was from Salvador. He fell in love with that woman, oooohh, back in the nineties. She wouldn't leave that house. She already had her ginseng business, so he just moved in there and stayed 'til he died. He's the one that taught my husband to hunt."

Soon María pulled off the road in front of a home that had begun as a trailer and grown by leaps and bounds of construction into a veritable complex. A maze of roofed porches, outbuildings connected by zinc-roofed breezeways, and sidings of various colors gave no clue as to where one might go to knock on the door. María turned off the engine and sat silently. Analía realized she had almost forgotten this method of approach, common in Mexico, of giving the occupant time to realize there was a visitor in the driveway. About two-thirds of the way along the hive of a structure a door rattled open, and the tallest, skinniest woman Analía had ever seen stepped out. Thick white hair hung from a low ponytail to her waist, over a flannel shirt and jeans. She raised an arm and waved her hand with far more energy than Analía thought could come from such a wraithlike figure.

María opened the door and waved back as she climbed out. Analía followed suit. "How are you?" María called out.

"Hey, girls," the woman called out, her voice also more powerful than expected. María and Analía climbed two short steps to a weathered wood deck. The woman grabbed María in a hug, hesitated, then did the same to Analía when María introduced her as Esther. Analía felt like a little girl again, since her head was level with the woman's elbows. "Y'all want coffee?" she asked. She led them back through the rattling door into her home.

The inside of the building was as puzzling as the outside. The walls and floors had the same unfinished look as the outer structure, as if someone had used whatever materials were at hand for their pure functionality. There were countertops made of plywood, storage shelves where each shelf was a scrap of a different pattern of wallboard, racks hanging from the ceiling made of every conceivable metal object – farm implements, hand tools, industrial-looking pieces from factories defunct fifty years ago. Wrinkled tan roots hung on the racks, and a warm breeze traveled across the room, carrying scents of earth and wood. In spite of the junkyard-style furnishings, there was an almost sterile feel in the space, as if it were a scientific research outpost. Analía stood inside the doorway and turned nearly a full circle, taking it all in.

"Don't worry, honey, you can't hurt nothin' in here," Esther patted her arm again. "Those're dryin' racks, for the 'sang, and all those buckets are ready to ship." She pointed to a batch of white plastic buckets stacked geometrically in one corner near another door. Analía smiled and blinked. Esther gestured to one wall, where two-by-four-framed gaps in the wall allowed a view into the next room. "That's the furnace room over there, with the fans."

She led Analía and María into another room, which resembled an office. Along the walls was a series of framed certificates, each a little dustier than the one next to it. She led them to the cleanest one, pointed, and declared, "That's my buyer's license right there. There's one for every year, going all the way back." Analía was reminded of the galax hunters in the woods, how they kept mentioning their permits. A bumper sticker on one filing cabinet read, "Mountain girls dig big roots." Esther saw Analía reading it and her face reddened a bit. "That was a gift, from the distributor's buyer. He used to flirt with me, after my husband died. Well, I guess he *thought* that was flirting." She rolled her eyes. "I was embarrassed to put it on my truck, so I put it where he would see it."

"You sell ginseng?" Analía asked.

"No, no," the woman said. "Well, yes, of course, but not to the public. I buy it from the hunters, and sell it to the companies that process it and sell it. You know, I'm like the people that buy the corn from the farmers and sell it to the cereal companies."

Analía felt weak. Jaime had found his place here. Instead of collecting eggs and selling them to stores, he had collected ginseng and funneled it into distribution. A thousand miles from home, he had continued to gather what people needed. She shook off the feeling and looked at María.

Esther opened a drawer, revealing dozens of small plastic baggies packed with seeds. "My good hunters," she said, "the ones that I know are doing it right, I give them seeds when they bring me roots. I tell them when they find a good patch of 'sang, that means that's a good growing spot, so when they dig some out, they should throw some seeds in and knock a little dirt over them. Just a little." She made a dusting motion with her fingers, like sprinkling salt. She looked at Analía to see if she understood. "That costs me out of my profits, for them seeds, but it's the right thing."

Analía nodded. She cleared her throat, thinking it was time to address a particular hunter. María took the lead and explained Analía's story. Esther's face passed through the stages Analía had become accustomed to: pleasantness at the mention of a brother, concern at the mention of him disappearing, then that serious determined look that people took on when they heard about her quest.

"Have you got a picture of him, honey?" Esther asked. Analía brought out her increasingly grimy photo, holding her breath.

Esther studied the picture. Finally she nodded. "Oh, yes, I remember this boy. He came in, oh, the last two years, I think. With some other folks." She looked at María. "With your husband, I think, right?" María nodded.

Analía wanted to know. "Did you give my brother seeds?"

"Oh, yes," Esther replied. "He had the makings of a good hunter," she elaborated. "He never brought me any tiny roots, and he was always asking about how to dry them right. It was pretty hard to explain, you know, he didn't have a lot of English. But he used every bit he understood."

"Do you know about his regular job?" asked Analía, afraid to hope.

Esther furrowed her brow for a moment, but her fabled bad memory held up this time. "Oh, sure, honey, last I knew, he was working for the Williams, cutting trees." She turned to María. "You know them? His brother's the principal down at the high school."

25
Full Circle

"I am sorry to bother you with this," Analía told Ricky. "I know you have many other things to worry about now." She did not know what was necessary to prepare for court, but Ricky had been tense and preoccupied.

"It's no big deal," Ricky said. "It'll give me something else to think about. And you can see where I went to school," he tried to smile. "I can skip a half-day of work. Nobody will die of a plumbing emergency in one morning." After all of Shelley's running around with Analía, he was glad to have a chance to contribute. They pulled into the visitor spaces of the high school. Ricky felt a little funny bothering the principal at school, but he figured Mr. Williams owed him one.

They went straight to the secretary, who greeted Ricky like an aunt who hadn't seen him since he was small. She called up the principal and soon they were sitting in his office.

"This is Analía Cuevas," Ricky said to the principal. "This is Mr. Williams, he had to put up with me when I was in school here."

"It wasn't so bad," Mr. Williams said. "I've seen you at the dances, haven't I?" She nodded. "You're quite a dancer."

"I practice a lot in Mexico," she smiled.

"So that's where you're from," he said as if he'd been wondering. He had, since he liked to know everyone in town and this mysterious person was the first brown face he'd seen at the dances. "By the way, Ricky, will you thank the band again for me for doing that fundraising night? I think all we did was get that woman more riled up, but a few students will be grateful for the money next year. I don't know what that woman's going to do next."

"Sure," Ricky said. "Glad to do it. I guess I might need a favor myself." He told Analía's story to the principal, leaving out the part about Anna Jessica. "So I reckon maybe Jaime worked for your brother at the tree service," he finished. "We'd like to go talk to him about it."

"Sure, Ricky, that sounds just fine. You want me to call him?"

"Could you?" He cleared his throat. "Um, I think maybe this guy didn't have a work permit, and I don't want Jimmy to feel like we're checking up on him."

The principal made a face and nodded. "I understand. Jimmy has trouble keeping good workers. I know he maybe goes outside the lines sometimes. I don't think he'll care. If this guy disappeared all of a sudden like you say, he'll be glad to know somebody's looking for him." They listened as the principal called his brother and explained what they needed. Ricky blushed when the principal described him in glowing terms, but he was happy that Analía overheard it.

"He says you should head over there right now, they're going out on a job in about 45 minutes," the principal said when he hung up.

"We better get a move on, then," said Ricky, and he stood up to shake hands.

"I hope you get good news, honey. That's a tough spot you're in," Mr. Williams said to Analía. She nodded again.

The tree service site reminded Analía of Mexico. Machines of indeterminate age and purpose sprawled around a gravel lot, and several Latino men in work clothes roamed among them, moving quickly and shouting urgently to each other.

"They look busy," Ricky said as they got out of the truck. "That must be the office over there," he pointed toward a short singlewide trailer behind a crane. "Watch your step."

Ricky knocked on the door, which rattled and threatened to fall off. "Yeah!" came a shout from inside. Ricky pushed the door open and peeked in. A man with an unruly mass of gray curls looked up from a scratched metal desk. "Oh, you're that kid from the school," he said, and jumped up, reaching out a hand. Ricky climbed up the two steps and shook it. Jimmy looked like the version of Mr. Williams that hadn't held together as well over time, with leathery skin and a soft paunch. Ricky introduced Analía.

Jimmy had other things on his mind, chain saws and mulch grinders. "Uh-huh. I was thinking after I talked to Mike. My guys'll know more about that boy than I do. He didn't have much English. I remember when he disappeared, though. There's one guy here that I believe used to bring him to work a lot. You should talk to him. Let's round them up." He went down the two steps in a combination of walking and falling and began shouting in the gravel lot.

"Very busy," said Analía quietly to Ricky as he came down the steps more carefully.

As Jimmy yelled, two men came over and began yelling in Spanish. Around the lot the others dropped what they were doing and came over, speaking in low tones amongst themselves. Jimmy explained Analía's search, and one of the first two guys said more Spanish. As he talked, all eyes settled on Analía. Then there was silence.

Jimmy barely paused before he prodded again. "Come on, guys, you all help this girl out." He delivered this order as if he were instructing them to chop a tree or stack wood. He strode away, leaving Ricky, Analía, and the group of workers staring at each other.

Analía waited for the awkwardness of Jimmy's abrupt commands to subside. "We came here because I heard my brother was working with you for a while," she said apologetically. A few of the men nodded. She shared the things she had learned about Jaime, and the men nodded here and there as her story coincided with what they knew. Ricky, taller than anyone in the group, was trying to look as small as possible, trying to assess what was happening while appearing nonexistent. Eyes landed on him periodically, questioning.

"He mentioned you a few times," said one of the men eventually. "He said you are going to college."

"I am hoping to find him so I can get back to school," Analía said.

There was a lot of standing around and very little talking, except for indistinct mumbles among the men.

Finally one of the two bilingual men relaxed. "We heard that the police caught him hunting for ginseng. We didn't tell Jimmy. We thought he got deported."

Another man corrected him in Spanish. "No, he got away. I heard he went to Georgia." There were louder mumbles, arguing over rumors. The bilingual man turned to her.

"We don't know. We were pretty worried, too," he said. "He never called in to work, he just stopped showing up. He didn't answer his phone."

Analía sighed. "Does anybody know who else he might have gone to stay with?"

"I can take you to where he lived," said one man. "When he first started I used to give him rides to work." There was another pause as everyone considered this option. With slow nods and small shrugs the men agreed that this worker knew him best. "I can show you after work," he said.

The bilingual man studied him. "Can you come with me?" he said to Analía. He started walking away. He seemed to be the leader in Jimmy's absence, so she followed him. Ricky scratched his head and followed her. The man led them to where Jimmy was leaning out of an open truck door, studying a clipboard. The bilingual man made a small arm motion that caused Analía and Ricky to stop several feet away from the truck. The man went up and spoke with Jimmy in low, urgent tones. Jimmy looked disgusted, glanced at Analía. They continued to mumble forcefully.

"Hell, just go do it now," Jimmy said. "Tell him to meet us at the site." He didn't look at Analía again as he started the truck.

"That guy, Roman, is going to take you there now," the man said as he led them back to the group. He gave Roman a string of rapid instructions in Spanish and the rest of the group split into two's and three's, matching themselves to other vehicles.

Roman stared at Ricky, appraising. "You come with me?" he said in a heavy, heavy accent. "Faster I drive. I bring you here after?" They both shrugged and nodded.

They crowded into a truck filled with dusty tools and plastic toys. Roman had been right when he said it would be faster if he drove. They zipped around curves and swooped through turns at junctions unmarked by any kind of sign. *Damn*, thought Ricky. *These boys know some roads even I don't know.*

"He tell me he live here a long time," said Roman. "Compañeros there know all of him."

After a while Ricky saw a familiar diner, and he realized where he was. *Oh shit,* he thought. His mouth went dry. A few more curves and then they saw it: a handcarved wooden sign with painted flowers and leaves. Roman was driving so fast no one could react before they arrived at the second sign, its arrows still pointing to Emma Lane and Emma Road.

Roman parked abruptly outside the trailer where Ricky and Shelley had taken Analía weeks ago, and he reached for his door handle. Analía put a hand on his arm, staring into her lap and shaking her head. Ricky saw her face and spoke up.

He shook his head at Roman. "We appreciate it, man. But, uh, we've already been here." He cleared his throat. "We, we don't need to knock on the door."

Roman, too, had seen Analía's face. He sat back against the truck seat. "You find this before," he confirmed. Ricky nodded.

Roman waited while Analía cried stoically in the center of the seat, sitting straight up with her head down, closed into her disappointment. Ricky leaned against her and said nothing. After a bit Roman started the engine and drove away, cautiously now, as if something might break in the truck.

26
Distant Relations

After Roman dropped them back at the tree service lot, it was still a weekday, and Ricky was still expected to appear at various homes and restrain the flows of water to their domesticated paths. He had no choice but to leave Analía on Sue's porch and drive away.

Analía stood on the porch, the sense of something unfinished preventing her from entering the house. Rest would be surrender. She couldn't just hide, the way she had after she found Anna Jessica. She realized that Nicole's inhospitality and the shock of meeting Anna Jessica had thrown her. She had run away from the trailer, utterly shaken by encountering an unexpected family member.

She had panicked and made a mistake there. Ana Jessica's bubbly spirit should be just as welcome here as it would have been in Mexico, where dozens of aunts and uncles and not-precisely-specified relatives would have celebrated this newest member "coming to the light." Cousin-uncles and aunt-mothers would have swarmed the house loaded with gifts and cakes. Analía grinned to herself imagining the surly Nicole set upon by such a horde. Then it saddened her that this hadn't happened. Jaime saw his first child enter the world without a parade of proud relatives to clap him on the back and slip him small wads of cash while passing a tequila bottle. Anna Jessica was born a year before he disappeared. He had never mentioned her. Was he afraid that if the family thought he put down roots here that he would never come home?

Bueno, now Analía knew she had a niece, the closest thing there was to a brother, and she remembered the way to Nicole's trailer. She stabbed at her phone and began watching the driveway. It took forever to get a taxi in this town, not like at home, but eventually one showed up and charged her two days' pay to drive out to the trailer park.

Nicole was as subtle as ever.

"You ain't takin' this baby," she announced before Analía had even stepped over the thin metal strip that served as a threshold to the trailer.

"Of course not!" Analía sounded indignant. "Right now you and I are the closest each other has to Jaime, and I thought we could talk."

"What good's that going to do?" Nicole whined.

"Maybe not much," Analía agreed. "But you must miss him, and so do I."

"Missing him won't bring him back."

"True. But looking for him might, and, Nicole, you must know more about his life than anybody else I've met. There has to be something useful you can tell me."

"He never did nothin' but work and come home," Nicole sounded as if she were complaining. "I'm telling you, there was no good reason for him to run off. He didn't do drugs, he didn't drink much, he got in trouble with the law a few times for driving without a license but that was it. He had no reason to take off." She sniffed.

"So he worked cutting trees..." Analía prompted.

"Yeah, for a while right before he disappeared. Before that he always worked in restaurants, that's where I met him, in a Chinese restaurant. He had been there a long time, he was an assistant manager. Then they sold the restaurant and the new owner was always on him about every little thing. He couldn't do anything right. That was a lie, they just didn't like paying him so much – you know, 'cause he'd been there a long time. He got sick of their crap and quit." It was the most Nicole had spoken at once, and the longest speech on the subject of Jaime that anyone had made in America. It was the tale of a person who existed and had common annoyances in life. The ghost she had been chasing had argued with a new boss. Analía was terrified to break the spell, like a partygoer at a séance that had turned scary but riveting.

"What else do you want to know?" Nicole asked. She seemed irritated at being forced to think about Jaime, but Nicole's animosity rolled in and out like waves on a beach, and Analía let it pass as if it presented no more threat than the waves lapping impotently at the sand.

"I was wondering if you could tell me exactly when Jaime left, or when you saw him last." She wondered if it was at the same time that he stopped sending money, or before or after. Whether he disappeared from both families at once might offer a clue.

"When exactly?" Nicole looked up at the ceiling. "Yeah, I remember. It was right after Anna J's birthday, at the end of October. We had a little party, it was on a Saturday. He took off Sunday morning and never came back."

It was the same month he stopped sending money home.

"And you never heard from him after that?"

"Not once."

Analía sat quietly for a bit. She looked out of the corner of her eye at Anna Jessica, flopped on a bean bag chair watching TV. She scanned the little girl's plump face, looking for a sign of Jaime. There was something familiar in the precise tone of her skin, and the languid way that she smiled at the cartoon characters. Analía pointed with her chin to Anna Jessica. "I think she has Jaime's ears."

Nicole rolled her eyes. "Of all things."

Analía remembered something. "Nicole," she began.

"Didn't you say you and Jaime talked about going to Mexico?" she asked.

Nicole looked wary. "Yeah."

"Do you think you ever would?" she asked. She studied Nicole, trying to imagine how to reach this person. "I wish our family could meet her someday."

Nicole sighed. "I was real excited about it. But I can't go by myself. I can't afford it, either. I don't have the money to be traveling all over the world."

"What if I visit again?" Analía asked.

"What do you mean?" For Nicole *this* visit was already too much.

"What if I come back? If I leave on time I can get more visas. You know, take pictures, bring pictures, tell her about our family in Mexico. She's *your* daughter, Nicole, I would never say otherwise. She has a lot of people in Mexico who might love her, too." Nicole didn't look too angry, so Analía went on. "We could keep in touch by internet, too. With Facebook." It felt ridiculously limited to Analía, but maybe that would make it unthreatening to Nicole.

Nicole's world had suddenly gotten too large. She was comfortable hanging around the trailer with Anna Jessica. On the other hand, it was a lot of responsibility, and what Jaime had told her about Mexico had been appealing. She got up and disappeared into another room for a few minutes.

She returned with a small tattered photo album and pushed it toward Analía. "If you find him, he's going to want this. It's his pictures. He looked at them all the time."

Analía opened the album. There were a few pictures from Mexico, even one of herself at twelve. She hadn't known he carried these photos from Mexico, protecting them from the coyote, the river, the sun. Here was a photo of Jaime holding Anna Jessica. He was older there than Analía had ever seen him. His arms were darker, his cheeks heavier, his forehead worn; he had grown into his face by passing it on. That was a *man* in this photo, a half-stranger. She felt Jaime evaporating from Nicole's future.

"No. When I find him, he's going to want you and Anna Jessica more than old photos," she said. She delivered the album back into Nicole's lap. "You hold that for him."

Nicole sighed. "Okay," she said, and moved the album from her lap to the couch, tossing it carelessly, as if she didn't expect to need it again.

"Do you have an email address?" Analía asked, sitting up straight.

"Why are we doing this?"

"If he appears we can tell each other?"

"He took off, Anna," said Nicole. "I had to deal with it, and maybe you should, too. Get on with your life."

He is the father of your child…

Didn't you love him at all…

He could be…

Anna Jessica deserves a father…

and the other half of who she is…

Analía let each of these internal temper tantrums roll through her head, one by one, with a placid expression on her face. Whatever Nicole had felt for Jaime had stiffened into bitterness. There was only one truth left that mattered.

"Your daughter is my niece," she said.

Nicole sighed again and found a notebook in the drawer of the coffee table. They set about their task of knitting a web that could hold together across a thousand miles and a well-guarded international border. Analía needed it to be as strong as real spider's silk, which for its thickness is mightier than steel.

27
Testimony

"They said *what?*" Ricky asked his lawyer. The office, a former bedroom in an old house, was so quiet he could the secretary tapping on a keyboard two rooms away in the former living room.

"They've put a witness on their list to testify about the medical importance of ginseng. Odd thing is, it's not a doctor, it's a patient. A woman who takes ginseng for some disease—"

"What's that got to do with me?" Ricky demanded, indignant. "I'm *getting* ginseng for her. Where's she think it comes from?"

Anderson nodded. "I think their theory is that she will create sympathy and that will influence the jury to want to control ginseng hunting so it remains available. That makes your, ah, uncontrolled hunting appear more serious."

"So she needs ginseng, but to hell—I mean jail—with the people who hunt it, right? Who is this woman?"

The lawyer leaned back in his chair, closing off. "Now, Ricky, you know you can't have anything to do with a witness for the prosecution. That's tampering, even more serious than your current situation. That's prison time, son."

Ricky scoffed. "I'm not a nut job. What do they do, they just find a random person who takes 'sang and say, come look pitiful at court?"

The lawyer cleared his throat. "I understand this person came forward. A concerned citizen. Not sure why the AUSA went for it. Could mean they feel their case is weak."

"It's not weak, man, they caught me with 25 roots in Pisgah." Due to the variation in weight and value as confiscated roots dried out in the evidence room, criminal charges were based on root counts. Hunters always tried to get roots out in one piece. Whole roots brought better money, since buyers liked to believe they were getting older ginseng. But it meant that a hunter who was caught with two-year-old roots got the same charges as one who ripped fifteen years of growth from the ground.

"So who is she?" asked Ricky again.

"Ricky, I—"

"I get it, Mr. Anderson. I have no interest in messing with a witness. But don't I have a right to know who's accusing me?"

Anderson tightened his lips and pulled himself back up to his desk. He shuffled files and opened one, going to a tab inside. He ran his finger down the page and said, "Okay, one Sophia Damaso." He studied Ricky. "You know her?"

"Sophia," Ricky repeated. "Ain't that the lady that's pushing for the scholarship fund? The one who thinks our band is the best thing since sliced bread but won't even speak to a single one of us? The lady that likes *traditional culture* so much?" Round spots of color formed high on his cheeks.

"I don't know," said Anderson. "I heard something about that scholarship fund. You think it's the same person?"

"I'm not sure, I think that's her," Ricky looked at his knees and shook his head. "Doesn't she have anything else to do," he said mostly to himself. "So what kind of time am I looking at?"

Anderson cleared his throat again and leaned forward. He folded his hands together and shifted in his chair. He had practiced the loaded pause and the slowing down to warn clients of the bad news to come, and give them a moment to prepare. He didn't hug or pat his clients, but he needed to convey that he didn't like what he was saying. "Well, Ricky, you know they're going to have your state court record to consider at sentencing. You've hunted out of season a few times; they're going to say you have a pattern of disregard for the law," he began.

"Those was for deer," Ricky interrupted. "Not 'sang. And I never took a doe out of season and we ate every bit of those animals. For the love of God, they have hunt days every year to cull deer that eat people's yards. We ain't runnin' out of deer." He shook his head again, as if he could say no to everything that was happening. "We ain't runnin' out of ginseng, either. Pisgah's full of it. If people need it so much for medicine, why can't they get that? We got acres of it that nobody can touch, it's just sitting there like gold in a bank window in front of people that need it. If that woman is so desperate, she ought to be thanking people like me for getting it."

"So you're a Robin Hood stealing for the ginseng-poor?" asked Anderson.

Ricky gave a disgusted look. "I ain't sayin' that. I'm just sayin' it don't make sense to let people pick the rest of the woods clean, like people do on private land, then keep this reservoir that nobody can touch. You know some people pick every plant they see. They don't know to pull the old ones and leave the young ones. Or they know and they don't care. Nobody gets hauled into court for that! It's like Pisgah's got ginseng in a zoo, where you can just look at the animals, but they're becoming extinct everywhere else, and the ones in the zoo don't get to hunt or get hunted like real animals. The 'sang in Pisgah is radio-tagged and DNA-marked, and it's never seen life outside the zoo. In real life, people hunt ginseng and eat it!" Ricky realized he'd gotten louder and louder. As an animal hunter he'd never shared the bloodlust of some of his fellow hunters, but now he was ready to tear the ginseng out of the ground with his teeth if it meant he could roam whatever woods he liked.

The secretary's tapping two rooms away had stopped. Anderson studied him calmly, recognizing that this aggression would not turn toward him. Ricky steadied himself and went on. "It's an artificial situation. Half the thing is locked up and out of reach, the other half is getting destroyed by overuse. There's no balance. That lady's 'sang is going to get more and more expensive, and she's not going to like that any better. Why don't she worry about those people that build all them look-alike houses? They got permits, building permits, to destroy *acres* of 'sang all at once."

Anderson scowled. No one expected a lawless redneck to back up his illegal activities with articulate wildlife management theory. Could he make this work in the courtroom? The first rule of litigation was: Don't confuse the jury. If the United States Fish and Wildlife Commission couldn't do better, could 12 bored jury members earning $12 a day make sense of this? An opportunity to argue something meaningful began to form, but it fizzled out.

"You're probably right, Ricky," he said. "It is a complex issue. But the whole resource management system is not on trial here. You're charged with breaking the law as it is written now, for the third—" He glanced at his file. "Fourth time."

Ricky huffed and nodded, resigned. So Anderson went on.

"Unfortunately, son, I think you're probably going to get six months to a year for this. I know it's—" he stopped because all of Ricky's anger had melted. Ricky's jaw was clenched now to hold back tears. Sometimes Anderson's job was watching grown men cry. He knew that plenty of men's tears in his office were the first of their lives, or at least since puberty.

"I know it's rough, Ricky. I'm sorry there's just nothing I can do to make it shorter. They're very strict about these things."

Ricky stared at the baseboards in the office. "I can't do that. I gotta be making money or my mom will lose her house. And I can't sit inside for a whole year. I ain't never passed a whole day in my life without being outside at least some of it, even if it's just to mow the yard." He paused. "Well, except for that 30 days I did before. But that was the county jail, we went out on the work program picking up trash. Rain or shine."

"You're going to have to find a way to do this," said Anderson. "There's no way to avoid it. You have time to get ready. Your court date's in December, take time to plan," he suggested. The lawyer's job also included reconciling people and their punishments, a shotgun marriage ceremony with a honeymoon nobody wanted to go on.

"How can I plan to walk away from my entire life for a year?" asked Ricky. "I'll lose my truck. I got a little money in the bank, but it'll barely help with the house payments. Mom lives on Social Security, that don't keep everything together. She can't never get caught up without help."

"It's a tough situation, Ricky," said the lawyer. "But you'll pull through somehow. You always have."

"Yeah," said Ricky. "So far." A few minutes passed in silence.

"Well, thanks," said Ricky, and he stood up. He nodded goodbye and left. Anderson watched him walk out the door. He remembered an old story in his own family. His mother's great-uncle had once gone to court for hunting out of season, represented himself, and somehow convinced the judge that he was innocent. The charge was dropped just before lunchtime, and according to the tale, as his uncle had left the courtroom among the other defendants and staff flowing out the door together, he had offered the judge some deer meat. The family legend didn't specify whether the meat was fresh or frozen. Anderson had never known if it was a story of the great-uncle's brazen stupidity or his forgiving nature.

Ricky sat in the truck outside the lawyer's office without

starting the engine. He thought of the day he and Analía met James Black Dog in the woods. He had heard that the Cherokee, or maybe the Navajo, believed you should never smoke indoors, that you had to make sure the smoke had a clear path to the spirit world. Similarly, bodies of the deceased were never shut up in closed rooms – there always had to be an open door, window, or smokehole so that at whatever moment the soul chose to depart, it could go freely. Otherwise it would get stuck and bring bad energy to wherever it was trapped. He'd never met a Navajo, so he didn't know if it was true, but it made sense to him. He was a soul on its own, with no wise elder to make sure he was stored correctly. He always had to keep watch over himself to make sure of his own path to the outside.

Shelley made fun of him on camping trips, because he would never sleep in a tent. Instead he put his sleeping bag right on the ground, padded with dry leaves. She teased that he was trying to be a macho guy, or maybe just the opposite, wanting to gaze at the pretty stars. He never bothered to tell her it was because he couldn't sleep in the confines of the nylon tent, feeling that it was no different from the plastic bags everyone knew better than to put over their heads. He could never fall asleep in a plastic bag. But two minutes of smelling the moldering leaves and hearing the twigs rustling over his head, and he'd be out. In the morning his sleeping bag would be damp with dew and he would emerge from it feeling like a deer coming out of its refuge in the brush. He would want to swivel his ears and twitch his nose in the slanting sunlight while the other campers slept in their nylon casings.

Thinking about waking up made him wonder how it would be to wake up with Analía. She'd told him about *palapas* in Mexico, open-air half-walled buildings roofed in straw. It seemed perfect to him: a stable floor and a sheltering roof, but only the gentle suggestion of walls.

Although there *were* jaguars there. Ricky guessed they would need a dog – and a gun – in there with them. He leaned back into the truck seat and tried to imagine one of these *palapas*, occupied by himself, Analía, and a dog that knew when to bark. They would have bright rugs strewn on the floor and maybe something cooking on a fire. He didn't know if fantasizing about Analía in a *palapa* would keep him through a year of jail. Could a man spend a year of his life with his body in jail and his mind in a *palapa*? If he'd never seen one?

28
Nothing Between You and the Sky

Ricky stood shoulder-to-shoulder on the edge of a small cliff with Analía, looking hundreds of feet down at the merest twinkling hint of a river at the bottom of the valley.

"It is so pretty…" she said wonderingly. Across the valley were blazing oranges and reds, golds as bright as a summer squash, the usual autumn show, which didn't happen in Mexico. Ricky drove past these views every day; this bounty was a given. He figured it was like being married to a beautiful woman: after enough years, you could concentrate on something else in her presence. It might take the attention of a stranger to make you take a good long look again. He smiled proudly.

"People come from everywhere to see that," he said. "Every year."

"What happened to that mountain?" asked Analía, pointing across and up at the bare trees on the other side of the valley.

Ricky looked, and thought, and smiled. "Nothing," he said. "It's just fall," he shrugged. "I like it when it's like this. See, down there at the bottom," he pointed, "down there it's still summer, all green and growing. Halfway up the mountain, it's fall, with all the pretty colors. And up at the top, the leaves have already fallen and it looks like winter. It's like you can watch time pass right here, see any season you want just by looking up and down."

"Like you can go back in time," Analía said, and tried not to think about things that might have been different.

"Or see the future," said Ricky. He sighed and turned around. He had brought one of Sue's old quilts, and he walked a safe distance from the edge and spread it over the rock. They lay down and watched buzzards circling above them as the heat from the sun-warmed rock seeped up into them.

"So the lawyer thinks I might have to do a year of jail time," Ricky said when the last of the buzzards had floated out of sight.

Analía still couldn't understand how someone could go to jail for digging roots out of the damp American soil. It was darker and richer than the sandy earth in Mexico, it smelled different, wetter, like something pleasantly rotting. Ricky had told her about the few real dangers in the American woodlands: the same rattlers that vibrated fear into the people back home, the coppery snakes with the wide triangular heads that hardly ever killed anyone, the black and brown spiders whose bites made hideous wounds and scars that you would live with for the rest of a long happy life after the bite. Compared to jaguars, scorpions, mesoamerican snakes, and the dengue fever that still claimed hundreds each year in Mexico, the U.S. was a promised land of natural safety. No wonder the Americans had been so successful here – the land they took from the indigenous people was of milk and honey relative to the deserts and stony lands of her home state. She could see how people like Shelley wanted to protect it, felt like mothers guarding this unthreatening, fertile piece of terra firma. But like mothers who feared letting their children play on swings, many of them needed to control the land rather than revel in its bounty. They wanted their land to be a spoiled child -- cosseted, unscratched. The parts they hadn't paved, anyway.

Analía thought about Jaime, who had spent most of his childhood roaming the *selva*, climbing trees, building forts with his friends. She had to believe he would have been just fine with the mild North American snakes and spiders. With all his joking about the bears, Ricky said people hardly ever actually saw one. She refused to think about the coyotes that people said had migrated to North Carolina.

Ricky was waiting for a response.

"It will pass sooner than you think," she said. In Mexico, when the odds were stacked against you, you tucked your head and waited like an armadillo in its shell. Endurance was a national character trait, honed by centuries of colonization and corrupt governments. You were always ready to fight each other over some perceived slight, but trouble with authority was simply to be outlived. It was a humble heroism few Americans appreciated. Or wanted to try.

She laid a hand on Ricky's cheek and repeated, "It will pass."

"I don't know, Analía," he said. "I don't know if I can do it."

"You will. And then it will be over and you will be right back here in the woods."

"By myself."

"I thought you like it that way."

"Not as much as I used to," he said. "And you'll be long gone, back in Hotwater, Mexico." He loved to joke about the name of her home state.

"I would stay with you, Ricky," she said, and met his eyes for a moment. "But after my visa ends, if they find me they will throw me out and I can never come back. I have to, Ricky. If I don't leave on time, I will never be able to get another visa. I will never see Jaime's daughter again. She will not know our family at all."

Ricky felt angry for a moment. It wasn't even *her* kid. But then he remembered his mom and Shelley, and he knew she was right.

"I'm sorry I couldn't find Jaime for you," Ricky said.

"It was not your job," Analía kissed him on the forehead.

"You did everything you could. And we did find him. He was in the woods, well, he went into the woods." She choked off a sob. It didn't matter whether he was disappeared on purpose or by someone else, he was still gone.

"Anyway," she said. "He left pieces behind. Anna Jessica...and, somewhere out there, is growing ginseng that he planted." She had told Ricky about the dealer's unprofitable method of preserving ginseng. "Some of him will always be here." Her eyes filled and she looked away. Ricky took her hand and tried to distract her.

"Are you sure you're leaving, Analía?" he asked.

"I have to, Ricky. I cannot quit college. I lost Jaime for college," she sobbed.

Ricky rolled over and pondered the sky. "When do you leave?" he asked. She told him the date that her visa expired. "I'm not going anywhere as long as you're here." He squinted at the moon that had risen early. "Tell me about the *palapas* again."

She laughed and wiped her eyes with her free hand. "What else can I tell you? They are not very complicated. *Vigas* – what do you call, beams? Some straw, that is all."

"Do you sleep on the floor?"

"*Ay dios*, no, I told you, there are scorpions and snakes." She widened her eyes to emphasize the danger. "Not like your little black snakes. You sleep in a hammock."

Ricky chuckled and nuzzled his face into her neck. "What if the snakes crawl up the ropes of the hammock to get you?" He mimicked the crawling with his fingers along her spine.

"Very sad for you," she smiled. "If they want you so much, just say your prayers and wait to die." She didn't move his hand from her back.

"Oh well, I guess it's not so bad to go in your sleep...But wait, are there two-person hammocks for married people?" He wrapped his other arm awkwardly under her.

"Only when you are just married and full of energy." She smiled. "When you are old you put your hammocks close and hold hands."

"Just hold hands?" he asked, and kissed her, which was followed by other activities her aunts would not have approved of.

A little while later Ricky got his clothes from beside the quilt and dug around in his jacket pockets. He found an old receipt.

"Have you got a pen?" he asked Analía.

"A what? You are going to write a news story about this?"

"A pen," he said again, sniffing her hair. "Or a pencil. Seriously." She twisted around and dug in her bag, then rolled back holding a pen out to him with her eyebrows raised. "You are going to write your name on me?"

"Not a bad idea," he said, and instead of taking the pen, he held the old receipt out to her.

"How about drawing me one of those palapas?" he asked.

"Still with the palapas," she said. "I thought I had distracted you from that. I have better paper." She reached into her bag again, there was a rip as she tore a sheet from a notebook, then she snuggled against him, pulling one edge of the quilt over herself.

"Can you see in there?" he said to the top of her head.

"I see what I need to see." The quilt lit up blue and he realized she had her cell phone for light. He watched the stars beginning to glow as she worked with the paper against his chest. Soon she reached up and handed him the paper containing a drawing of a small building resembling a gazebo. She had added a setting sun in the background and a single hammock inside. Along the bottom were written the words, "*Te amo.*"

Ricky folded the paper and reached over to put it in the pocket of his jeans. "That's just what I needed."

29
Passive Resistance

Under pictographs of the four directions and the seven clans of the Cherokee gathered a judge, a clerk, a bailiff, many lawyers, and even more residents of North Carolina accused of defying the laws of the United States of America. The Assistant United States Attorney was a tall, thin man with a buzzcut who looked like a friendly banker in his serious blue suit. He announced to the crowd that he would call the calendar. His voice was trained to fill this large space and he required no microphone to reach the far corners. As he called out names, people in the crowd stood and said the names of their attorneys, or they said guilty, or not guilty, and notes were taken of their responses. Sometimes they said nothing, and an attorney up front stood at the same time and said, "I represent so-and-so." It resembled a more formal version of roll call in school.

"Richard Morgan," said the AUSA, and Anderson rose looking back at the crowd, waiting for Ricky's tall form to unfold.

Nothing happened.

Anderson's eyes went to the floor and whoever was paying attention saw a slight shake of his head and a forlorn set to his mouth. But he raised his eyes to the judge and stated evenly, "I represent Mr. Morgan. No information." It was courtroom shorthand for "I have no information or excuse to offer for my client's absence," or as the lawyers said to each other, "I don't know where the hell he is."

The same had occurred once or twice already during the morning, and even the crowd knew the routine by now. The bailiff called out twice more, "Richard Morgan, Richard Morgan," and continued, "Appear as you are ordered." But that was a formality, too, just another step required before the judge issued an order for Ricky's immediate arrest.

Which the judge did. Perhaps because Ricky was not the first that morning to ignore his summons, or perhaps in his zeal to protect the tiny homunculus of the forest, the judge declared that the bond on this order would be $50,000. An amount usually reserved for those who had violently assaulted actual life-size humans.

Anderson noted this in his file. Ricky was his last client that morning, so he went straight out the door to his car, and drove home. He did not advise his secretary of his whereabouts. But he did drink half a bottle of whiskey on his porch, in the chair beside the rack containing his grand-uncle's old deer rifle.

The government's witness left the courtroom more agitated than the defendant's lawyer. The prosecutor had explained that no new court date would be set at this time; that Sophia would be notified when Ricky was re-arrested. He said that could be months away.

Sophia was furious at the absent guitar player. His disregard for the law seemed bottomless. She stomped out to the parking deck, desperate to calm her nerves. She glanced off at the mountains in the distance and knew what she needed to do. Being in nature always made her feel better than any therapist could.

Her hike began as a march as she strode into the woods. After a few hundred feet she was breathing more deeply and the stress from the courtroom was fading. The soft thud of her footsteps on the ground was a cadence slowing her own heartbeat. She finally remembered to look for gold on the ground along the trail.

She had chosen a hike that was a circular path, and she made it back to the parking lot without seeing a single ginseng plant. She climbed into her SUV and prepared to go home. A sense of futility hovered but she pushed it away. The case would go on. The officer was probably right about finding ginseng: it would take practice. There was always the danger of eating the wrong root. She stared out the windshield at the trees, the green mass that she knew had different components but still appeared indiscriminate to her. Suddenly a big chestnut-colored bird flew over the hood of the car, startling her. She had just caught her breath when she heard a baby scream.

She twisted in her seat, trying to see in all directions at once. *How could a baby be screaming in the woods? The safest thing would be to start the vehicle and drive away.* She heard no other voices. *Wouldn't there be an adult with a baby in the woods? Oh God, what if someone was abusing a baby in the woods?* She could never forgive herself for driving away.

Her shaking hands pulled the pepper spray from the glove compartment. She took a deep breath, wanting to scream herself.

As soon as she opened the door she could tell that the sound came from off to the left behind the vehicle. It sounded so close, but she could see no one. Then, movement in the weeds, down low. She clenched her fists and shook out her hands, rattling the pepper spray, trying to steel herself. The movements continued and the screams were more frantic. She would have to go over there. She decided to swoop in fast, sprinted toward the movement, then changed her mind and crept closer. No way was there any person in those weeds, there just wasn't enough room. Maybe it was an animal attacking a baby. She took a breath and ran again toward the weeds, waving her arms and shouting garbled words. She swung her arm through the weeds and kicked at them with her feet. Another chestnut shape rose from the weeds and clutched at her. She ducked away from it and nearly fell. The hawk corrected its course and rose away from her in a whoosh of feathers, screeching a protest.

The baby was still screaming at her feet. She pawed through the dry weed stalks and found nothing. There was no baby here. The noise quieted a little, but she poked deeper into the weeds and located its source, a handful of soft grey-brown fur. The baby rabbit had a gash in its neck leaking a slow, steady stream of blood. Its eyes were wide. It didn't move when she lifted it, even when she brought it to her chest, smearing her sweater with blood.

"Oh, you poor little thing," she crooned. It didn't struggle as she carried it to the SUV. She was able to hold it with one hand while she flipped items around in the back of the vehicle. She dumped a new pair of shoes into the floor and padded their box with cotton gauze from her emergency kit. She set the rabbit in the box. She put the lid on and got in the vehicle, where she fastened the seat belt directly over the passenger seat, then ran the lap belt around the box to hold it steady.

During the forty-minute ride back to town the rabbit didn't make a single noise. At a stoplight she pecked on the navigation system and set it to direct her to the nearest veterinarian. As she listened to the soothing GPS voice she finally had time to wonder if wild rabbits carried diseases.

She carried the shoebox in front of her like an offering into the veterinarian's office. That and the look on her face made everyone in the office turn to stare at her.

"I—have an emergency," she declared, losing steam. The receptionist cocked her head and made no move to take the box.

"What have you got in there?" she asked.

Sophia extended her arms further with the box. "It's a baby rabbit," she said. "A bird attacked it."

The receptionist blinked. "You took it from the bird? Is it your rabbit?"

"No, it's a wild rabbit." Sophia thought it was an odd question for an emergency. She let her experience in the insurance industry guide her. "Don't worry, I'll pay for whatever it needs."

"It's not that," said the receptionist. "We're not allowed to treat wild animals."

"What? Then who does?"

"Well, wildlife rehabilitators. You're not supposed to catch or keep wild animals. Let me get the doctor." She disappeared through a door behind the desk and the other assistant quickly looked down at her computer. Sophia's heart rate had risen again. She set the box on the counter and risked a peek into it. The rabbit hunched in a corner, eyeing her. The blood on its neck was drying, no longer flowing.

She got as close to the second assistant as she could from across the counter. "I know there are rules, but this little rabbit is hurt. You have to help him," she begged.

A plump woman in a white coat came out of the door behind the counter, looking annoyed. She glanced around the empty waiting room and relaxed a bit. She looked Sophia over for several seconds and said grudgingly, "Let me see this rabbit."

Sophia pushed the box toward her. "Don't you have a Hippocratic oath for veterinarians? He's hurt – well, I don't know if it's a he. But can't you help him?" The doctor opened the box, peered in, shut the lid, and turned away, carrying the box.

"Don't lecture me about a Hippocratic oath," she said patiently. "Don't you know you're supposed to leave wild things in the wild? Follow me."

Chastened and relieved Sophia trotted around the desk and followed the doctor to an examining room. The doctor smeared ointment on the rabbit's neck, and prepared a hypodermic needle.

Sophia jumped at the sight of the needle and nearly grabbed the rabbit. "You're not putting him to sleep, are you?" she cried.

The doctor proceeded with the shot. "This is an antibiotic," she said. She felt around the rabbit's tiny body. "This is a flesh wound. This rabbit is old enough to be on his own. He'll be fine."

"Oh, thank you so much!" breathed Sophia. "That's wonderful of you. How do I take care of him?"

The doctor worked another minute silently, then put the rabbit back in the box and closed the lid. She looked at Sophia appraisingly.

"You don't," she said. "It's against the law to have possession of this rabbit if you are not a licensed wildlife rehabilitator. Are you a licensed wildlife rehabilitator?"

Sophia slumped. "You need a license to take care of a hurt animal?"

"You do. And we don't have anyone in town who's licensed who does rabbits. Squirrels, deer, hawks, even snakes, but not rabbits. Rabbits are hard, even for appropriately trained people. They're very sensitive to stress. They can literally die of stress. Their hearts give out. Even experienced rehabilitators have a very low success rate with wild rabbits."

"So he's doomed? What am I supposed to do? Just let him die?"

"I'm supposed to tell you to turn him in to the wildlife officers."

"Oh, I know one," Sophia said, brightening.

The doctor pursed her lips. "The wildlife officers are not rehabilitators, they don't have time to mess with this. They'll dispatch him."

"Dispatch." Sophia felt a little faint.

"Therefore, because of my *Hippocratic* leanings as a veterinarian, I am going to assume that you found this rabbit on your very own private property. Perhaps you were hunting him, failed miserably, and had a change of heart. I am assuming you did *not*, under any circumstances, remove a wild rabbit from public lands." The doctor was among those lucky few humans with the muscle control to raise only one eyebrow, and she did so, looking sternly at Sophia.

Sophia inhaled and gave that panicked look that children give when caught putting Scotch tape on the cat. She thought of the rabbit in the box, crouched in the corner with the greasy ointment on his neck, and had a fierce urge to grab him and run. She shrunk into herself a little bit.

"Thank you. Ah, what should I do with him?" she asked.

"Because of the stress issue, he needs to be let loose again as soon as possible. The minute you see a good scab on that wound, you put him back outside, you hear me? And you'll let him go in a place where he'll have a fighting chance." She explained what to feed a wild rabbit, that he should be freed near a water source, perhaps on the edge of a field near some woods, and Sophia heard about half of it. "Meanwhile, put him in the quietest place in your home, and don't pester him. Don't pet him. Don't love him to death."

Sophia carried the rabbit in his box back out of the veterinarian's office and wedged the box into the floor of her backseat, wanting to look over her shoulder for the forest ranger swooping in to arrest her. She made certain to come to a full stop before turning out of the parking lot, and drove home with one eye on the road and one on the speedometer. She knew from her days in the insurance business that a nervous driver was a dangerous driver, but she couldn't shake the fear. It would be just her luck to hit a license checkpoint with an illegal rabbit in her vehicle.

In her driveway she wanted to slip the rabbit under her coat, but she reminded herself that he was in a shoebox, and people bought shoes every day. So she grabbed her purse and the box and pretended she was coming home from a day at the mall.

The veterinarian had said to put the rabbit in a quiet place, so she set him up in an old cat carrier in the guest room and went outside to look for his dinner. "Grass and what you'd normally think of as weeds," the vet had said. Sophia prided herself on keeping her tiny patch of land free of what people thought of as weeds, and ended up going across the road to an empty field to gather a miscellaneous batch of greens. She stuffed them in the carrier, where they took up nearly all the room aside from the water bowl and the rabbit himself, who eyed her guardedly from the farthest corner of the carrier. She couldn't resist a tiny smoothing of his fur.

She needed a cup of tea. The wasted morning in court, the bird attack, and her new status as a criminal wildlife rescuer had taken a toll. She settled into her favorite chair with the tea and laid her head back against the flowered fabric. Usually she would call Gale for whatever support she might need, but she didn't know where to begin to explain all that had happened. She figured that if she was going ahead with this underground rabbit-saving, the fewer people who knew about it, the better. Gale would only increase her fear of getting in trouble, maybe even call her a hypocrite.

She suddenly felt very alone, more alone than all the other times she had felt alone. She consoled herself that alone was perfect right now, that she could be here in solitude with this rabbit and no one would be the wiser. She couldn't shake the sense that she had just done the very thing she was condemning others for. But she couldn't just leave a poor injured animal to die in the woods. She was doing a good thing. And she would end it the right way, by putting him back.

She thought about that. She would risk getting caught by putting him back. She would be conspicuous strolling out into Pisgah National Forest with a shoebox.

Sophia turned these thoughts around in her mind, seeing

herself in the federal courtroom alongside the ginseng poachers and the marijuana dealers. She imagined maybe she could just keep the rabbit instead, but another round with the internet proved that he didn't look like any breed of domesticated rabbit. She would be stuck with an illegal rabbit for – how long did rabbits live? The internet advised that it was far too long for her to feel this guilty. She fell asleep rolling the dilemma around in her mind without reaching a conclusion.

While she slept, somewhere in Pisgah National Forest, a hungry hawk perched on a poplar branch, watching the ground, humbly and heroically enduring the wait for a meal.

By morning the rabbit had eaten every scrap of the weeds that Sophia had pulled for him. She was spending more time than she could have imagined sneaking across the road to refill his cage. She wondered if anyone would notice her carrying all these yard cuttings into the house. What would she say? *Crafts,* she told herself. *I'll say I'm making a wreath.* She sat down on the bed beside the rabbit to think more about her ethical dilemma.

She had broken, and was still breaking, the law. The veterinarian and her internet research were clear about that. But every time she wiped out the rabbit's cage, she wondered how she was supposed to leave this tiny creature to be ripped up by a hawk. Or hand him over to a ranger to be "dispatched."

All the legal options ended with a dead rabbit. But how could helping a vulnerable creature be wrong? She wasn't going to eat him or sell him; she wasn't doing this for personal gain. She was hiding this rabbit for altruistic purposes, like one of those families who hid Jews in Germany. It was civil disobedience. She just needed to stay out of sight until it was over. She hoped the next few days would pass quickly. What was a "good scab," anyway?

30
The Hand-Off

"Come on, it won't be so bad," Ricky pleaded as he and Shelley crept down the porch steps of Sue's house in grey pre-dawn light. Sue's fall planting of chrysanthemums was already in beside the steps, signaling the death of summer. The dogs snuffled around their feet without barking, curious but sensitive to Shelley and Ricky's stealthy manner.

"Why do I need to go deer hunting?" Shelley asked.

"Why'd you bug me to take you to the range all those times?" he asked. "Plus, I might be in jail for a year, remember? I'm on borrowed time right now. They could pick me up any minute."

"I went to target practice because it was fun," Shelley retorted. "The deer aren't going to overpopulate and take over in one year," she grumbled. "Seriously, the world will survive if you skip taking a couple deer." She paused. "I'm not trying to say it's okay, I feel bad for you, you know that. But I don't have to get your deer. I'd have to buy another license anyway, it's not transferable. Sue can buy groceries for one winter. People will probably give her meat, knowing you're in jail." Being the pitiful family that other people would take care of made her want to scream. She threw a bag of snacks into the truck and slammed the door, forgetting she was trying to be quiet. "We'll be okay, Ricky."

"Listen, you're the one who's so proud of taking care of the land. Bears kill deer sometimes. Them coyotes love nothing more than a good slow deer. There ain't nothin' wrong with shootin' a deer and eatin' it. You scared?"

That taunt usually worked. In theory Shelley was perfectly happy to hunt a deer and have a venison steak dinner. She'd rather eat an animal that lived a free life in the woods and died quickly in good health than one that suffered in a box for its whole life and died in terror. But she couldn't help seeing awareness in their eyes when she looked at them through the scope. They surveyed the landscape while they chewed, their ears moving like antennae. Once, she saw one look up and down the road at Sue's house before crossing. They passed by a few times a week, and often sprang up from nests in the fields when she went out to her car in the mornings. Hunting them would be like shooting a neighbor she had seen come and go, but didn't know personally. That would make her the quiet neighbor who flipped out one day and shot the family next door.

But Ricky was right, it was cowardly to rely on others to do your dirty work. So she had dragged herself out of bed at a ridiculous hour.

"You get to see the sunrise," Ricky wheedled.

"The sunset is just as beautiful," she said. *And better timed for enjoying*, she thought. Ricky rolled the truck down the driveway and out into the morning.

They didn't go far, just down the road to where the Millers let people park to cross their land into the woods. They were quiet as they traipsed through the briary overgrowth and into an opening among the trees. Quiet was required for hunting, so there was no sound but their footsteps and an occasional brush of fabric, or a sniff in the cold morning air.

Ricky's tree stand wouldn't hold them both, but he knew a spot where they could hide in vines that covered an old fallen tree. They settled in. Shelley figured people went hunting and fishing so they could sit peacefully in the woods or by the lake, with fishing merely an excuse for doing absolutely nothing. And/or drinking. The mountain version of meditating, with a few or many beers and the possibility of a good meal at the end. *Everyone would meditate if they got grilled trout afterward,* she thought. She snuck a sideways look at Ricky on her left.

He sat with his gun across his lap, his hands resting loosely, one over the stock and the other over the barrel. He gazed unfocused into the middle distance, blinking slowly. There was an alertness in his face, and she knew he was listening intently. He had told her once that you could use your ears just like your eyes, directing them to attend to one place or another. She knew that right now he'd be tuned into the farthest distance he could, listening for the rustle of dry leaves that meant a deer was walking or pulling at a twig as it chewed. He'd be measuring the height of noises he heard, to discount the incessant scrabbling of squirrels and birds in the branches. Too much noise at ground level would be a deal-breaker, as it would mean another hunter or a bear nearby.

"Quit starin' at me," he said in an undertone, not a whisper. The sibilance of whispers carried much further than a baritone murmur.

"Sorry," she breathed.

Hours could go by just like this, and they did.

Ricky lifted the gun soundlessly and moved it toward Shelley. Their eyes met, and he raised his eyebrows a millimeter. She looked down at the gun, and reached for it. A joint in her wrist popped from the hours of inactivity, the sound loud in the silence. They both froze. Ricky's eyes softened and wandered as he listened, then he nodded slightly twice and blinked. He moved the gun further in her direction, and she took it. She slowly and steadily moved her hands and fingers into place and raised the gun near her face. She raised her eyebrows at Ricky and glanced all around, asking, "where?"

He looked past her, off to her right, and lifted his chin, staring into the woods, still unfocused, letting his eyes wait to perceive movement in his peripheral vision. A twitch on the other side of Shelley caught his eye, and when he stared at it, he spotted the dark line that appears sometimes along the edge of a deer's ear. Shelley followed his eyes.

She was sideways to the deer, and it was on the wrong side for a right-handed shooter. She would have to twist more than ninety degrees to aim at him. Scooting around on the ground in the leaves, there was no way she could turn enough without the deer hearing her. Ricky's position was even worse, with her between him and the deer. Nevertheless, she started moving, trying to roll her butt on the ground rather than slide.

Ricky put a hand on her knee and when she looked at him, he shook his head once. They both waited, immobile, for the deer to move. It ambled a few steps in the right direction, and Shelley pivoted as it moved. The deer came into her sights, and she stopped breathing to steady the gun. She thought "pull," and felt the electrical signal from her brain die out on its way to her finger on the trigger.

Ricky said nothing. He breathed soundlessly. He was motionless. The deer stepped lightly into the underbrush and its steps faded.

"Shut up," murmured Shelley preemptively.

"Okay," Ricky continued in the deep undertone. "I'm not giving you shit, but why not?"

"We can talk about it later," Shelley said. "You want the next one?" she asked. She held the rifle out to him.

"Sure," Ricky assented, silently taking the rifle. They sat waiting until rustles in the leaves stirred off to the left, at about 10 o'clock to their position. Shelley was motionless this time as Ricky set the rifle to his shoulder, the sound absorbed by his thick jacket.

Crack! exploded into the stillness. Ricky leaped up. Once that sound was made, the deer was either hit or gone, and every moment counted in tracking down an injured deer. He started in its direction.

Shelley got up more slowly and trekked after him.

"I'm pretty sure I hit him," Ricky called back over his shoulder. He stopped her several feet away from the deer.

"He's down," he said quietly. "I must've made a pretty good shot. Give him a few minutes."

The deer made choked gurgling noises. Shelley listened, everything in her wanting to race over and save it. She felt disgusted, and wanted it to die soon. She wanted to scream, and cry, and cover her face with her hands, but she did none of those. She didn't wail, "What have we done?" She stood turned so that Ricky couldn't see her face.

He put an arm around her and said, "This part will be over soon. We're going to use it, Shelley. It's the way of things."

She said firmly, "I know." The deer quieted, and they walked over to it. It was lying on its side, and they both stared at its chest, looking for movement.

"You know it might kick you, right?" Ricky asked.

"I know," she said. "But I think it's done." They stood behind the deer's head and prodded his shoulders with their feet, softly and then more firmly, but he was still.

"Well, that's the hard part," Ricky stated. "He's kinda small," he said. "He'll be easy to carry out." They heaved the deer up and carried its warm, pliable body through the woods for a while.

"You okay, Shelley?" Ricky asked eventually. "I know you

don't like hunting."

"I don't not like it," she argued. "I just...it's hard to see them as beautiful living beings and as dinner, even though I know they're both."

"Well, the tomato plants are pretty, aren't they?" Ricky said. "And you rip the tomatoes right off and eat them."

"I don't think the tomato plants are smart enough to look before they cross the road."

"So you only eat dumb things? You better hope the Indians were wrong when they said you become like what you eat." He laughed. "Things get a pass if they're smart enough?" He reflected a moment. "Reminds me of that scholarship program."

"Uh, what?" she said.

"Look, if you're smart like us we'll let you live, if not, you're dinner. That *is* the same thing, isn't it, if we don't eat the brightest?"

Shelley scrunched up her face. There was some kind of logic in there, but it didn't fall right into place.

"You eat pigs. Pigs are as smart as dogs," Ricky continued, interrupting her attempt to straighten out her thoughts about intelligence and prey.

"I don't kill the pigs, damnit."

"Somebody does!" He wrestled the deer to a different position, grunting.

"I didn't say it was wrong, Ricky," she said appeasingly. "I don't think it's wrong. Just maybe it's not right for me."

"You eat the meat."

"I just feel like I *know* the animals," she said. "You know I've stalked them around the woods since I was a kid, trying to see how close I could get. Sometimes they let me get real close."

"They can tell when you're hunting," he said. "They can feel it. That's why they let you get close. It's a lot harder when they know you're after them."

"So what do you think when you shoot them?" she asked. "You see their eyes, you know they have feelings about the world. Do you think, ha, I got you? Fuck you, little deer, 'cause I want a steak?"

Ricky snorted. "When I'm shooting them, I'm mostly thinking, hold still, hold still. To myself and them. I have to breathe right, and they have to hold still. And don't go around telling people this, but after I shoot them, I think, thank you."

"Yeah," Shelley said noncommittally.

"When mom throws out corn for them, don't you think they're grateful for the food?" said Ricky. "So I'm grateful for my food, and I eat it."

"Yeah," she said again. "Maybe I like to feed animals and you like to feed people."

"You didn't feed my black snake, either, when I had him," he teased.

"Yes, I did. I gave you two mice that I caught in the live traps, from the kitchen, for him."

"Yeah." He thought for a moment. "You killed those mice, you know." He lifted an eyebrow at her teasingly.

She laughed this time. "No, I didn't, I fed them to the snake." She smiled, waiting for him to attack that reasoning.

He wasn't laughing anymore. "So, I'm feeding the deer to my mom! Should I take it to her on a leash and tell her to chomp onto its neck with her teeth? That's a much worse death for the deer. And you're back to the idea that whoever eats it is the one who killed it. I win!" He raised a fist. "Or do you want to wait around for them to die of a disease? Can't even eat them, then. That would be like waiting for the tomatoes to rot and fall off the vine. You're perfectly happy once they're dead. You watch me skin them, you cook 'em."

He warmed to his lecture. "If they died of disease, the bacteria would be killing them. They'd suffer a lot more." He paused. "Look, Shelley, you live and you live, and then something gets you. You want all the deaths to be peaceful and painless? A good clean heart shot is pretty damn close in that department, better than a lot of things."

"I don't disagree!" she half-shouted.

"So why don't you do it, Shelley?"

"I don't like the celebration," she said.

"What celebration?"

"You know, all the 'whoo-hoo, I got an eight-pointer.'"

"You want all the food-collecting to be grim?" he asked. "When you pick tomatoes, you're out there going, oohh, look at this one, oohh, this one smells good, ooohhh, look how red. You're havin' a pretty good time. Maybe you're not bloodthirsty, but you're sure as hell tomato-thirsty."

"Some people enjoy killing too much," she argued back. "Those creeps who get all hopped up about blowing things away and leave beer cans all over the woods. They have no respect. It's repulsive to enjoy killing a sentient being. It's like they hate the deer. It's sadistic."

"Those aren't hunters. What they're doing is not hunting. No more than them canned trophy hunters on TV." He turned away from the deer and spat on the ground. "If anyone would kill a deer respectfully, it would be you," Ricky said wryly. He stepped along grinning at the ground, imagining her bowing to the deer with her hands folded, imploring it to *please, kind sir, honored deer, fall down and die now, for my freezer is empty. Don't be scared by the growling, it's only my stomach.*

"I just don't know how to love an animal, then kill it, then feel grateful toward it!" she said. "It's practically schizophrenic!"

"It's schizophrenic how much you love deer steaks but you won't pick one yourself."

"Look, Ricky, I'm happy that we're gonna eat this deer," she said. "Okay? Just...maybe this is not my role. You know, nobody's ever had a society where everyone hunts. Some people do other things. You know? 'Hunting and gathering?'" She let go of the deer with one hand and made an air quote. "It doesn't mean I don't appreciate what you do. It doesn't mean I judge it. I just...don't do it...you know, some animals are hunters, some animals are scavengers."

Ricky smiled oddly. "Sure, I guess everything has to be what it is." He took a few more steps and shifted the deer. Shelley took a step to the side to keep her shoe out from under the slow red drips they were leaving behind.

After a while she said, "I guess I don't want to be the scary predator. I don't want the deer to hate me. I think they know they're dying."

"Don't you know you're dying?" he asked. He took a few steps. "Do you hate the bacteria that are going to eat you when you're dead?"

There was nothing she could say to that.

They walked along for several minutes. Shelley, out of habit, mentally catalogued plants that she saw, feeling inconsequential.

"Live and let live don't work," said Ricky eventually. "You want to take care of the woods, but you won't let them take care of you," he said. He didn't know why he couldn't just let this go. "You can't just give and give. You have a right to take something once in a while."

31
Wolves at the Door

"Somebody's at the door!" Tim hollered from the shower to Analía. She was already headed that way. She opened the door. Two federal marshals in uniform stood on Sue's porch.

"Where's Ricky Morgan?" one marshal asked without preamble.

Analía blinked. "I don't know," she said, which was halfway true. Could she get in trouble for not telling the police Ricky was out hunting? She didn't know exactly *where* he was hunting, so it wasn't a lie.

Tim appeared from the bathroom, his hair uncombed and his clothes wet, as if he hadn't used a towel before putting them on. He stepped around Analía and squared himself in the doorway.

"What can we help you with?" he growled.

The second marshal reached for his handcuffs as the first one took a step forward and asked again, "You Richard Morgan?"

"I'm his brother," Tim said. "Ricky ain't here and I don't know where he is."

"That right?" said the marshal. "You got some ID?"

Tim was frightened for a moment, but he got lucky. His wallet hadn't fallen out of his pants in the bathroom. He handed his license to the marshal, who glared at it.

"Sure do look alike," he said, looking steadily at Tim.

"Did I mention we're brothers?" Tim said, staring back. "See where it says Morgan on that license?"

"If you want to get smart—" started the marshal, when the second marshal stepped forward.

"What about you, little lady?" he asked, looking at Analía. "You have papers?" he asked. Supreme Court rulings proclaimed that he wasn't supposed to ask random people about their immigration status, but he wasn't anywhere near a court right now.

"I have student *permiso*," Analía said, her voice fading and her English deteriorating from nervousness.

Tim moved directly in front of her and leaned toward the marshals. "I told you, Ricky ain't here," he said, louder than the first time. "You got some kind of warrant for the house?"

"What would we find if we did?" asked the first marshal.

"Let's see it," Tim challenged.

"We can get one if we need it," said the marshal.

"When you got it, bring it," said Tim, and pushed Analía out of the way as he shut the door. They stood still behind the door, looking at each other.

"We're going to find him," called the marshal from the other side of the door. "You're not helping him." Tim put a finger to his mouth and placed a hand on Analía's arm. They stood silently. Analía swallowed.

The marshals turned and went down the porch steps, muttering between themselves and laughing to show that their confidence was intact. Tim relaxed his shoulders and studied this woman. He didn't know whether to be angry at her for leading Ricky astray, or angry at Ricky for putting her at risk. He shook his head and went back to the bathroom.

The next evening, Shelley was almost too angry to go hear the band. Ricky kept going on with his life as if there weren't a sword hanging over his head. She knew he was smarter than this. Was he so crazy about Analía that he wouldn't leave her to go to jail? He was more upset that the marshals had scared Analía than that they were after him.

Maybe she wasn't angry at Ricky at all. She figured that Sophia woman would be at the dance. Ricky said she was coming to court against him. Would she have the nerve to show up to dance to music played by someone she was trying to put in jail? Would she call the cops when she saw Ricky? Why was Ricky still going if that was a possibility? The whole thing just got stupider and stupider, with everyone running blindly forward like a bunch of sheep. No, Ricky and Sophia were more like two goats, determined to butt heads until one of them ended up bloody. She figured it would be Ricky, since the Sophia goat had the law on her side.

And what about herself? Here she was in the house, picking out clothes, looking for Analía so they could decide who would shower first. Then they would all head toward the high school like they expected a party.

Where the hell *was* Analía? Shelley checked the living room, the spare room, the porch. She stood outside Ricky's room for a minute and listened. She didn't hear anything, so she held her breath and opened the door. Empty.

"Hey, have you seen Analía?" she asked Sue in the kitchen.

Sue bowed her head to the sink, where her hands were buried in soapy water. "Ricky's cleaning that deer y'all got. Why don't you see if he knows where she is?"Shelley got two steps out the back door before she stopped dead. Ricky was out at the edge of the woods, with the deer strung up between two trees. The dogs were lying under one tree, and though she couldn't see from this far away, she knew the look they would have in their eyes.

There was Analía, *helping*. Ricky was slicing meat from the carcass, and handing it off to Analía, who organized the cuts on a piece of plywood laid over two sawhorses and covered with a plastic tablecloth. Analía's movements were efficient and smooth as always, and even Ricky seemed graceful from this distance.

Shelley froze for a moment, then turned and went back in the house. She walked past Sue without stopping and ordered, "Tell Ricky to take Analía to the gym with him." She took the first shower for herself, and left the house alone before Ricky and Analía even got back inside.

Shelley took the longest way she could think of to the high school, driving up and over Allesee Mountain. Allesee was considered a minor mountain; it was unmarked on most maps; few people knew its name, or that it had a name. A former site of Cherokee winter ceremonies, it hid now in plain sight. She hid with it for an hour, asking herself why Ricky and Analía cleaning a deer felt like treason, or shunning. She had been replaced in a role she didn't want in the first place.

When she got to the gym, Willie Blankenship's cancer poster was back, the quilts still hung on the walls, dancers swirled in their intricate patterns. Sophia was nowhere to be seen. Shelley was surprised to think that maybe Sophia knew better than to show her face. After a few dances, Shelley calmed down and joined in, pretending everything was just fine.

The band members felt so bad for Ricky that they let him do whatever he wanted, so he and Analía spun their way through an unusually high number of couples' dances. Her hip and his arm, his shoulder and her shoulder, their hands, slid into place every time as if programmed. He was surprised to find himself undistracted by where that hip, those shoulders had been just a few days ago in the woods. Instead it felt like a ritual they had been performing since grade school. She was always right where he expected her to be.

Louise and George, having danced thirty years' of couples' dances, moved their feet automatically as they watched the young pair.

"He's so much taller and bigger than her," said George. "It oughta look funny, oughtn't it? But it don't." Louise shook her head.

"Y'all look good together," called George to Ricky as the two couples passed near each other. Ricky and Analía both blushed.

"Makes me a little sad," said Louise. "Those two are headed in different directions." She laid her head on George's shoulder, where it fit.

The fiddle player noticed the police first. He pointed them out to Jack with his eyes, and leaned back as if to stop playing, but Jack put his head down and drove a bit of fury into the reel. A few of the older dancers recognized the change in pace and looked their way, puzzled, moving less certainly but keeping up on autopilot. Other dancers heard the awkward note as the backup guitar player regained his composure. They smiled pleasantly toward the band, thinking they had made a rare mistake.

Two county deputies stood watching the dancers, looking uncertain. At the start of their shift they had received a request from the federal marshals to check out the known hangouts of a certain federal fugitive, but when they saw the name on the warrant, they had dropped the papers on the table behind the dispatcher's desk. They stayed in the station for one more round of coffee and football talk. Now they ambled across the gymnasium floor as if they were about to choose partners.

But the dancers knew the deputies never danced in uniform. Nudges and whispers went through the crowd like lightning, and the couples twirling near the stage drew tighter together. The police attempted to work their way discreetly through the mass of bodies, but each time they moved toward the stage, another smiling couple bumped them off course.

Another pair was being bumped along on the far side of the gym. Amid the hurried music and the mumbled words that sounded like "police," Ricky and Analía found themselves scooted further and further around the side of the stage. Ricky paused and looked into Analía's eyes, then let go of her and disappeared out the side door they used for cigarette breaks.

She stood there alone in the crowd, holding her own hands, tears forming in her eyes, until George appeared and slid his arm around her waist. "Don't want to look like somebody just abandoned you here, now," he said, and gently whirled her back into the dance. Louise slipped away on her own through the spinning stomping crowd.

"I guess he's not coming back tonight," said Shelley, sitting next to Analía on the stage after the music ended for the night. Louise, George and a few other dancers made themselves busy near the front door, sweeping and folding up chairs. The drummer and the fiddle player were gone, and Jack was slowly carrying gear out to his truck. Analía nodded pensively.

When all the other gear was packed away, Jack plucked Ricky's guitar off its stand and stashed it in its case. He stood there holding the case and the stand for a moment, looking around. Then he laid the case gently on the stage behind Shelley.

"'Night," he said quietly. Shelley nodded. He turned and left carrying the stand.

"How will he get home?" asked Analía.

Shelley shook her head. "Don't know. Walk, I guess." She looked around the gymnasium and slid off the stage. She had to climb halfway back up to lift Ricky's guitar without scraping the case along the floor. "Let's get out of here," she said and started walking without waiting for confirmation. Analía followed her.

32
Days Missing

When Analía woke up the next day, Shelley was gone. She checked Ricky's room and wandered through the house, smelling no cooking and none of Ricky's shampoo. It wasn't her regular work day, but she took a bus to the store. Shelley was there stocking cat food, almost throwing the bags onto the shelves. She glanced up at Analía and shook her head.

"I haven't heard from him," she said, warding off questions.

Analía ignored the subtle rebuke. "I found his phone in his jacket pocket." She sighed. "So I guess he cannot call us. How long do you think he will be gone?" she asked, risking Shelley's ire.

"Well, he probably knows better than to come home," Shelley said. "I guess they're looking for him now."

"Where will he stay?"

"I don't know," Shelley shrugged awkwardly and stood up. "He's probably staying with somebody in the band, but he can't stay one place too long or they might get in trouble, too. I don't know how he's getting around."

Analía slumped. "Now we have to look for him, too."

Shelley glowered at her for a moment and dropped her eyes. "I guess I kind of thought we'd gotten past having our men running from the law. So much for progress." She clenched her jaw. "He'll turn up," she assured Analía. "He'll have to deal with this sooner or later."

Shelley didn't mention to Sue or Analía that when she put Ricky's guitar away in his room, the door of his gun cabinet wasn't closed all the way. She opened the cabinet door, and the empty space inside seemed to jump out at her. His entire life savings of guns had vanished. Shelley didn't invite Sue and Analía to join her in wondering what in the hell he was out there doing. Turning himself into a hermit outlaw living off rabbits in the woods? Shelley would let Tim discover the guns missing next time he went looking for cartridges.

Time passed without Ricky appearing. Shelley and Analía sat on the porch and watched for him. Shelley waited with her nose in the shiny new copy of *Sustainable Medicinals* that had arrived from her online order. Analía propped a magazine in front of herself with her travel paperwork hidden behind it. She counted the days left on her visa, having no way to tell if they were enough to see Ricky again. Every development put new weight on the scale opposite her choice to return to Mexico. Jaime, Ana Jessica, Ricky. School, the rest of the family, home. No scale had ever been built that could weigh these for her and give a true measure.

They called his supervisor and all the band members, but no one had seen him. Analía sat on a chair holding Ricky's phone, and Shelley sat on the steps with Sue's dogs. She leaned against their shaggy fur that always smelled like the time of year. Now in the fall, if she buried her face in their fur, it smelled like dead leaves. In the winter, their fur held a sharp dryness that she thought of as the smell of cold. Springtime brought the scent of wet mud, and their summer perfume was cut grass. They always smelled like the land they lay on. But where would Ricky smell like now?

Somewhere during the waiting, she forgave Analía for doing

what she herself couldn't. And Ricky for letting her.

Shelley was in her parents' old car, but she was driving. Her dad's Army dog tags rattled in the console, instead of hanging from the rearview mirror. She was coming home from a class, but she had no memory of it: couldn't picture the seats, couldn't see anything on the board, didn't have any notes. She wound her car around the curves on Willard Stuart Road, but when she turned at the red barn, the road to Sue's house became an on-ramp that put her on the highway one exit before the gas station. The car was gone, and she was walking, a pedestrian prohibited on the interstate. It might be safer to climb over the concrete barrier and go up the hill through the woods.

Maybe Louise could leave the store for a minute and give her a ride. Why was she in such a hurry to get home? She wasn't hungry; she didn't have to pee. She needed to tell them about Ricky. No, they already knew. There was an emergency waiting at Sue's, some crisis that needed her. How could she be ready if she didn't know what the crisis was? She would show up and everyone would expect her to fix it, but her backpack had disappeared with the vanished car.

She jogged down the exit to the gas station, and the off-ramp led straight into the parking lot of the Catholic church. Someone had disconnected all the roads that led to Sue's house and tied them in knots. But she hadn't noticed any construction: no mounds of bare red clay shoved aside, no trucks spewing black smoke, no stench of fresh-baked asphalt. How long had she been gone?

If she had come to the Catholic church, the emergency at Sue's must have something to do with Analía. If Jaime was in danger, and she didn't have her backpack, Analía would never forgive her. She didn't want to face Analía if she was going to let her down.

She could wait in the church until she remembered what the emergency was, and then she would know what to do. Then maybe one of the roads might lead home. She pulled on the handle of the eleven-foot-high door and went in. The rack of candles in the back corner had grown, stretching itself all the way around the nave and the altars, soaring up the curved walls of the dome. Every candle was lit, covering her in a heaven of flickering pinpoints, but the pews were in soft darkness. She walked up the center aisle, and saw that now the benches were upholstered like the kneeling pads. They were covered in fabric with a winding vine and leaf print in every possible shade of green. She lay down on one and fell asleep with her face tucked against the wooden back.

When she woke up Shelley realized it was Sunday. She rolled out of bed and headed for the kitchen. Sue came around the corner from her bedroom looking stricken.

"What's wrong?" Shelley asked, still confused about the emergency in her dream.

Sue shook her head slowly and handed Shelley a wad of cash. "It was in my jewelry box. He must've snuck home and put it there. I guess he knew I would look in there eventually." She sniffed. "He left a note. It just says 'I'm sorry, I hope this keeps up with the house payments for a while. There's 'sang drying in the shed. Shelley will know when it's ready and where to sell it.'" She looked up at Shelley accusingly. "After I found it I called Mary at the bank – you know we went to school together – to check on his account. She logged in and says he cleaned it out Friday." She grabbed Shelley's arm. "You can't tell anybody she told me that."

"I know!" said Shelley. She laid the money on a coffee table and sank onto the couch. "I thought he was selling his truck to get ready for jail. I guess he needed the money." *He must've sold all his guns, too,* she thought to herself. "It's too bad we didn't think to ask her if Jaime had a bank account."

"He left something for Analía, too," said Sue.

"He's acting like he's never coming back," said Shelley, without thinking. Sue's face crumpled. "He's just being dramatic," Shelley said quickly. "He'll come back and take care of things sooner or later." She hugged Sue. "You know he will." The thought of Ricky coming back and going to jail didn't make either of them feel better, but it was better than not knowing where he was. "He can't hide out forever."

"He wanted to be with that *girl*," Sue said, and shook her head.

Shelley hugged her again. "He knows her date to leave is coming," she patted Sue's back. "He'll be back."

Sue lost it again. "To go to jail for a *year!*" Neither of them wanted to imagine it. After the 30 days he did in the county jail, Ricky had come out pale, jumpy, short-tempered. For a year-long sentence, he would be sent to a state or federal prison, hours away, with murderers and rapists as cellmates. What would he be like after that?

"I got him some seeds," Sue said, wiping her eyes. Shelley looked puzzled. Sue pulled a tiny Ziploc bag out of a drawer in the coffee table and stared at it, rubbing the plastic film with her thumb. "I bought an ounce of ginseng seeds. I tried to tell him we could plant our own. He didn't like it. But I wanted to plant 'em with him before he goes to jail. He'll have something to look forward to while he's in there. I thought maybe I could write to him about how they're doing." She choked up again. The plants would forge themselves in the sun and snow and rain while Ricky slept among clanging bars and flickering fluorescent lights.

Shelley sighed. "It's a good idea, Aunt Sue. What did he leave for Analía?" she asked.

"It's Analía's business," insisted Sue. "It's a note. It's folded and taped."

"I don't care," Shelley retorted. "Who does he think he is?

She has bigger things to worry about." She stood up and reached for the note and Sue pulled back. They tussled like schoolchildren fighting over a cookie.

"What's wrong with you, Shelley?" Sue was trying to put the note in her pocket. "It's not meant for you!"

"Give me that damn note!" Shelley demanded again, quitting the fight and putting her hands on her hips. "Where does he get off running away? Now she's lost both of them." And she began to cry, but not for Analía. Ricky wasn't a goat after all, he was a man clutching the railing of a sinking ship. She went back to her room without coffee or breakfast. The application packet from State was lying on her desk, a map of a country she could never visit. It might as well have been a brochure for a trip to the moon, for all the likelihood that she could sign up. She couldn't abandon Sue with the mortgage payment and Tim, who only worked when he felt like it.

Shelley stayed away from the kitchen when Analía woke up. She let Sue give her the note in private. But when Analía headed back to her room after breakfast, Shelley couldn't contain herself. She jumped from her bed and accosted Analía in the hallway. Analía was wearing one of Sue's old Christmas sweaters over her pajamas. As the year had cooled, she had taken to wearing layers, dressing as if it was later than it was.

"What was in that note from Ricky?" Shelley asked.

Analía pulled the note from her pocket and handed it to Shelley. It *was* private, but Shelley was the best friend she had in a thousand miles.

Shelley was surprised that Analía surrendered it so easily, but she overcame the sense that she was intruding and opened it. It was a drawing of a gazebo and a campfire. At the bottom, it said *Te amo* in Analía's flowery script, and below that, in Ricky's unchanged-since-fourth-grade scrawl, *Te amo.*

Shelley stormed back to the kitchen, where Sue was leaning

on the counter with a full cup of coffee.

"Come on," Shelley said, pulling on Sue's arm.

"Where are we going? I have to get ready for church."

"We have more important things to do," Shelley said. "Go put on your yard clothes."

"They take ten years to grow, Shelley. We don't have to do it right this minute," Sue protested.

"If they take ten years to grow, we have to get started now. You change and I'll get dressed and get a hoe. You can still make Sunday school."

"Not right now," Sue said. "Damn it, my boy is missing and I don't have time to mess with a garden!"

"Damn it, Sue, he walked off on his own," Shelley said. "He wasn't kidnapped. He knows how to take care of himself, better than most of us. He can bitch about grown 'sang, but you *know* once it's growing he'll be interested in it." She sighed. "Okay, I know this will be like building a model race car, not the same as going to a real race. But he still won't be able to resist it." People who loved something always caved eventually to symbols, icons, tchotchkes of their beloved. If she were being honest, she would have to admit she was a little enchanted herself with the idea of having her own ginseng. She could never tell anybody, but she would know. "At the very least, we shouldn't let the seeds go to waste."

They threw on old shoes and walked through the morning-wet grass that needed mowing. Shelley carried the hoe and lectured Sue on what kind of spot they should find to put the seeds.

In the back woods it was chilly, the trees still cradling the night air in their branches. Sue hugged herself and followed Shelley, who muttered "North is there…" to herself as she held branches back for them to pass. She eyed the woods like a surveyor, calculating. She peered out of the woods toward the neighbors, toward the road, checking sight lines, and found a spot from which she could see nothing but leaves in every direction.

"Don't clear it first," she instructed Sue. "We don't want to make it look like anyone's been here. Try not to break off twigs or step on other plants while we're working."

Sue smiled a little. "I feel like I'm hiding stolen treasure," she said.

"More or less," Shelley said. "We should spread the seeds out, in several spots. Up along there, maybe," she pointed to a small hillock. "We can start here." She showed Sue what to do with the hoe. "We're not burying the seeds, just use the edge of the hoe to make a little scratch, and then brush that little bit of dirt back over with your hand. If the seeds fell on their own in the woods, they wouldn't be buried."

"I've planted wildflowers before, Shelley," Sue said.

They skimmed their way among the rhododendron and sassafras bushes, scratching and patting the earth. When they shook the last few seeds out of the bag and stood up to stretch, the only sign of their passing was a meandering trail where the dew had been brushed off the foliage and there were no sparkles in the patchy sunlight.

33
The Spirit of Wilderness Past

That evening Shelley was at the gas station and Sue joined Analía in the vigil on the porch. A red pickup pulled into the driveway, and the dogs, instead of standing on the porch barking a threat they wouldn't back up, tumbled down the steps wagging their tails.

"Well, look who's here," said Sue, her face brighter than Analía had seen it since Ricky disappeared.

The driver's window was down. A burly man with a beard leaned his head out and shouted, "Hey there, hot mama!"

Sue stood up and waved but her face hardened a bit. "I think he's drunk," she said, almost without moving her mouth.

"How are you, Bob?" she called out. Then said quietly to Analía, "This is my old friend Bob Mackey. He used to be a forest ranger."

The man got out of the truck, and his walk might have been taken for merely idiosyncratic, but Analía had uncles who walked that way when they were being very careful not to tip over. She looked at Sue nervously.

"Should I call someone?" she asked.

"No, no, if he didn't kill anybody getting here in that condition, he won't hurt anybody now," Sue said. She went down the steps and put an arm around Bob as both a greeting and a steadying force. She reached back with her foot to shove the truck door he had left hanging open.

"Whozat l'il lady up there?" he asked, pointing his chin at Analía.

"That's Analía," said Sue, trying to keep him upright. "She's... a friend of Shelley's. She's staying here for a while."

"Cute," said Bob. "Nah's cute as you!" He grinned and grabbed Sue in a bear hug.

Sue laughed and wrestled him partway off. "Not in the yard, Bob," she said cheerfully.

"Then lez go'n the house!" he offered. He stumbled to the top of the porch steps and gestured toward the door as if inviting Sue to his own home. Sue laughed again.

"It's a mess in there, Bob," she countered and maneuvered him into a porch chair. "Did you come all the way from Morganton in this condition?" she asked as she tried to get him straight in the chair.

"Naw, I didn't start out this way," he scoffed. "It was a long ride." He remembered why he made the trip and turned to her. "Susie, I heard about Ricky takin' off." He reached clumsily for her hand. "One o' the old rangers called me. I'm so sorry, Susie." His eyes cleared for a moment as they met hers.

She looked away. "I just don't know what to think," she said. "This is just going to make more trouble." She shook her head faintly. "He can't run forever."

She turned to Analía. "Why don't you make Bob some of that powerful coffee, Ana?" she suggested. Analía nodded and went inside.

"I wasn't sure I'd see you again, either, Bob," Sue said. She knew better than to try to have a real conversation with a person in this state, but too many emotions at once carried her past that wisdom. Bob lolled his head back against the chair, still holding her hand.

"I know, Susie. I was just tryin' to start over. Reckon I didn't go far enough."

Analía crept out and put a mug on the table next to him. She looked at Sue and started to go back in the house but Sue let her eyes drift to an empty chair so Analía sat and looked away toward the yard. She knew that a semblance of normalcy could go a long way with someone entering the morose stage of drunkenness.

Bob sat staring at the cup. "Ain't nobody but waitresses brought me a cup of coffee in a long time," he said. "You know them little white cups they got in all the diners. I seen a lot of them." Sitting made him more lucid, as if not concentrating on staying vertical freed up brainpower.

"Where're you staying?" Sue asked.

"Oh, I got me a little place, ain't much." Bob said, waving a hand to assure her of the unimpressiveness of his residence. "Apartment in a house. Got Koreans upstairs, some kind of Mexicans next door. Guatemalans, they say. I don't know. They're alright...quiet."

"I bet you miss your cabin," said Sue. She had dinner once at the cabin in Pisgah National Forest, provided to rangers by the Forest Service. Bob had bought a crockpot and tried his hand at roast beef. The roast beef was barely edible, but the creek running alongside the cabin and the raccoons at dusk had made the meal worthwhile.

"So much traffic over there." Suddenly he grinned. "You shoulda seen me at first. I wasn't used to it and I was always in the wrong lane. I never heard so many horns in my life," he chuckled.

"Every day I wonder what I'm doin'," he went on. "I make good money, and my place don't cost much, but what am I savin' up for? Get up, go to work, come home, eat something, sleep in my little box under the Koreans beside the Guatemalan Mexicans. It ain't really a home, it's a nighttime storage unit for people. Gotta drive ten miles to go fishin' or see a river. And when you get to the river, it's got a paved parking lot and it closes at dark." He laughed. "First time a cop came along and told me the river closed at dark, I thought, what? How do they close a river? Do they put the cover on it?"

"You could always come back," said Sue.

Bob stared off past the trees at the edge of the yard and shook his head. "No place is good anymore. One's too full, the other's too empty."

Sue was silent and Analía watched Bob pass out in her peripheral vision. Sue leaned her head back and watched the sky turn from aqua and pink streaks to blueberry and crimson to navy. She wondered which was which in Bob's statement. Was Morganton too full of strangers and rules, or too empty of connection to cherished things? Was home too full of memories, or too empty of the people in those memories? Finally Analía said, "He is lost, too."

"I guess he is," Sue said quietly. "He's been like a pinball bouncing around in a machine since he got divorced and left the rangers. Doesn't know what to do with himself."

Not long after Bob Mackey passed out, Analía went into the house, headed for bed. As she placed her clothes neatly on the chair in the spare room, she kept seeing Bob stumbling from his truck. Comfortable as it was, her new home resembled his. They were displaced people, living in the remnants of homes designed for intact families. They were remnants of families.

She sat on the bed and pictured how she might look from afar, if that Google Earth satellite that Shelley complained about could zoom in on her. One woman from far away, temporarily sheltered here, in this house, on this road, surrounded by Americans and their struggles, their goals and controversies. She had been drawn up into Shelley's search for a path into her future, she had watched Ricky try to fight his way through a world that didn't fit him. And all the while she herself in stolen moments had crept around the rural ghettoes and underground businesses of this country, following the tracks of a brother who had always been one step ahead of her. Jaime, escaping, had laid down a child in his path for her to pick up and tend to, to distract her while he snuck away to some mysterious older brother activity.

It was clear to Analía that Bob Mackey had lost his family, left his land, and was wandering unanchored in unfamiliar territory. It wasn't the cool night breeze coming in from the yard that chilled her as she realized the same was true of herself. Her passcard to America was running out. It was time to go home.

Explaining that to her mother would not be as easy as explaining it to Ricky. She stayed still on the bed a long time, holding the phone. Eventually she found herself trying to explain the national forest hunting regulations to her mother, who had grown up in the *sierra*. Her mother got this crossed, and declared that politicians with money were the same everywhere, and Analía let it go. Close enough. Her mother would understand being unable to fight a force such as that. Rich people's selfishness was one thing her mother would not expect her – or Jaime – to overcome.

"You need to get back to school," her mother ordered. "When you get another visa you will look for Jaime again."

"Of course."

"You have things to do, *mija*. You come home. Jaime is fine or he is with God," her mother said. "With God he is fine, too." She coughed. Neither of them would mention the third option, that he was somewhere hurt or in distress.

Analía put down the phone and sighed. Her mother probably already had something on the altar in the house for Jaime, encircled by trinkets and candles. Analía would never be able to look at it without seeing an altar to her own act of abandonment. Before she even got home, Jaime would have transformed into a beloved martyr of the family.

She flopped back on the bed, her mind turning to those grander martyrs, immortalized on stained glass in churches, who had given up their lives for the souls of others. Had they wanted to be heroes, or would they have preferred to go back to their houses and pat out tortillas on the *comal* with their aunts and cousins? Did the martyrs want to be saved themselves? Did they wish someone would sneak up to them in the middle of the night and say, *hide under this blanket, come away with me, and no one will ever know who you are again?* If they had run away in a moment of weakness, would their freedom have been too sweet for them to return and finish their tasks?

"I'm going to need a favor, Shelley, and it's a big one," Analía said as Shelley watched her pack.

"Another one?" Shelley joked. Since Ricky left her sense of humor was still there, but everything came out sounding meaner than she meant it to. Her banter was now laced with anger that seeped up from below. She kept needing to apologize. "Just kidding, you know. I'm happy to."

"This is big, Shelley. I do not think that Nicole is reliable. Do you think you can keep up with her?"

"Oh, sure," Shelley said. "I think you're right about her, but she won't go far from her family. Her mom's worked at the hotel for years. She'll be around."

Analía nodded. "I need to be able to find out about Ana Jessica. You're going to have to be friends with her. I have made her an email and a Facebook account." She handed Shelley a page of notebook paper with usernames and passwords.

"Friends?" Shelley looked skeptical. Analía was one hell of a planner. She always looked so calm and peaceful, but like Sue said, watch out for the quiet ones. The wheels were always turning in Analía's mind, calculating how to get from here to there. Shelley wished her own path could be so clear. "Fine. Our family's between babies now anyway, I guess it will be fun to have one to play with."

"I will be back," said Analía. "I will not lose the part of Jaime that I still have." She sniffed and flicked drops away from her eyes. "Maybe I can get a longer visa. Maybe someday Anna Jessica can visit Mexico. Maybe when I come back Ricky will be home." She cleared her throat. "You have helped me so much, Shelley. I know it's too much to ask, but I need you to help me stay in contact with her. We can email. I have all of Nicole's information, but if it changes, you have to help me. I am scared to lose her, too." She looked down.

"Analía," Shelley began. "Do you think Jaime…" she lowered her eyes and scratched her head, unable to say it.

"Jaime what?" challenged Analía. Shelley met her eyes without speaking.

Analía stared at Shelley defiantly. "I think he is ashamed," she said. "I think he is embarrassed to tell us what happened, that he started a family here, that he was chased by the police. I think he is hiding because he feels he is a failure. He will call home when he is…stable again."

Shelley squinted at her. "That seems…" she inhaled deeply. "Odd," she sighed. "Do you think he would let everyone worry like that?"

Analía squinted back. "That is what I think," she declared with quiet forcefulness.

"Okay," half-whispered Shelley. "Don't worry, I'll do everything I can to keep up with Nicole. Sue will, too." She cleared her throat. "Are you going to be able to go back to school without Jaime paying for it?" she asked.

Analía shrugged. "I'm going to," she said. "Somehow." She

looked around the room for things she might have forgotten. "I can tell everyone I worked in the United States. That should help me get a job." She slumped. "I have to finish. If I do not graduate, then Jaime is lost for nothing."

Shelley knew that Analía's education was weighted with the same load of hope that her own education carried. Were they autonomous people or just vessels of aspiration for the less fortunate?

"Doesn't it feel selfish to go on without Jaime and Ricky?" Shelley asked.

"They are not children," Analía said quietly. "They will show up when they are ready. They are just putting it down." Shelley made that face that Analía knew meant she had missed the English. Were Jaime and Ricky insulting the police? Or had they laid down some burden that they carried?

"You mean putting it off?" Shelley asked. "Delaying?"

"Yes, delaying."

"What do we do after college, Analía?" Shelley asked.

Analía inhaled and sighed. "It's for *something*, Shelley. It's supposed to teach us to do things. It's supposed to make us stronger, because we know more. We're supposed to have more choices."

"Are choices better? Maybe college is just a way of telling us that what's around us isn't good enough. You know, the mechanic isn't good enough, the farmer isn't good enough, running a store isn't good enough. Then you graduate and start looking to change everything, because nothing is good enough. All you've learned is to pick the whole world apart, piece by piece." She stopped and shook her head. "I already have my choice."

Analía studied her for a moment. "You have half your choice, Shelley. You know the plants part. But you said you have no idea how to make a living at that. That can be what you figure out in college. How to make the rest of your choice. You don't have to change while you're there. Just get the papers you need."

"I can't leave Sue," Shelley said. "I can't run away, too."

"You are not running away," Analía protested. "No more than Jaime ran away from Mexico, or me, when I came here. It is not another country." She inhaled. "It is the same state!"

Shelley interrupted her. "Nobody can make me leave." She looked up at Analía. "*You're* going home." It was an accusation, the whine of a jealous child.

"I am going home so I can come away again. Maybe you go away so you can come home again, only better."

"Um-hm, better. 'Cause I'll never be good enough here." Shelley's eyes had never looked so hard.

Analía rolled her eyes. "Not better. *Más poderosa.*" Shelley gave her the look. Analía searched her brain. "More...powerful."

Analía sat down on the bed next to Shelley. "What do you want, Shelley?" she asked.

Shelley looked up into the distance.

"I want Ricky to come back and hunt 'sang on the weekends, maybe with Jaime. I want Bob and Sue to sit on the porch and drink iced tea. I want the band back together. I want the right people to stop leaving and the wrong people to stop changing everything and go back where they came from. I want everything to be different." She was crying. "So much is gone, I can't go too."

Analía nodded. "I know, Shelley, but you can't wish about the past. Your only hope is forward." She sat down and neither said anything for a while.

Later that day Analía stood in a line alongside one more bus, carrying the same cloth bag she had arrived with months ago. She wondered if she would be riding with the same lady driver who had dropped her off with good wishes, if she would be recognized, what she would say if the woman asked if she had found what she was looking for. The man in front of her stepped up onto the step, and Analía stood still.

Jaime had come to this place as a son, and left as a father. Analía had tried to convert herself from sister to detective, but fate made her an archaeologist. She had assembled the signs of Jaime: addresses, mail, traffic tickets, photos. She had linked him to other known peoples: counter-tenders, coworkers, fellow hunters. She found his living descendants: a daughter and some ginseng plants in unrecorded locations. She had a solid collection of artifacts, a web without a spider.

Analía watched her feet as, one by one, they removed themselves from the American asphalt, leaving no marks. The yellow line at the top of the steps, the one you had to stand behind while the bus was moving, was the beginning of Mexico. She passed over the two rubber-padded steps of no-man's-land in between and became a daughter and a student again.

The lady driver was not at the front of the bus. Instead the driver was a man, middle aged, who had the look of someone beginning a long dull day at work. He stared out the front window as the passengers climbed up the few steps and turned past him. He didn't even have to check their tickets, as that was done at the station. Analía figured that the world had the compassion to turn its eyes away as she started home in defeat. Someone watching from a distance might not see that she had not quit yet.

34
The Only Answer to Lightning is Thunder

Shelley rambled around Sue's place. The house was so much emptier it felt as if they were planning to move, but there was no exciting new home waiting for them across town. Ricky's door was closed. Echoes bounced from the furniture in the spare room, which had only ever been augmented by one cloth bag of Analía's things.

Time was vacant, too. Her classes and shifts left gaps, which Ricky's shenanigans and Jaime's trail had formerly absorbed. She followed Sue around whenever they were both home, inventing chores. The house was cleaner than it had ever been, the porch swept, the dog bowls washed. Shelley was considering sorting the screws in the jars in the shed. If Ricky didn't show up soon, they would be reduced to sitting in the woods and watching the ginseng sprout.

The knock on the door surprised her, but not as much as what she saw when she looked out the window. That woman was here. On her very own front porch now, with the fading evening light barely silhouetting her.

Shelley ducked back behind the door frame, and imagined throwing a bucket of water right out the door onto Sophia. She remembered Ricky's shotguns. Too bad he took them, or she could grab one and stand on the porch and say, "Git off my land." The thought of enacting *that* stereotype made her happy enough to smile almost pleasantly as she squared her shoulders and opened the door.

"What can I help you with?" she said, not sounding helpful at all.

"I'm very sorry to bother you," Sophia began. *Sure as hell you are*, thought Shelley. "I know you don't want to help me," said Sophia, "but I'm not asking for help for me."

"That's good," said Shelley.

Sophia's shoulders fell and she exhaled. "Look, I understand you're studying biology in school," she began.

"Botany, actually," said Shelley. "But biology's a requirement." She tightened her lips and shifted from one foot to the other. "What is it that you need?"

Sophia held out a shoebox that Shelley hadn't noticed she was carrying. "There's a rabbit in here. He's hurt. I don't think I can take care of him. I thought maybe you would know how."

Shelley squinted at the word rabbit. Her instincts kicked in. She leaned out a little and reached for the box. "Where'd you get a rabbit?" She lifted a corner and peeked in at the rabbit.

Sophia looked away. "I found him. A hawk was trying to eat him. He just needs a few more days of care and you can let him go. He eats quite a bit. I bought that for him." She pointed to an opened bag of rabbit food that she had set on the porch before knocking. She didn't want to rat out the veterinarian, so she didn't say more.

"So why don't you just *take care of him* a few more days? I thought you liked taking care of things. You know, watching out for the traditions and wildlife and all." Shelley realized that she might be about to lose her temper. She didn't want to scare the rabbit, or leave him in Sophia's care, so she walked carefully away from the door and put the rabbit in Analía's old room.

Sophia had the manners not to step through the open door. She had made the trip across town nervously, having programmed the address from court documents into her GPS. Now that she was here, she was afraid to get any closer. She was pretty sure that contacting the family of the defendant she wanted to testify against was against the rules, too. She was literally down a rabbit hole of unethical behavior. Shelley reappeared.

"You want me to clean up your mess, is that it? You know that rabbit's illegal, don't you? And you can't get caught with it, 'cause you're such a straight arrow. I mean hypocrite. So you bring it to somebody else to take the risk, 'cause you also can't stand to just let it die, right?"

Nobody in this little southern town had ever talked to Sophia the way people talked to each other up north. She was shocked, and almost in tears. "I'm sorry," she whispered. "I just can't do it. The stress is making me sick."

"So – me? Why would you bring it to *me*? Don't you think I'd just *love* to tell everybody you illegally possessed wildlife? Why wouldn't I run straight out to tell absolutely everybody about you, especially your forest ranger friends?" Shelley paused and glanced toward the spare room. "Come to think of it, how do I know this is not a trick? Is one of your forest ranger friends going to stop by here as soon as you leave and write me a ticket for having this rabbit?"

Sophia shook her head vigorously. "No, no, I just don't want him to die. And...and I can't do it. I wanted to, but I can't." Her eyes met Shelley's for a brief moment, and she turned and nearly ran back down the steps. At the bottom she stopped and turned. "I haven't told anybody. Please just take care of him and let him go when it's time." She squinted at the woods. "I know *you* can do it."

"That rabbit's going to get eaten by something sooner or later," Shelley said from the porch, Ricky's voice echoing in her head. "Are you happy?" she asked.

"How could I be happy?" retorted Sophia, tears returning. "Everyone hates me over the scholarship program that's for their own benefit. People are still stealing ginseng. What am I supposed to be happy about?"

"Well, you got one criminal out of the band, didn't you? Thanks to your meddling, there's one less poacher in Pisgah. And now you saved a little bunny. I guess you're a hero, aren't you?"

Sophia wilted. "I was just trying to help," she began, looking at the ground.

Shelley sighed forcefully. "Help, help, help," she said. She looked up at the treetops, as if they might step in to back her up. "Why'd you even come here if you think it's so full of problems?"

"I don't think it's full of problems. I *love* it." Sophia looked genuinely puzzled.

"*How do you know?*" Shelley came down the porch steps. "Are you sure you've even seen it? From what I know, you don't talk to anybody unless it's to tell them what to do. Except that other woman that comes to the dance with you, you spend all your time with her. We don't know her, either." She sat on the bottom step. Sophia looked around herself for another place to sit, but she finally plopped on the far end of the step, after brushing the back of her pants with her hands, in anticipation of dirt.

Sophia glanced at her SUV as if she might want to drive away. She turned toward Shelley. "I don't know how to talk to people here. Every time I try, it goes…wrong. It ends up awkward."

"That's what happens when you're new to a place. You should probably listen for a while, instead of talking." Shelley was asking herself why she was talking to this woman. It felt like a betrayal of Ricky, but on the other hand, if anything she could say would get this woman to leave him alone, it would be worth it.

"So just shut up and go along with things?"

Shelley rolled her eyes. "Maybe just ask why things are the way they are before you say they should be different."

"But no one has any answers. The answers don't make

sense."

"They do to us. You should keep listening 'til you see it."

"So I should just change everything about myself to fit in?"

"Maybe if you know how it makes sense to us, you'll know whether your suggestions make sense. If they do, you can explain it to somebody and it will make sense to them. And it won't be awkward."

Sophia did not look pleased with Shelley's suggestion.

"You were trying to help me, too, about college, right?" asked Shelley.

"Of course," Sophia said. She felt a bit less discouraged. "There are so many good things here, so much potential, like you, you seem smart and I just want you to succeed."

Shelley was nodding along, then she stopped and held Sophia's gaze. "I'm not potential. I'm a person. Don't you care why I picked community college in the first place?"

"I guess it would have been for financial reasons...and maybe all colleges seemed the same to you?"

Shelley forgot all about trying to help Ricky and a long string of curse words ran through her mind. *How dare this woman be right about anything?* Sure, she missed the whole angle about leaving home, and a lot of other stuff, but the bits she got weren't wrong.

The two of them sat on the step, flanked by Sue's chrysanthemums, and some time went by. Each having made a small successful parry, their next steps could be quite dangerous. Finally Shelley set that conversation down and opened a new one.

"Hey, you said you were sick. I heard you take ginseng for some disease that you have. Ricky had some drying when he left, it's about ready. You want to buy some? It's a whole lot cheaper this way."

"Is that the ginseng he stole from the national forest?" Sophia asked.

Shelley raised her chin slightly and looked at Sophia sideways. "No. They took that. It's locked in a box in a building somewhere. It's going to go bad way before the case is over. We won't make any money and it won't be anybody's medicine." She lifted her eyebrows at Sophia. "That ginseng is lost."

Sophia sighed. "I just wanted to protect it." She made a soft fist and set it on her knee. "I wanted to do something *good.*"

Neither the treetops, nor the chrysanthemums, nor the lichen clinging to the undersides of the porch steps could speak up for Shelley here. "I believe you," she finally said. "But you can't protect it by locking it up, any more than you can protect wildlife by stealing a hawk's dinner, or protect the dancing by making a bunch of rules." Shelley said. "You protect things by becoming part of them, by adding yourself to them. You have to make them stronger, not smaller."

Sophia shifted on the step. "I'm not sure I'm ready to buy ginseng from a poacher. I mean, I'm sorry, I know he's your family…it just doesn't feel right."

Shelley shrugged. She thought to herself, *You might not buy it from us, but you'll still need it.*

"Just a minute," Shelley said. She left Sophia on the steps and went around the house to the shed. She felt like a traitor again, but she remembered Ms. Brown feeding Analía at the church picnic. Ricky had left her in charge of his ginseng while he was missing, so she figured she was entitled to make her own decision here. She came back with three of the smallest roots and held one out to Sophia, who frowned at it. Shelley sat down, tore off the tip of one root, and put the piece on Sophia's knee. "Just eat that little bit. It doesn't taste so great, but it's good for you. Which you already know."

Sophia chewed the ginseng tentatively and made a face. Shelley raised her eyebrows and nodded. "Yeah. Here." She put the other small roots in Sophia's hand. "You can have that. Eat it, don't waste it."

Sophia swallowed and looked at the roots in her hand. "Thank you. Thank you for taking care of the rabbit."

Shelley nodded and stood up. Sophia did the same and went to her vehicle.

Shelley went up the steps as Sophia's engine purred into action. The cat slipped into the house as she entered. Shelley made sure the bedroom door was closed to keep the cat away from the rabbit, which, at least for a time, was hers to tend. She went to Sue's desk in the kitchen corner and dug around. She found the piece of notebook paper with the barely legible phone number, yanked her cell from her purse, and tapped.

"Yeah, hello," said a voice soft with beer.

"Hey, Bob," she began. "It's me, Shelley, you know, Sue's niece?"

"What? Oh, Shelley, yeah." He ruminated. "What's wrong? Is Sue alright?" Concern thinned the beer fog somewhat.

"Oh yeah, everything's fine. Everyone's fine, except, you know, Ricky hasn't turned up. Uh, I'm just callin' to see how you're doin' down there…I heard you stopped by."

"Yeah, just missed home I guess."

"Hey Bob, could I ask you something? It's kinda personal." Alone in the room, Shelley made the gestures of reticence, her shoulders low and her eyes darting to the floor.

"'Course, I guess."

"So, Bob, I was just wondering, do you think you'll ever come back home?" Shelley realized Bob might think Sue put her up to this. She needed to clarify. "I promise, I'm not asking for Sue. You and Sue are your own business." She paused. "I was just wondering, now that you're there, with the good job and everything, would it feel like giving up to come back? You know, would it feel like you failed, or wasted your time moving there?"

Bob was silent for so long she thought he had fallen asleep. "I guess some people might see it that way," he finally said. "But I don't think I do." Shelley heard some rustling, and the small whoosh of gas as a carbonated drink opened. She heard gulps. "I think it would just feel like coming home."

"But do you think you *will*?" she asked again.

"Why's it matter?" he asked.

"It just does, Bob. Everybody keeps disappearing." She looked at the blank slates of the night-dark windows of the kitchen. "Everyone says that going away for school and jobs and money is a temptation. But I think it's the other way around. I think the temptation is to just keep running away and hiding while people change everything you love until you can't recognize it anymore." She was silent for a while, too.

"Sorry to bother you," she said. "You take care down there, okay?"

"Sure, Shelley. Tell Sue I said hi, okay?"

Shelley clicked off the phone and looked around the kitchen where she'd eaten most of her meals since her parents died, and plenty before that.

She had hoped she could just stay home like a tree with the poison ivy growing up all around, or the acid rain falling on it. She could just wait passively, entertaining herself with wildflowers the way the fallow farmland did, until it got bought up by developers. But she realized that if she stood still, she would get hit by lightning, or be run over by the bulldozers that never stopped coming.

The tree and the land had no choice but to stand there and take it. She was going to have to be like the coyotes that ate people's cats, like the bears who trashed people's barbecue grills. Both risked getting shot to push back at the boundaries, to reclaim what they could from the encroachers. She would have to come out of the woods and remind people that she had been there all along. Her mere crossing would be taken as a threat as she crept through land where she wasn't welcome.   She would have to make herself vulnerable to the potshots of irresponsible hunters.

Shelley went to her room and gathered the papers from NC State. She piled them on the kitchen table with her laptop. The cat gave up on sniffing the crack under the bedroom door and settled on the next chair over while Shelley poured a fresh Diet Coke. She sat down, pulled up the university website, and clicked the online application button. She started at the top: "Name...Address."

Isn't that what it's all about, she thought as the keys clicked.

Epilogue
Engraved Invitations

It was very late in the evening several weeks later when Shelley drove home from a shift at the convenience store. Some nights she would make the turn into the driveway without looking, then turn her head quickly, hoping to see Ricky's truck in the driveway. It was a game she played with herself, even though she knew the truck was sold and she had a feeling Ricky wasn't coming back. This evening disappointed her, as had all the others. She sighed, got out, and went around to the mailbox.

Analía's graceful script beamed up at her from a red- and blue-edged envelope, addressed to her. A letter from Mexico, with foreign stamps that Sue would want to keep. She skipped to the chair under the porch light and began reading.

...I had hoped that when I returned, I would find that Jaime had made his way back here as well. I have not seen him yet, but I still carry the hope that one day he will show up. I imagine him traveling hidden through the rest of the U.S. and Mexico, maybe working for food, sleeping in a different place each night, one day closer to us. Every night I pray that he is safe and has enough to eat. I will not allow myself to imagine anything else.

I have other news, big news, Shelley, and you must pay attention, because I cannot say all of it. I am afraid even to send it in email. I can only tell you that I am married now, and it's too soon to be sure but I think I am expecting a child…

Shelley's heart wrenched, thinking of Ricky, but she continued reading.

…I am very happy, but my family would be scandalized if they knew that I saw my husband take off his belt the very first day I met him. I hope you understand, Shelley. If there is ginseng in Mexico, I have the man to find it.

Shelley leaned back in the chair and looked up at the darkening sky. She pictured Ricky's six-foot-plus frame among the diminutive Mexicans, his pale Irish-derived face bright red from the sun. She thought of the miles and miles of undeveloped land in Mexico, and the years Ricky would have to explore and learn it. Someday he would know every inch and creature the way he had known these woods. And no one was likely to bother him for hunting anything he needed whenever he needed it.

Not for many years, at least.

Now Sue would have no choice but to keep up with Nicole, since that made Anna Jessica Sue's…granddaughter-in-law? Grand-niece by marriage? It defied labels, but the thread that ran through Ricky in Mexico to Analía through a missing father to a little girl across town would hold. Wait, Sue might be a grandmother! Shelley grinned. Forget the stamps, Sue's scrapbook would be filling up with passport photo receipts and airplane ticket stubs. Tim would gripe about staying home to take care of the dogs, then start emailing Ricky recipes for armadillo.

After a while, she looked through the rest of the mail and found an envelope with the colorful NC State seal. She had heard that thin envelopes like this one were bad news, because it only took one page to say no. She propped the unopened envelope on the porch rail, facing her, and eyed it suspiciously. Had she been too big for her britches, as her grandmother used to say? Would the decision, after all, not be hers to make?

The single page in the envelope began with the word, "Congratulations." Later paragraphs said that she had been granted a merit scholarship, and that she should expect a great mass of paperwork in a later mailing. She did some quick math in her head and figured that if she worked double shifts all this coming summer, she could leave Sue enough to pay off the rest of Ricky's lost bond.

She sighed again, happily, and looked out over the porch rail to the dry stems of the wild purple asters that had come up when no one took over mowing after Ricky left. Beyond the edge of the roof, the squirrels were flinging themselves from branch to branch in the oaks, burning up the last of their energy before tucking in for the night. Her eyes rested briefly on the blackberry bushes, underneath which the rabbit might be busy insinuating himself into the existing rabbit population. She lifted her gaze to the darkness of the woods on the other side of the creek, where a coyote might be sleeping off a dinner of disoriented rabbit, dreaming of fat slow deer. He might be curled right on top of Sue's ginseng seeds. Below him the seeds' enzymes would be dancing with water molecules, their cells dividing, packed together like twins in a womb as they embarked on their years of arduous growth.

She took in a deep slow breath, trying to absorb the land that she would see only in the summers for the next few years. Soon she would be gone too, disappeared, and probably lost more than once. But she would be back, and she would not be uprooted.

With deepest gratitude...

To the ginseng people who shared their time and wisdom: hunters, buyers, poachers, protectors, users – the whole *panax quinquefolia* community, that thin but far-reaching web.

To the Guatemalan ginseng cooperative in Avery County, NC, for joining my people in appreciating our precious woods and their gently hidden secrets. I never succeeded in tracking you down – like ginseng some days, you were too elusive for me – but your willingness to learn our ways is the only reason this book ever happened. Sometimes it's the things you don't find.

To Janie, Cynthia, Carla, Lori, Kelly, Ricardo, Tony, Cathee, and all my other friends who repeated, "of course you can write a book" over and over for more years than I will admit to.

To Bambi for life-giving sustenance, even when I didn't deserve it.

To Julio, who listened patiently to every iteration. Sometimes what you're looking for comes along.

About the Author

Victoria Lyall is a native of Appalachia, and lives there still.

Made in the USA
Columbia, SC
22 December 2023